THE BLESSED CURSE

REN SYLVAIN

For Damian

May you always know where to find me.

TABLE OF CONTENTS

Prologue

Red blood- human blood- dripped down King Aneurin's cuirass. The horned owl embossed upon it used to be bleached white when he was young, but it was brown now, stained with old gore and new.

Three hundred years he'd been cursed with wings and feathers. For a year longer, he'd been cursed to kill anyone who loved him. And the feathered horns upon his head bore the weight of the crown he'd vowed to wear until he fulfilled the destiny he was owed by the blood that enchanted his veins until he was twenty-five.

Disgust ripped through him as he tore off his greaves and tossed them onto the stone floor of his throne room. What sort of fate was being an Ambrosius, blessed with the magic aphrodisiac of a divine destiny if the curse of a madwoman was enough to steal his glory?

And he'd been fool enough not to slit his own throat and end it all. Too much of a coward.

No—he wasn't a coward. Just vain enough to think he could outwit a curse.

"My lord," the steward Godfrey said from the double doors that led into the audience chamber. "I have news from Senden's Branch."

King Aneurin hissed, and shook his head. *Not now. Please not now.*

"What is it?" A subtle trill echoed in his words, avian and owlish.

Godfrey cleared his throat. "Two Ambrosius infants were slain in the chaos last night. Twins."

King Aneurin froze. Centuries passed, and yet every year the hunting of the Destined continued. He was powerless to stop it.

But every time he tried, he only made things worse.

He'd gone into Senden's Branch to kill the ambrosia hunters there. He killed as many as he could. Those who consumed the blood of the divinely blessed could not be suffered to live. But as a drop of blood slid down the back of his hand and dripped onto the floor, he knew it didn't matter what he did. So long as he tried to protect his people, to be the king they deserved, more would die. It was Eugenia's curse—Aneurin could never be loved unless she was there to love him, and she was long dead.

"Both were blessed?"

"Yes," Godfrey confirmed. He looked at the ground. "Their mother is here."

Aneurin removed the iron helmet from his feathered brow and let it drop from his hands to the floor with a resonant *thunk* that echoed through the chamber. As the vestiges of noise faded away, he said, "Bring her to me."

The woman had light brown skin and mournful brown eyes that blazed at him as Godfrey and a number of King Aneurin's guards escorted her in. She pointed at him as she said, "You killed them."

Aneurin stood before his throne, knowing better than to sit upon it in front of her as if he were a king worthy of his crown. He knew he wasn't. He damned himself and his entire thousand-year reign when he made the bargain that gave him feathers.

Should have slit my own throat when Eugenia cursed me. Let a more deserving soul carry the weight of this cursed crown. How stupid of me to think I should carry it for a thousand years.

"I grieve your children, madam," he said out loud. "If I could take their place in Della Mortis's embrace, I would."

"My babies," the woman sobbed. But when she glared at him again, there were no tears on her strong-featured face. Only wrath. "Why haven't you saved us?"

Aneurin looked out the window. At the yellowing hills of his palatial property and the distant ribbon of forest that separated him from the town of Senden's Branch. The sky was dark though it was early afternoon, and he was glad for it. He hated when the sun shone light on all his failures.

On the poverty. On the illiteracy. On the trafficking of ambrosia and those whose hearts pumped it, and all the other horrors that he'd been unable to quell since King Octavian died and Lord Aneurin had ascended his throne.

"I have done all I can," Aneurin said. He closed his eyes intending merely to blink, but his exhaustion caught up to him. He had the body of a feathered terror, but inside, he was a weary old man desperate to claim his rest.

"You have done *nothing*," the woman cried.

"What is your name?"

The woman clamped her mouth shut, her eyes widening. "Marie Chordstreet."

"And the names of your children?"

The woman narrowed her gaze. "Luc and Emenette. They died because you sent the hunters into a frenzy. They were *desperate* and they broke in my door because of *you.*"

Aneurin staggered back, looking to Godfrey with a slack-jawed expression.

Godfrey stared back, but broke first. He swallowed hard and said, "His Majesty will stand the cost of their funerals. I will—"

The woman screamed. "No! He will do nothing! Because nothing is what he is."

Godfrey chewed on his upper lip and turned away. Aneurin's heart sank.

"You are nothing in life. You will die nothing. Oh, valiant King Aneurin, noble King Aneurin is what we're taught about, but you are no good king, sir," the woman spat. "You would serve us better if you'd just stayed in your nest and stopped pretending to give a damn about us."

The king hated that he was trembling. "I'm sorry."

The woman cleared her throat and spat the phlegm onto the floor at his feet. "Your impotence killed my babies, and a thousand babies before them, and a thousand more babies tomorrow. Take that with you when you have the decency to die."

"Madam—" Godfrey started.

"I'm leaving. I never want to see another tax collector at my door, Lord Aneurin. I will not pay a single crown to you. We will forget you like you have forgotten us."

After she was gone, Lord Aneurin said, "Godfrey."

"Yes, my lord."

Bloodshot green eyes met Godfrey's own. "Once that

woman survives the trek back to her house, close up the gates. Keep them manned. Any who seeks an audience with me may be allowed entry, but the palace is closed to all other business."

Godfrey opened his mouth to speak but seemed to think better of what he was about to say. "When shall we notify the other regents we will be ready to receive them?"

Aneurin flared his wings and lifted his chin. "Never."

And unlike every other word spoken in the throne room, which echoed like an elegy at a funeral, this one command fell to the floor like a stone and was still.

Aneurin did not speak again for two hundred years.

Now

Chapter Two

At first, the echo of footsteps behind her didn't bother Calla Renaud. She kept moving through the cobblestone streets of Senden's Branch, the middling village she had lived in her whole life. Familiar streets, streets she called home though she rarely traversed them.

The footsteps became louder, faster. Calla quickened her pace. Almost there.

But her pursuer was running. They'd turn the corner and catch her any second. She broke into a sprint, gathering her skirts in her hands and racing for the corner. She stumbled on an uneven stone, and a shadow crossed into the street behind her.

With a whimper, Calla lunged down Reca Street and burst through the door of the tiny three-room house she shared with her father. Breathless, she slammed the door behind her and fastened all seven of the deadbolts. Then she flew to the windows and lowered the bars over each one of them, padlocking them in place. It wasn't until she had fully secured the house that she turned to look at her father, who stood at the kitchen counter, a knife in one hand and a carrot in the other.

"What happened?" Peter Renaud said, setting the carrot down but keeping his grip on the black handle of the knife. His honey-colored eyes, so like her own, were creased with worry.

"Someone was following me," Calla said.

"Man or woman?"

"Does it matter? The streets were almost empty. I thought it was safe, but it wasn't." She slid down the wall and rested her head on her arms. "I just wanted to pretend for one day that I wasn't a threat to myself. Or to you. Just one day."

Peter sighed and set the knife down. He crossed the room slowly, not wanting to startle his precious daughter. "You'll be free in just five years," he said, crouching and putting his warm, calloused palm on her knee. "That's almost no time at all."

When she finally lifted her head to face him, her eyes brimmed with tears. "I don't want to live in fear. I'd like to go for a simple evening walk without fearing for my life. I hate my blood. I hate magic. I hate destiny. I don't want it!" Then she wept, she wept *hard*, for she had dared to hope, and hope was lost.

Peter was quiet but his hand never left her knee. After a long while, when her sobbing turned to softer whimpers, he said, "I forgot why we pray to the twelve gods a long time ago. The promise of glory is not worth the price paid by the ones entitled to grasp it. But that doesn't mean you were wrong to hope."

Calla sniffed, then wiped her nose on her sleeve. "I don't want to be stuck in this box for the rest of my life. How am I supposed to conquer the world if I don't even know what the world looks like? I want…I want to be safe enough to look at the stars. To find the sea. To stand still for one moment when I'm not confined within the walls of a dilapidated house. It's a prison, Papa. How—how can I be fit for destiny if I don't even know for sure whether my next breath is my last?"

Peter sighed and sat on the floor, grasping his daughter's hands. "I think—"

He paused, and within that pause, Calla heard it. A scratching on the door.

"I'll kiss your pretty neck and then I'll tear it out with my teeth," a man said through the crack in the wood. "I'll taste that ambrosia. I'll drink it all the way up until your glory is *mine.*"

"Look at me," Peter whispered. "Look at me, not the door, Calla. Only at me."

Calla stared at her father but visibly winced as the man began pounding on the door. Again and again he threw himself against the rotten wood, but it held.

"We will wait him out," Peter whispered. "There's only one thing left to do."

Calla whimpered, her grip tightening on his hands. "They'll come for me eventually. I always knew it would be like this. I was stupid to go out again. I almost got caught last time and I'm so—"

With a sigh, Peter drew closer to his child, though she was a woman grown. "We can try what no one else has tried. In three days, at first light, we will go to King Aneurin. The Strix Lord will know what to do."

Calla scoffed. "How? He hasn't given a damn about Lorana Vale in centuries."

Peter poked her nose. "Praying to the gods is useless, but we know they exist because King Aneurin exists and none but the gods could conquer death like he has. You must have faith. When the well is dry, my lily, dig deeper."

Dread seeped into her bones like water flushes the cracks in a foundation and brings down a house. She shook her head. "Why should he keep me safe? He hasn't concerned himself with anyone in Lorana Vale for centuries."

"I will ask him to protect you. I will be on my knees. And if he refuses, I will call him a coward."

"He'll kill you," Calla whispered, shaking her head again.

"He won't. You are very beautiful. I bet he takes one look at you and begs you to stay."

Calla snorted in disbelief. "Or he'll tear out my throat with his beak or whatever he has. Maybe he's just a giant pigeon perched on an enormous nest."

Peter shook his head. The pounding on the door stopped long ago. "No, Calla. I think this will work. And if he refuses outright, well...five years isn't awfully long. You've made it twenty so far."

Chapter Three

The palace was grander than Calla thought it would be. She expected something like one of the old novels her father brought her—a manor so haunted, cobwebs draped from the gargoyles perched on the roof. Skeleton guards standing watch at the gate. But instead, a handsome man no older than twenty greeted them as they rushed up the path to the iron gate.

"Hello, villager," he said. "What business do you have with the house?"

"House?" Calla scoffed. "This—" she gestured wildly at the building "is not a house. A manor if you're being precious, but *that* is a palace. A well-maintained palace."

The guard's eyebrows raised, and he looked over his shoulder at the white stone of the four-storied edifice behind him. Gold columns held up a massive veranda, way high up on the fourth floor. Calla thought she saw a flutter of black and white wings, but she couldn't be certain.

The guard turned back to Calla and Peter, chuckling. "I'd certainly hope so, Miss. We have all worked very hard for a long while to make sure our Lord Aneurin is comfortable. He is a stickler for protocol, and that means everyone must do their jobs or face his wrath."

Calla's stomach sank as she looked again at the veranda. She was *sure* she'd seen wings. *Enormous, grizzly bear-sized wings.*

Peter stepped forward. "Sir, we want to see the Strix Lord. I know it is strange and I dare say, *shocking* that we would presume to do so, but the matter is urgent. I promise the request won't take more than a minute."

The guard looked genuinely surprised. He looked at his companion who wore a similar expression of shock. "Lord Aneurin doesn't grant audiences because no one requests them anymore. Not for two hundred years. I don't recall what the protocol is for this." He looked again to his companion, who shrugged.

"Please," Calla said. "This was our last option. Our last hope."

The guards cringed as a piercing owlish trill echoed through the courtyard. "Well, there's that. You've just been granted an audience, and we are going to be scrubbing the bathrooms for the next twenty years for detaining you."

They moved to open the gate.

"That…sound…said all that?" Peter asked nervously.

The guards laughed. "Oh yes. And other things too. By the time you walk through that door, you'll find the entire house is assembled. You got your audience with the king, and almost everyone who works for him."

Ripe anxiety flooded through Calla's veins, mixing with the

ambrosia in her blood.

Destiny.

The closer she drew to the doors, the more terrified she grew and she almost fled.

"Are you sure, Papa?" she murmured as they ascended the steps.

"He knows we're here, Calla. If we leave now, we'll be considered rude."

She squared her shoulders and reached to push on the door, but it was pulled open before she got there.

Inside, she found a magnificent marble staircase. It swept up to a first landing that had a backdrop of a tall window through which the sunlight made the gold flecks in the marble of the rest of the room glitter. The long running carpet that led to the stairs and up it was surrounded on every side by perfectly postured servants in clean uniforms. There wasn't a speck of dust to be seen.

A few steps up the staircase and a little to the side, a lone man stood. Blond hair was combed neatly back, longer on top than around the sides. A short, manicured shadow of facial hair lent his face a certain dignity. He watched her enter, a skepticism written on his face that made Calla want to hide, but also a curiosity that drew her sight to him. An overwhelming urge to befriend him took over but she had other things to think about.

Everyone was silent as Calla and Peter stepped to the foot of the staircase.

Heavy footsteps fell as someone descended the stairs above. Calla thought her heart couldn't beat any harder; that she couldn't be more afraid of what was coming. Hope and despair both kindled flames in her heart, one white and one black.

The creature that stepped onto the landing was the most magnificent beast Calla had ever seen. Clearly masculine, he was tall with the body of a man, wearing a finely tailored shirt, vest, and jacket embroidered with gold thread. Tightly fitted black trousers were tucked into tall black leather boots that reached his knees. Two enormous wings towered from his back, the dappled feathers black, white, and gray.

But his face was what made Calla take a staggering step forward, catching his vibrantly green eyes. A man's eyes, despite being surrounded by black and white feathers. The entire top of his head was feathered thus, and on top were two feathered tufts like horns. But he had the nose and mouth and cheeks of a man, flesh mostly, but feathers crept up his neck and covered most of his jaw line, but not his chin.

The Strix Lord Aneurin, King of Lorana Vale. And he just stood there, looking at them.

The man on the stairs spoke first. "Lord Aneurin Roran welcomes you to his home. What business do you have with the king?"

Peter looked to his daughter, but her gaze was fixed on the creature. He cleared his throat and began his plea. "My name is Peter Renaud. My daughter, Calla, has been chosen by one of the Twelve. For twenty years I have kept her safe, but the magic of the destiny she will achieve if she makes it to her twenty-fifth birthday has grown too potent. She is no longer safe in Senden's Branch. She was followed home by a man who threatened to violate her, not just for the ambrosia in her blood, but her beauty as well."

"She is an Ambrosius," Lord Aneurin said.

Calla's eyes widened at the softness of his voice. How could a lord as callous as he was rumored to be sound so gentle?

Peter nodded. "Yes. The power in her blood will grow more

attractive as she ages to those who are willing to kill for it. Until it is fully absorbed, she is in mortal peril."

Lord Aneurin said nothing. The man on the stairs said nothing. The chamber fell silent, but Calla's heart beat fast.

Peter fell to his knees. "Please, my lord king. Keep her here, behind your gates, behind your soldiers. Defend her and keep her safe until she is free to claim her destiny."

Lord Aneurin shifted his gaze from father to daughter. Calla's mouth parted when his eyes met hers. Again, silence reigned as they took the measure of each other while she silently pleaded, and he silently considered.

She broke first. "I will not trouble you, my lord. I don't have many skills, but I can keep out of the way. I've hidden for most of my life. A home so vast as this shouldn't be difficult to hide in."

Lord Aneurin's wings flared with a flutter of feathers, and the man on the stairs looked at him. With a trill, the Strix Lord turned away and retreated up the stairs.

The man on the stairs raised his eyebrows and exhaled through his nose before he descended the stairs. "Your plea has been heard, Mister Renaud. She may stay until her twenty-fifth birthday, as you desired. But you may not return here. You may not write to her. No one must know she is here."

Peter's face fell as Calla shook her head. "No, Papa," she said. "I can't last five years without you."

"You must, Calla lily. I will be fine." He turned to the man. "Will *you* write to me occasionally to let me know how she fares? Just that she is safe, if she is happy? I will not respond, I swear it."

The man clasped his hands behind his back. "I will, Mister Renaud. Now say your goodbyes."

The rest of the staff turned away to resume their duties, leaving the room empty save for Calla, Peter, and the head of staff.

Tears dripped down Calla's face as she embraced her father. "I'm afraid," she whispered.

"Lord Aneurin will protect you. Do not fear him," Peter replied into her ear.

"I am not afraid of him. This is a grand house, but it is still a prison. And what if I cannot trust the obedience of the staff?"

Peter kissed her hair. "I know, my girl. But it's just a few years, and then you'll be free. Stay strong for me." He kissed her forehead, then her cheek. "I love you, Calla lily. I always have, and I always will. Especially now that I'm not feeding two, I can afford to eat more so I'll live longer."

Calla laughed incredulously as he released her. "I love you Papa. Use your new wealth to buy meat every once in a while. Would do you good."

Peter smiled. "Aye, a fine marbled steak would fortify me."

The blond man cleared his throat. "It's time, Miss Renaud."

Calla kissed her father one more time. "You're free now, Papa. Don't worry about me. I'll be brave."

Peter Renaud smiled. He was still smiling when he left the house. Whatever happened to him now was his own fate, even if it wasn't as grand as Calla's would be.

"My name is Godfrey Fontaine," the man said to her as her father left. "I am the steward of this household. I oversee things, and I am the point of contact between the staff and His Grace. I will serve in that capacity for you as well. If there is something you need to communicate with him, tell me and I will deliver the message. Follow me."

Calla nodded and allowed him to lead her through the palace. Glowing sconces illuminated even the innermost halls, and there were vases on every table and cart they passed. But no flowers. No fern or ficus added any greenery to the corridors and vast, finely furnished rooms he led her through.

"Is there no garden?" Calla asked.

"Of course there are gardens. Behind the house. His Lordship will show them to you. You will bathe and allow Delilah to dress you, and then he will meet with you. He won't say much, but he would take the measure of you. You may tell him of any questions or concerns, and he will send me with his responses."

"Delilah?"

"The servant I have assigned to you."

A servant assigned to her? Calla couldn't imagine what that would feel like, to be attended to and waited upon. And it was curious that Lord Aneurin wouldn't speak to her himself. Did the owl-man consider himself too good to speak to peasants like the Renauds? She figured she was lucky he'd said as much to them as he did instead of speaking through his steward.

"Is he...kind?" she asked tentatively.

Godfrey took a deep breath. "He is noble. Before he conquered time, he was kind and brutal alike. He has a code that has sustained him for five hundred thirty-one years. He will not be *intentionally* cruel to you, but you may find your interactions with him rather one-sided if you have any at all beyond the one you will have today. Has this tour given you an idea of the layout of the palace?"

Calla realized she hadn't been paying much attention beyond admiring the rich tapestries and fine art hanging on the walls, the gold-trimmed bannisters, the perfect orderliness of the place. "I'm sorry, Mister Fontaine. But if I'm allowed to look around, I'll learn. I—"

She swallowed the lump in her throat.

"I haven't been free to wander someplace new. Not for my entire life. I'd like to wander. None of the staff will try to drain me, right?"

Godfrey halted in his tracks and looked at her. "Of course not, Miss Renaud. None of us will ever give any inkling that we intend to do you harm. And you may call me Godfrey. I will be spending the most time with you of all of us here."

She smiled weakly and they resumed their tour. He led her back an alternate way to a narrow hallway that let out under the staircase. Up the stairs they went, all the way to the fourth floor.

"Lord Aneurin's rooms are on the direct opposite side of the house, on this floor. You may *wander* near his suite, but do not disturb him. He won't answer you and you will risk his displeasure. If you see him in the hall, you may greet him but do not detain him, and *never* touch him."

Calla nodded. "I wouldn't presume to touch a king, even one who does not rule."

Godfrey looked at her askance. "Do not criticize him for his absence. There are reasons for it. We do the best we can."

He stopped before a door with the head of a lion emblazoned in gold on it. "Welcome to your room."

Calla's jaw went slack as she ventured into the place she'd sleep for the next *five years*. The bed was enormous, and she could tell from the puffiness of the blanket on top that it was comfortable. She'd been sleeping on a straw pallet her whole life, and now she had a *bed*. Four posters supported a white canopy and draping curtains. There was a white vanity with a matching, cream-cushioned bench. An armchair, a fireplace, three end tables, and a wardrobe—all finely crafted and painted. A broad window stretched along the far wall with gauzy white curtains and goldenrod drapes. A tapestry draped from another wall. The image upon it was a door illuminated from beyond by a rose-colored light.

Calla had never imagined the luxury of such a room.

"I…I expected to be put in a closet or something," she breathed, running her hand along the blanket on the bed. "This is too fine for someone like me."

Godfrey chuckled. "You are our first guest in hundreds of years, Miss Renaud. We would put our lord to shame if we offered anything but the finest. My room is on the second floor. It has a fox on the door. If you need assistance in the night, come and I will help you. Do not worry about waking me."

She blushed nervously. "I wouldn't dare to disturb anyone. I meant what I said. I'll keep mostly to myself. Is there…are there things to do here?"

Godfrey nodded. "Anything you'd like can be obtained, though we have a vast library and a chess board. I can play with you if you'd like, though I am busy, and we'd have to schedule it in advance. We have several instruments, though they may require tuning. If that is the case, let me know. And there are the gardens. You are permitted to go anywhere as long as you don't cross the wall that borders the property."

He paused then realized something strange. "You have no bag with you. Shall we send for your things?"

Her blush deepened. The formality and consideration with which Godfrey had treated her thus far was better than she imagined ever being treated by a stranger. "I don't have any belongings. All I have is what you see."

Godfrey's eyes widened. "Miss Renaud—"

"—My father is a good man. Do not judge him. It's my fault we were forced to live in poverty. It's just the way for families with an Ambrosius. *My* fault. Not his."

Godfrey pursed his lips and gave her a look that scolded her for lashing out. "I was not judging your father. I just worry you're going to be too proud to accept it when we remedy your lack of a suitable wardrobe."

She blinked at him. "What do you mean 'remedy' it?"

Godfrey laughed. "Oh, Miss Renaud. You are the guest of the King of Lorana Vale. You must look the part, and you will be free to take everything with you when you go."

Calla set her jaw. "I'm not too proud to accept that. But you must let me be of use."

The steward waved his hand. "If you think of a way you can serve, let me know. But we are full up on staff here."

A pretty young woman with blond hair and brown eyes entered the room. Her apron was clean and pressed, her hair arranged in a bun on top of her head. "Hello, Miss Renaud. My name is Delilah. I will clean your room and help you dress and bathe. If you fall ill and want to take your supper in your room, I will fetch it for you. I will hem your clothes and repair your shoes. I am here to serve you."

Calla staggered backward until she was sitting on the edge of the bed. She felt like she couldn't move, could barely breathe. What if this was a trick to punish her for her audacity to ask Lord Aneurin for help?

"Mister Fontaine, you must know that I did not come here to be waited upon. I will work for my stay, I will sleep in the kitchen, I don't care."

Godfrey opened his mouth as if to speak and so did Delilah. But Calla pressed on.

"All I want is to be protected from harm and enough food to eat to keep me strong and alive."

Godfrey gave her another stern look. "We know, Miss Renaud. But you were brave in coming here, and it is His Lordship's pleasure that you are treated with the same respect as we give him."

Calla shook her head. "How do you know that? Because he made those sounds?"

Delilah stepped forward, her hands clasped in front of her. "Because he said you are to stay with that sound, Miss Renaud. After so long, we know the king well, and we can anticipate his whims. He's already waiting on the stairs. We must be quick."

Godfrey nodded, smiling slightly. "I'll leave you to it. After your appointment with Lord Aneurin, you will dine with him and then the evening is yours. Delilah will help you turn down for the night at nine, but you may stay up as long as you wish."

With that final word, Godfrey left and Calla was pulled into the bathroom to be bathed and prepped for her first real encounter with Lord Aneurin.

Chapter Four

Calla peered at Lord Aneurin who stood in a ray of light from the window high on the wall above the front door. He watched her as she stood before him in a borrowed lavender-colored dress, rubbing one arm with her opposite hand.

When their gazes met, sorrow washed over her. Such sad green eyes. Sadder even than she imagined hers might be. A reclusive king, a mysterious lord… he must have been as lonely as she was.

Wordlessly he turned away, leading her out of the front of the building. The breeze ruffled through the feathers of his wings, and she watched the dance of shades of black and white as it did. Around the palace all the way to a vibrant, bursting garden with flowers of every kind and hue, and the whole time, he said nothing.

Through the flowers they walked, up a hill to a bench that

looked over the land to the east. About halfway to the horizon, she spotted a wall, just beyond a wide strip of forest. The border of the palace grounds.

"I will not harm you," Lord Aneurin said quietly. "I have no desire to drink your blood and my staff are loyal and will obey my command to protect you. You are safe here, so long as you keep your distance and respect the rules." His voice was just as gentle as it was in the house.

"I will, my lord. Your Majesty? I don't know what to call you."

A sharp exhalation from his nose, and he said, "'My lord' is fine."

Calla looked around, back at the manor which seemed too far away. "Godfrey told me about the library, I'll likely spend a lot of time there, if that's okay. He said you have instruments, but I can't play. Could never afford a tutor I could trust. But I noticed there are no flowers anywhere in the house. Why?"

Lord Aneurin looked to the east and said *nothing*.

She tried again. "If I'm going to be here for so long, I'd like to see some flowers. Perhaps I can try my hand at flower arranging, and then after I find my destiny I'll become a *florist*. A safe, quiet life. I would just need a steady supply of fresh flowers of all sorts, some ribbon and vases to put them in. I think that's all you need to become a florist. I've always been too poor to be able to buy flowers."

With a turn of her head, she watched Lord Aneurin, wondering if her rambling was annoying him. The corners of his lips twitched. He flashed her a glance and gave her a nod. Then he turned and walked away.

Remembering she was to dine with him, she followed him back to the manor and into the dining room, where a simple meal was already served. She sat at one end of the table, he on the other. And they ate in silence.

When she woke the next morning, Delilah was already there, sliding dresses into her wardrobe.

"I have a small frame," Calla said from the bed. "And no one took my measurements. But maybe that's for the best. I ate more last night than I've eaten in the last three weeks combined."

Delilah glanced over her shoulder. "These are for you to borrow until we can have new ones made. They were the queen's." She shuddered. "Not Her Ladyship, Lady Eugenia, may her soul rest. But Lord Aneurin's mother. She was slight, like you. They are a bit old-fashioned, but no one will see you in them except us, who remember what clothes are supposed to look like."

Suspicious of Delilah's nervous tone, Calla murmured her thanks and rose from the bed. "I like the pink one. It's not garish like I always imagined pink dresses would be."

The servant pulled out the dress in question and looked at it. "It is a delicate color. I remember once, there was a party and three courtiers wore bright pink, thinking they should because it was a spring party. When the queen showed up in this..." She laughed and moved closer to Calla. "Everyone instantly compared her dress to the ugly ones. The poor girls fled the party in shame. This was before Lord Aneurin was born, you see."

Calla brightened. "Well then maybe he hasn't seen this dress worn before. Something new for him to look at since he's been cooped up in this castle for who knows how long."

Delilah smiled and helped her dress. She fixed Calla's long, dark hair to be swept to the side and knotted at the nape.

There was a box on the vanity. When she opened it, Calla

was surprised to find several simple gold chains with even simpler pendants. Opal, emerald, even a diamond. "I've never worn jewelry," Calla said. "I can't borrow this, it's too fine."

Delilah shook her head. "Those aren't to borrow. They're for you to keep. There's no use for them here. Who would wear them?"

"I can't accept," Calla protested.

"Ignore His Majesty's wishes at your peril, Miss Renaud."

Grimacing, Calla selected the opal necklace and fastened it around her neck. The reflection in the mirror didn't look like herself. It looked…like she was someone. For most of her life, she'd assumed her interests and desires and personality would magically bloom at midnight on her twenty-fifth birthday, like magic. She had no conscious concept of who she was besides poor and hunted.

The only things she'd ever relied on were her love for her father and her love of books. The only sources of what meager education she had. It was never safe enough for her to go to school, but at least Senden's Branch had a library. A rarity in the Vale.

"Time for breakfast, Miss Renaud. Lord Aneurin is already there. He will wait for you to arrive before he begins to eat," Delilah pressed, opening the door to the bedroom.

Calla took one last curious look in the mirror before jumping up and following her servant to the dining room.

Lord Aneurin sat at the end of the table. One arm rested on the tablecloth while his hand fiddled with the spoon in the sugar bowl. He was *bored*, and Calla could tell. But when she entered, he sat up a little straighter and immediately began ladling a serving of porridge into his bowl.

"Does my lord not eat pastries?" Calla asked as she took her seat. "I'd have thought an ancient king would be far more indulgent."

Godfrey, who stood by the door eyeing her peculiarly, said, "After five hundred years, Miss Renaud, you learn to eat to live, not to live to eat."

She chuckled and shrugged. "Oh, I'm used to eating simple fare, Mister Fontaine. Oats are nearly all we could afford most of the time. I only ate vegetables on Tuesdays and Thursdays, and fruit only every other Sunday. Meat was once a month. It was porridge, porridge, porridge all the time for twenty years."

As she spoke, Lord Aneurin watched her. He didn't begin to eat until she put the first spoonful into her mouth.

What she didn't say was that she did have one indulgence. Sweetened tea with milk. But when the tea was poured into her cup, there was no milk, and Lord Aneurin took no sugar in his own, so she drank it black and bitter.

After breakfast, Lord Aneurin stood up and left. Calla looked at Godfrey who stood with his hands behind his back, saying nothing. When she left the dining room, he followed. She wandered from room to room with the steward as her shadow. In the corridor before the sunroom, she whirled on him.

"I thought you were busy, Mr. Fontaine. Am I to be kept under guard?"

Godfrey shot her a withering glance and gestured to the door to the sunroom. "If you please, Miss Renaud."

She relaxed her clenched fists and pushed through the door.

Inside the sunroom were wicker chairs and sofas. Tables with glass tops. A shelf with a number of books and pamphlets on it. A cart with wine and glasses and several little pastries and fruits. But that wasn't what caught Calla's attention. In the middle of the room, before the great glass wall that overlooked the garden and distant forest, was a long table. And on it were hundreds of flowers. A rainbow of color. Bunches of baby's breath and ferns and reeds. Dozens of vases of every size and shape and spools and spools of ribbon. There were even charms attached to delicate wires.

Calla spun around to face Godfrey. "He actually listened to what I said," she whispered. "I was joking! Well, not really, but I didn't think he'd go through all this trouble."

"No trouble at all, Miss Renaud. Please, enjoy yourself." He turned and left her alone in the sunroom.

Calla slowly approached the table. She picked up a blue rose and sniffed it. It still smelt of dew. She set it back on the table and picked up a lily. She had just the idea.

She worked for a while, experimenting with different colors and flowers until she felt *a presence* enter the room. Vibrations on her back set her heart racing and she immediately spun around.

Lord Aneurin stood in the doorway, his hands in his pockets. He didn't look like a king. He looked like a shy bird, but also not a bird because of the cut of his jaw and his gentle mouth.

"Hello, my lord. Would you like to see what I'm working on?"

The Strix Lord hesitated but took a few tentative steps into the room. The closer he drew, the more confident his gait became until he stood at the end of the table. Still quite a distance from her, but close enough to see her hands.

"I have never done this before, and I have no eye for, you know, art since I have never seen any. Except the art here, but I haven't taken a closer look yet. But to *me*, at least, I think these colors look nice together."

She gestured at the white vase with yellow lilies interspersed with spires of blue delphiniums.

Lord Aneurin tilted his head, and the movement sent a shiver of self-consciousness down Calla's spine.

"Well, the lilies are the focal point. Since they're so bright. But I thought the delicacy of the blue ones would sort of serve as a contrast. And then the green fern leaves are just to bring some diversity to it all. I don't know. Maybe I should take them out." She reached for the closest one, but a low trill sounded from the lord of the house.

She turned sharply to face him, her hand freezing midair. "Does that mean no?"

He met her gaze and gave a single shake of his head. When she smiled, he turned away and briskly left the room.

Calla didn't see him at all the rest of the day.

Chapter Five

The next day, Godfrey was strangely quiet. The stillness of the house was even more pronounced as he said nothing at all to her. At breakfast, Lord Aneurin ate and left. He came to see her in the sunroom, but he didn't draw close. He left as soon as she turned around to face him.

The same the next day.

And the next.

She couldn't bear the silence. Instead of going to breakfast, she penned a letter to her father.

Papa,

I wish you were here with me. King Aneurin and his staff are honorable and hard-working and nothing but polite when they talk to me. But I am an outsider here. Talking to me seems distasteful to them because they so rarely do it. Even Godfrey, the head of staff, treats me with a polite contempt. I do not think they want me here. The king himself does not seem to resent my presence, but he spends no more than twenty minutes a day with me. Most days, anyway.

I don't know if they'll let me send this to you. But I miss you and I love you. I'm just finding it so hard to be brave.

Love,

Calla Lily

Sighing and full of dread, Calla folded the note and went in search of Godfrey.

She found him in the study overseeing the polishing of a tea set that must have been as old as Lord Aneurin was. "Mr. Fontaine?"

Godfrey turned to look at her. "Good morning, Miss Renaud."

No inquiry about her health or state of mind. No comment about the weather or her dress or the letter in her hands. Nothing at all.

"I know you said I cannot write to my father, but could you please let me just this once? I—I just need someone to hear my thoughts. It's been days since anyone has had a conversation with me. Please."

Godfrey didn't even turn to face her when he said, "I'm afraid that isn't possible."

Anguish crumpled Calla's expression as if her features were made of tissue. "Please, just this once. I swear I'll never ask again."

Godfrey looked at her askance. "No, Miss Renaud."

With a frustrated groan, Calla whipped around to try going above the steward's head. She wasn't optimistic about her chances of finding Lord Aneurin since she missed breakfast, but he was in the sunroom. His pale, elegant fingers brushed the various ribbons on the table, almost as if he were waiting for her.

"Your Majesty," she said as she entered the room.

Lord Aneurin's wings flared as he looked up at her.

She held the letter out to him. "I want my father to read this. He is not an impulsive man, but he is the only one in the world who cares about me and I want him to know my thoughts because no one here will hear them, much less heed them. If you are as noble as Mr. Fontaine said you are, please find a way. Please...please allow it."

The king took the letter from Calla's hands, stepping backward when their fingers brushed together. He read the letter, his eyes narrowing. Pursing his lips, he folded the letter back up and shook his head as he offered it back to her.

Calla's heart sank. "Please, my lord. I've never gone so long without a conversation. My whole life, I at least had my father to talk to. But here...here, I have no one."

Lord Aneurin took a deep breath, shook his head again, and left the room.

Calla collapsed to her knees and wept. No one entered the sunroom all day, even as her crying turned to sobs that no doubt could be heard throughout the first floor of the palace.

She didn't bother to wash her face before dinner, allowing her teary red eyes to speak for her as she picked at her meat pie. When the first glass of wine was poured, she looked at it disdainfully. It offended her that a luxury indulgence such as wine would be offered to her on a day spent in so much misery, as if their cruelty could be forgiven.

"Please, my lord. Have Godfrey send my letter with his own. That's all I ask," she begged again.

Lord Aneurin dropped his fork on his plate and left the room.

But Calla had no more tears to cry.

At breakfast, Calla said, "If someone doesn't talk to me, I'm going to die."

Lord Aneurin, as usual, said nothing.

In the sunroom, Calla did not expect him to come, figuring she'd annoyed him enough with her request. But he did. He stood beside the table watching her arrange a tableau of purple and blue flowers.

"One time, my father brought me black tulips from the market," she said. She smiled sadly. "They were so beautiful. The way the petals contrasted with the gold ribbon used to tie them…it was like magic. When we think of beauty, sometimes we think of red roses or doves or the sunrise or a pretty girl. Silk and silver, elegance and sophistication. But beauty can be dark too. There are many forms of beauty." She sighed. "Only Della Ros knows how many forms there are."

Lifting her head to look at him, she realized he'd moved from his place at the end of the table. Now, he was right beside her, studying her face with an intelligent shrewdness that made her blood heat.

"Please, my lord," she whispered. "Let me send a letter to my father. Or let him send just one to me. Even one sentence. Or have Godfrey relay the message to him and bring me back his response. Anything. Please. *Please, my lord.*" She wiped a tear away as he stared at her.

Aneurin's eyes softened for a moment. His hands twitched at his sides.

But without a word, he turned and left.

Calla ran to her room and threw her old cloak around her shoulders and ran for the wall around the property. Behind her, she heard the shriek of Lord Aneurin's owl-call. She looked over her shoulder and spotted his tall wings on the veranda, pacing. Again, he shrieked. She ran and she ran, but at the wall, she teetered as she stopped abruptly instead of vaulting over it, almost falling over. She turned again to look, but Lord Aneurin was gone from her view.

The loneliness was so pungent in her chest after not hearing another voice for days. Before her twentieth birthday, she always had her father, and when he was at his shop, she could sit by the door and listen for passing townsfolk as they bantered about their day. She'd sit there weeping with her hand on the door, praying her scent didn't drift through the cracks.

She couldn't go back to that life. At least here, she could go outside. She sat on the ground and leaned against the wall, watching the clouds. She'd never had much opportunity to look at clouds, and she took great joy in observing the different forms they took from day to day.

She sat there until Lord Aneurin swooped down, landing on the ground after flying to her. He stood before her, his hands at his sides. She just looked at him. "I need someone to talk to," she said. "Or if you won't speak, just…sit with me. If not you, then Godfrey or anyone who has the time to spare. And if no one has the time to spare, put me to work with them so I can at least *be* around someone. Anyone."

Lord Aneurin said nothing.

"Please," she croaked, her voice hoarse from trying not to cry.

He said nothing but offered his hand.

"Godfrey said I'm not to touch you," she said.

Lord Aneurin looked over his shoulder and shrugged, offering his hand again. Then he gifted her with four words.

"It'll be our secret."

She looked between the set of his jaw and his offered hand. Gingerly, like she was afraid he was going to bite her, she slid her hand into his. Her eyes widened when she found it was warm. He pulled her to her feet and then dropped her hand and turned away, walking back to the palace.

"Certain I will follow you?" she called after him.

He stopped and looked over his shoulder and trilled a warning.

Resigned, Calla trudged after him.

Aneurin

"You will speak to her," Aneurin told his steward as he helped him undress for bed.

Godfrey grimaced and folded the king's clothes over his arm to take to be laundered. "She isn't one of us. Making her comfortable here could put her in danger. She has not yet asked about the nature of the curse."

Aneurin rolled his eyes. "She's never had anyone to talk to besides her father. I allowed her to stay to protect her from the world's cruelty toward Ambrosius. Including the risk she is to herself if her isolation gets the best of her. I do not worry the curse will take her if she's friends with you. Only with me."

Godfrey hummed. "I suppose you're right. She's never had anyone she can trust, besides her father. I do understand why she wanted to write to him."

Aneurin tilted his head and untied his cravat. "For some

people, having a devoted father is enough."

With a nod, Godfrey took the fabric from him. "But you don't think it's enough for her, not when she cannot speak to him."

The king spread his arms to allow Godfrey to unbutton the fastenings of his vest and shirt so he could pull them off. "You will befriend her. Prove to her she can trust you. Be for her what you are to the rest of the staff."

"Yes, my lord." He moved toward the door as Aneurin pulled on his sleep pants. He hesitated. "Your Majesty, I don't believe a father is all a person needs. Not for an Ambrosius and not in a place like the Vale. Isolation means death."

Aneurin exhaled sharply through his nose. "For a woman whose hope is louder than her voice, you're right. But you and I both know that the opposite is true for me."

Chapter Six

Calla

When Lord Aneurin returned to the breakfast table two weeks later, he seemed more at ease. He gestured for her to sit closer to him at the table, the seat nearest his instead of at the opposite end. He still didn't speak to her, but it was better to be within a couple feet of another person, bird or not.

Calla had begun to work in the garden in his absence. A space in the garden was allotted to her for whatever bushes and blooms she wanted. She kept it wild, not as cultivated as the rest of the garden. She decided that next year, she'd ask Lord Aneurin for a bench so she could sit and enjoy the blooms she worked so hard on.

She spent all day in the garden preparing her plants for the heat wave an elder from Senden's Branch sent word about. Sunburnt and aching, she picked at her dinner, too tired to eat.

Godfrey said, "Miss Renaud, if you don't eat, you will fall asleep before dark."

She laughed and pointed at him. "If I eat I'll fall asleep here at the table, Godfrey. If I hope to make it to my room, I'll just stick to water."

Godfrey chuckled. "Very well, Miss Renaud. If His Lordship has no objections, I'll see to it tomorrow's breakfast is a heartier meal than you're used to so you can rebuild your strength."

Calla smiled.

When she turned to look at Lord Aneurin, she found he was staring at her. "Am I a mouse, my lord? You look like you're going to eat me."

His fork was in his hands, lifted as if he were in the middle of taking a bite, but he was frozen. His avian face, lined with those beautiful feathers, screwed up with something akin to fright when she'd met his gaze. With a clatter, he dropped his fork on the plate and lurched to his feet. At over six feet tall, he towered over the table and Calla felt the first twinge of fear. She'd almost forgotten what it felt like. "I do not eat mice for sustenance," he said.

Calla brushed her hair at her vanity. The only light was from the small oil lamp on her bedside table which cast an intimate glow to the room that somehow made her feel even lonelier.

She'd sent Delilah away hours ago—as soon as she was in her nightgown. It was her time of the month and she didn't want to burden anyone with her melancholy. Since she'd arrived at the palace in April, she'd become reclusive every month like clockwork. Even Lord Aneurin seemed to sense it, standing farther away when her mood was not right for company.

It was strange to her that during her menses she would long

to seek people out, rather than huddled in fear in her wardrobe, hoping the scent of her blood didn't leave the single bedroom she shared with her father. It vexed her that she could not make up her mind, though she knew it was only because of the twenty years she'd spent alone.

Movement in the mirror's reflection caught her eye. Far behind her, the light coming from under the door revealed a pacing shadow. She heard no footsteps, but someone disturbed the lamplight from the hallway beyond her bedroom door.

Calla set the brush down on the vanity and slowly padded to the door. She rested her head against it, ear pressed against the painted wood, and listened.

Low owl-like trills sounded as Lord Aneurin sighed. Another trill, another sigh. More pacing. She could hear the footsteps now. She wanted to open the door to ask him what he wanted, but she didn't.

It would scare him away. So, she just listened.

The pacing and the trilling and the sighing continued until finally, he groaned, and she heard his footsteps recede in the direction of his own chambers.

The next day, he stood a little closer to her at the arranging table. But when she turned to him, he fled.

And every night, he'd return to her door. They never spoke. He never knocked. But she took to sleeping on the floor by the door just in case. It was a secret dance, and she had no idea if he even knew he had a partner.

Chapter Seven

Aneurin

"Is she sleeping all right?" Lord Aneurin asked his steward as he helped him dress. "She has seemed tired."

Godfrey fastened the buttons of the doublet that allowed the garment to accommodate the massive wings on Aneurin's back. "No. She's been sleeping on the floor for the last three weeks."

Aneurin whipped around to face him. "Why?"

Godfrey shrugged. "I have no idea. But every morning Delilah has to step over her because she's on the floor with a blanket and pillow, her face next to the crack below the door."

Aneurin's face fell. "Ensure she's comfortable. It's not for us to question her eccentricities. Being an impoverished Ambrosius cannot be easy."

"As you say, my lord."

After Godfrey went to bed that night, Aneurin returned to Calla's room. Now that he knew she was aware of his nightly visits, he couldn't bring himself to allow his shadow to cross the door. Far too dangerous. So he sat on the floor, his head against the wall.

Knowing she was inches away was enough for him. It had to be enough. If it wasn't, she was in mortal danger.

He did not return to her room again.

Chapter Eight

Calla

Two weeks before her twenty-first birthday, Calla went to bed in a *rotten* mood. All day she'd stewed as Lord Aneurin refused to say anything to her yet again. Almost a year, and he'd said nothing to her. Nothing at all besides that one sentence about mice. Godfrey spoke to her, but only terse sentences apart from random quips, but each joke made her hungry for more. Everyone, *everyone* in the house kept her at a distance.

But the way Lord Aneurin stared at her was really starting to piss her off. He wouldn't even speak to Godfrey when she was in the room. And he'd stopped visiting her door at night. They'd never spoken, never acknowledged it, but he'd grown bored of it and had stopped and that little intimacy she'd grown to rely on was *gone*.

She tore herself out of her bed and wrapped a thick fur-lined robe around herself. Not caring how she looked, she stalked the hallway to Lord Aneurin's room, her vision red, her ears steaming hot.

With clenched fists, she disregarded every warning Godfrey had ever given her. She pounded on Lord Aneurin's door. "A year," she shouted. "I've been here almost a fucking *year* and you won't talk to me! Why am I being punished?"

To her surprise, he opened the door. Still dressed in his fine embroidered doublet, even still wearing his belt. The only thing different about him was he was barefoot.

And yet he didn't say anything.

Calla clenched her fists again, itching to hit him. Just to get *some* reaction out of him.

"Your servants speak to me. Sometimes. They're very kind, but you are a *monster*."

He looked away but returned his gaze back to hers just as quick.

"Am I not even a person to you that you won't even address your staff in my presence? Am I *unfit* to hear your voice, *Your Majesty*?"

Lord Aneurin tilted his head, the way a bird does. He said in a low voice, "I find your silent company sustenance enough. But if you would prefer I not offer you mine, I will not."

Calla's lip curled and she threw a punch straight for his face, but he caught her hand. He held it, inches from her target, and their gazes met.

Her mouth fell open. So did his. As his eyes went wide, he dropped her hand and slammed the door in her face.

Calla gasped and fell against the door, sliding to the floor as she leaned against it. And she could hear him do the same on the other side.

She slept all night at the door of the king's chambers. When Godfrey found her in the morning, he scowled and lifted her to her feet. "I told you not to disturb him," he growled in her ear as he pulled her to her room. He threw her into her chamber. "Stay here until I come for you."

He returned an hour later, calmer and quieter. She should have known then that something was wrong. He said only, "You must not trouble him, Miss Renaud. He *needs* you to be stoic about this. If you're not..." he trailed off. "Just don't do that again."

For fifty days Lord Aneurin ignored her. No matter how she railed at Godfrey, no matter how she wept as loneliness crushed her heart, the king did not return to pace in front of her door.

Desperate and pale after weeks of biding her time, Calla waited for Godfrey to go to bed. She'd rather die than be so isolated and she had to speak to the lord of the house, to get him to understand.

The corridor was dark, the oil lamps turned low for the night. On silent feet she padded to Lord Aneurin's room. She put her hand on his door, her whole body pressing up against it. "I much desire your silent company," she said softly. "If that's all you can give me, I gladly accept."

The next day, he appeared at her side as she arranged flowers. He picked up a blue rose and handed it to her. When she turned to look at him, plucking it from his grasp, he put a finger to his lips. She smiled.

Every time he entered the room, Calla knew. Aware of his presence, like a silent hum only she could hear. Some days he would just watch her arrange flowers, but other times he handed her a marigold or a rose or a spray of baby's breath. The moment she said something, however, he fled with a flutter of the feathers that covered his body.

He never spoke, he never touched her, always keeping his distance. But he was there, silent and watching. Always watching, though his gaze turned away when she looked back.

Calla lost track of the days she spent at the palace. Her relationships with Godfrey and Delilah developed, but still, her loneliness grew as well. Every ounce of intuition in her body urged her not to get her hopes up. The steward grew more tense with her, coming to see her every morning and telling her to mind her manners and remember the rules, even when she hadn't broken any. Delilah stopped encouraging her to look nice, often tying her hair back into austere knots and braids instead of letting it flow around her shoulders.

She could have endured it if only she knew what she'd done wrong.

Eighteen months together, and she could barely look at him, even when she knew he was looking at her. She wasn't afraid, she just didn't see the point. The less she thought of him as a living, breathing person, the more content she was to pretend he was a ghost.

The fire in the library's hearth flickered and crackled. She read by the light of it, peering at the pages of her book. Lord Aneurin paced the room in front of her, seemingly discomfited by something, but Calla didn't bother to ask what caused his restlessness. She was just glad he was still in there with her instead of having fled after twenty minutes like he usually did.

She watched him over her book for a while. He'd cross the room to the window and stare out of it, then look over his shoulder at her. She averted her gaze before his eyes adjusted to the light. Then he would pace again. Every few minutes, he'd sigh and trill, but he still said nothing.

An urge to comfort him grew in her heart and then, quietly

so as not to startle him, she read out loud.

"'No fair maiden, I assure you,' Calonetta jeered. 'To say I am fair is to imply that I won't gut you, and I surely will, you bastard.'

The pirate lord puffed out his chest and brandished his sword. 'I don't want to hurt you, but I will if you don't leave. This is no place for you, fair maiden or not.'"

Lord Aneurin stilled his pacing. He did not turn to her, but he cocked his head as if he were listening.

"Calonetta grimaced as she unsheathed her own sword. 'I will not flee like a coward. I will go into the depths of hell with you. If you try to go without me, I will chase you. Do not tell me how afraid or weak I am. I will prove my courage.'

Captain Bismarck lunged for her shoulder, but she parried it. 'I have more to worry about than *you*," he barked. 'Sit down or I'll tie you to the mast!'

Calonetta roared as she thrust her weapon at his neck, the tip drawing just a trickle of blood. 'I will go with you,' she panted, her eyes wild. 'For my heart will break if I allow you to go alone.'"

Lord Aneurin took a seat in an armchair across the room. The giddiness Calla felt was like an explosion of color in her heart, but she hid it by reclining on the sofa and holding the book close to her face. She read the rest of *Captain's Bounty* late into the night.

On the last page, Lord Aneurin noticed her words becoming slower as the book drooped in her hands.

"The boundless… sea… called…" she said softly, and then the book fell to her chest.

Chapter Nine

Aneurin

The Strix Lord had known the woman was going to fall asleep when she reclined, though he was surprised by how long it took.

Her voice was soft, like his, because like him she hadn't had much occasion to speak. But her voice was still harder than his was, more impatient, like she was running out of time. Perhaps she was. There are very few Ambrosius who live long, happy lives. She was doomed the moment she was born and whatever god chose her flooded her veins with ambrosia.

And that thought made Aneurin incredibly sad.

So he listened to her read, and after she fell asleep, he risked smiling. But he did not move. It was close to midnight, and the library was dark, so dark even the shadows that had danced all night on the ceiling above their heads had been swallowed by it.

But there were a few red embers in the hearth. Aneurin told himself he would wait until they went out, and then he'd find a blanket for her and leave her be.

But long past the death of the futile embers he still sat and watched her form. The moon rose and with its ascension, light came through the windows. Not much, but enough to illuminate her face.

In repose, she was even more beautiful because her face lost that desperate anguish that plagued her every day.

They were alone. He could. But Godfrey would scold him for it if he found out.

Five hundred years since his wife died, five hundred years since he'd touched a woman. Except for that infuriating moment where he had intercepted her punch. But that shock of contact had caused an ache that hadn't left him in months.

Sinking to one knee, he bent over her. He held his breath and pressed his lips against her forehead.

She stirred and Aneurin flapped his wings to throw himself back, his heart racing. But she merely rolled over and nestled her face into the back cushion of the sofa.

Relief flooded through him. She was a deeper sleeper than he thought.

A sound from the window made him turn his head, and he saw frost creeping around the bottom third of every pane. It was cold in there already, and with the fire out, it was just going to get colder.

It couldn't hurt. It was kindness, yes, and his kindness was cursed to hurt anyone whose heart was inspired by it. But she was asleep. She'd never know. *No one would know.*

But he had to be quick. The cold would wake her if he

waited any longer.

As gently as he could, the King of Lorana Vale slid his arms underneath Calla's warm frame and scooped her up. He carried her from the library and up the stairs. Slowly, so as not to wake her.

No other place to look but forward, for if he looked upon her in his arms, his heart would stir. No room for fatal mistakes.

Calla's door was shut, but not all the way. He quietly nudged it open with his foot and swept inside her room. He rested her gently on the bed, grateful Delilah had turned down the covers already.

Damn, she was still wearing her shoes. Aneurin slipped them off her stockinged feet and set them on the floor before pulling the covers over her.

His heart raced so fast, and he regretted every moment he'd spent looking at her. He shouldn't have. He shouldn't have put her at risk. But at least he'd have five hundred years to remember how kind she was to him when he was nothing more than a beast.

"Five years is not enough time with you," he whispered, leaning over her.

Her eyes snapped open, and Aneurin froze. It was impossible to move even as she reached to brush against the feathers along his jaw. Her eyes searched his, her brow furrowed as if studying something she'd never seen before.

"Do you want me to stay?" she said.

Aneurin's soul plummeted to the depths of his belly as he reached for her, his hand caressing her cheek like she caressed his.

One torturous moment later, he pulled away, his wings tensing. Something was caught in his throat and he had to swallow it before he said, "I could not ask that of you. Your destiny awaits."

Then he was gone.

Chapter Ten

Calla

Fourteen days without Lord Aneurin's presence, but Calla thought those days were more than double in number. She had an idea that he was embarrassed for confessing to enjoying her company, but she couldn't understand why. He'd been a reclusive lord for hundreds of years, and he'd spent the evening being read to by someone who felt just as alone as he did.

It was a *good* thing he was grateful. The Strix Lord would be more like a Pigeon Lord if he was such an entitled brat.

The truth was, she'd enjoyed reading to him. The companionship was pleasurable and so acutely different from the isolated silence she'd endured for twenty years.

After yet another breakfast without his magnificent wings blocking the light from the windows, Calla sighed and went to the sunroom to arrange more flowers. At the door, she collided with Godfrey. Seizing the moment, she grabbed his arm to halt his hurrying steps.

"Is Lord Aneurin all right? He didn't take breakfast again," she asked softly. "Did something happen?"

Godfrey brushed some dust off the lapels of his jacket. "His Majesty seeks solitude, Miss Renaud. He is a man of few words, but when those few fail him, he immerses himself in meditation and silence until he finds new ones."

Calla's eyes narrowed. "You call him a man, but men don't look like that. Men don't live forever, cannot reign over the land for hundreds of years. He is something else, like the rest of you. All of you have lived far too long to be human like the rest of us in Lorana Vale."

Godfrey smiled and bowed his head. "It's about time you asked about this. I congratulate you on your manners, Miss Renaud. I did think you'd bring it up far sooner." At her puzzled expression, he chuckled. "When the change first took us, King Aneurin Roran was but a man."

"A *human* man?"

The steward shrugged. "Yes, though not anymore. Now he is the first of something new, and probably the last. There are few who could love a creature such as he has become, and none should."

How callous. Unease growing in her stomach, Calla rubbed her arm. "Surely one of the women who work for him who knew him before the change could love him. He shouldn't be so alone. He's too gracious, too kind."

Eyebrows raised, he shrugged again. "The curses that plague him were born of loyalty and kindness, Miss Renaud. His wife, Eugenia, loved him well and he loved her, though she was not a gentle soul. He never once betrayed her, behaving far better than his father Octavian did before him. When Eugenia fell ill, however, she feared that after she was gone his kindness and grace would inspire someone else to replace her in his life. She cursed him and that kindness. Anyone who dared try to replace her in his life would die. To avoid such a fate, he sought out the god of beauty, Della Ros, and asked him to make him so hideous no one would ever want to be near him. Della Ros agreed to change his appearance, but in return, Aneurin must rule Lorana Vale for a thousand years. To protect us, his staff, Lord Aneurin agreed. He is not even permitted to leave the Vale. Every time he has tried, he cannot break through the invisible barrier that keeps him here inside. But Della Ros was not too cruel—he also enchanted us, his household, and blessed us with eternal youth so he would have familiar faces to spend forever with. If he rarely speaks to us, it is to keep us from loving him too well. Do not question his love. We know, for his silence proves it."

Stunned, Calla shook her head. "But…" She laughed skeptically. "But why doesn't anyone know that? He's a bird mixed up with Della Ros. All of you look like you're not older than thirty. Why is the legend of Lord Aneurin only that he is callous and cold? The village would pity him rather than fear him."

The corners of Godfrey's lips turned down. "Ah, lass. You're not listening. Lord Aneurin does not want to be beloved of his people. He keeps his distance from them, and *you*, for your protection." He patted her cheek with his hand, his green eyes sparkling. "Only a little more than three years left until you're free."

Brushing her hair out of her face, Calla sighed. "Last year I barely had a birthday. Can we, you know, do something this year for it? Let my father come, or at least…"

Godfrey folded his hands. "You want a party."

"A party!" Calla gasped, throwing her hands in the air. "I've never had a party. I want to dance, I want music." Her voice dropped low, as if she were telling a secret. "Anything so long as it's different."

Godfrey sighed.

Calla woke up every day with a curiosity that revitalized the destiny in her blood, which would surge from the moment she opened her eyes until she arrived at the breakfast table.

And then her blood slowed, and slowed, until her eyes drooped and exhaustion overwhelmed her. And the way no one spoke to her was the cause.

But despite never saying anything, Lord Aneurin's presence always filled the entire room—even when the door was behind her, she knew the moment he entered, somehow sensing him. At first, she'd reacted instantly, turning around to greet him as soon as she felt him. But eventually, she learned to resist that urge.

He never moved right away. He entered the room and watched her until she reacted. But he always seemed disappointed when she did, as if she were taking something from him by acknowledging him. It was only after his face fell that he'd move closer, coming to the table to look at the flowers, standing behind the sofa to read over her shoulder while she held a book. He watched her read or arrange flowers or plant bulbs in the garden, or strum on the harp he'd hired someone to teach her to play. But never for more than twenty minutes at a time. Inevitably, he left. Sometimes he nodded his head at her before he fled; other times he merely turned away and left the room.

Days turned into weeks. Weeks into months. And Calla worried that he wouldn't even see her on her birthday.

On the twenty-second day of April, her twenty-second birthday, Calla woke up to Godfrey staring down at her. His face was mere inches from hers.

Yelping, she reached for a pillow and slammed it into his face. The steward staggered backward, his blond hair mussed by her assault. His green eyes flared wildly. "Have you lost your fucking mind, Miss Renaud?" He patted his hair back into place.

"Have *you*?" she snarled, pulling the covers up to her chest. "Why are you watching me sleep?"

Godfrey fixed his collar and sighed. "Lord Aneurin is expecting you. He has commanded a special breakfast served and he wants you to eat it while it is still hot."

At his name, Calla thrust herself out of bed, scrambling for the wardrobe. "Where's Delilah? I need to dress."

Godfrey cleared his throat, but Calla didn't hear him. She tore through her closet, discarding every dress she found lacking.

It's all right to want to look nice. It is my birthday and I can do almost anything I want.

Even in her mind, she sounded desperate.

Godfrey cleared his throat again. Whipping her head around, Calla hissed, "*What?*"

He pointed to the foot of her bed. On the cream-colored quilt was a gray dress with black and yellow lilies expertly embroidered all over it. "One of your gifts. He would like you to wear it. For another present, after breakfast you will take a walk with him around the grounds. You may speak to him, but do not expect him to reply or answer any questions. He has sworn he will not." Godfrey hesitated. "You will be alone with him. None of us are going to accompany you. If he gives you a direction, heed it."

At first, her delight was like a ray of sunlight piercing a cloud to illuminate just one spot on the ocean of her melancholy. But the light shifted and became more ominous than blessed, and delight transformed into worry. Every time Lord Aneurin bent a little, giving her a little more attention, a little more happiness, he shut himself away for days, weeks, months. Allowing her to speak to him for however long it took to traverse the grounds was an enormous gift. One she didn't know if she could afford to accept.

"He doesn't have to do that," Calla said. "Tell him I will only go if he promises not to impose his isolation on himself again. If he doesn't promise, I don't want to eat with him and would prefer to have breakfast alone. If he's there when I come down, I will consider the promise made."

Godfrey's lips turned down and he rolled his eyes. "You ask too much of him, Miss Renaud. He has already given you more than he's given anyone else in five hundred years. If you're not careful, you will put yourself in grave danger, and I fear—" He closed his mouth, nervously swallowing the saliva pooling under his tongue. "I fear he would be wounded beyond all hope of recovery if anything were to happen to you. He would never forgive himself."

Calla considered that the curse was a matter of degree. After all, the servants clearly cared for him and it wasn't like she was in love with him. She didn't know him. He didn't know her. She couldn't imagine loving someone without being able to ask them what their favorite color was, or their favorite book.

Even those little things were too intimate. Any idea of inquiring about them must be discarded. Calla knew that. But she also knew that she would risk harm if only it would break up the tedium of her everyday life. Especially if it meant proving to Lord Aneurin that curses cannot be maintained by the dead and beauty is the most subjective quality in the world.

Deep in her heart, she suspected Della Ros knew that when he transformed Aneurin into such a majestic, devastating creature, someone was bound to find him beautiful.

"Tell him or I will not come down," Calla said.

Godfrey sighed. "Miss Renaud—"

She groaned in exasperation. "Has anyone ever even been hurt by the curse? From what you said before, Lord Aneurin went to Della Ros right after his wife died. It seems you're all afraid of something that might not be real."

An ominous shadow passed over Godfrey's face. "His Grace didn't go to the god of beauty until the power of the curse was revealed."

Calla trembled as she felt the blood drain from her face. "What happened?"

The steward scoffed, adjusting his stance as he fretted with his waistcoat. "Sarah Hanover was a scullery maid who was in love with him before Lady Eugenia died. After Her Ladyship succumbed to her illness, she snuck into his chambers. She proclaimed her love for him and asked him for just one night. That she'd never ask for anything more from him, and she would leave at first light."

Shrewdly, Calla eyed Godfrey. "He doesn't seem the type to be easily seduced."

He laughed breathlessly. "He never has been, even within the urgencies of adolescence. But his is a passionate love when it is given, and while he'd loved his wife, he was unwilling to take the chance. All he offered Sarah was his benediction, kissing her forehead and calling for the guards to escort her to the village with a purse of gold so she could start a new life doing whatever she wished."

"And then?" Calla asked, blood pounding in her ears.

Sorrow flashed in Godfrey's eyes. "She never made it. An Ambrosius fleeing a pack of ambrosia hunters stumbled upon her and the guards. Knowing it would be Lord Aneurin's will that the Ambrosius be protected, the guards tried to defend them both, but there were too many of them, and most were at the peak of their intoxication. The guards were overwhelmed. Both the Ambrosius and Sarah were lost."

Calla nodded, her eyes on the beautiful gown she was supposed to wear. Still unwilling to concede. "It could have been a fluke. She was probably young. Was Lord Aneurin handsome as a man? There were probably lots of women who loved him. Men too. He can't know that her fate was his fault."

That darkness still lingered in Godfrey's face as he cleared his throat. "He was very beautiful, Miss Renaud. If you think his heart is radiant, believe me when I tell you his visage matched. A mop of raven-black hair that curled just under his ears. Eyes the most startling shade of green. A jaw chiseled by Della Ros himself and the most elegant features you could ever imagine. A more accurate portrait of nobility and grace you couldn't find. Just like his mother. And despite his youth, his skill in battle was legendary before he'd reached his twenty-sixth year. It is not just his feathers and wings that people fear now, but the distant memory of how much blood he can spill when he is crossed."

Calla met his gaze. "So he was kind and pretty. That doesn't mean he can't have some bad luck."

"Then I will tell you about his squire," Godfrey sighed. "Young Aluard loved him fiercely, perceiving him to be a hero the likes of which we haven't seen since before the gods retreated to their hidden valleys. He wanted a piece of Annie's glory. His Grace did not try to relieve him of the notion, but instead encouraged it, impressing upon him a code of nobility strongly weighted in favor of honor and justice. Aluard would have undoubtedly been a great man had the curse allowed him to live."

Calla didn't blink.

Taking a deep breath, Godfrey continued. "As you might

have guessed, Aluard fell in battle trying to save His Grace. An enemy tried to sneak up on him from behind while he was distracted by his engagement with the ambrosia runner lord who'd been plaguing the Vale for months. Aluard jumped in front of the man's blade, taking the slash that was meant for Lord Aneurin's back."

His lips turned down in sorrow. Then he added quietly, "He was avenged. Lord Aneurin took no prisoners."

Calla nodded again, her hand drifting over the embroidered lilies. *Exquisite craftwork.* "People die in battle, Godfrey. He cannot blame himself for coincidences."

But Godfrey noticed that she didn't meet his gaze and he scoffed.

"Even so. After that, he pulled away from us, and we pulled away from him. We told him what we needed, he provided. He gave us orders, we obeyed. Other than the affairs of the Vale, he didn't speak to us much for five hundred years. Until you came."

Furious tears stung Calla's eyes. She was not convinced the curse was real. All she allowed herself was a moment to soak in her frustration before she glared at the steward. "You seem to love him. You're not dead."

He smiled with a greater benevolence than any Calla had ever seen. "Miss Renaud, I may appear to be the same age as my lord, but I love him as a son for I was there when he was born. My love has not proved to be a threat to Lady Eugenia's memory as the inspiring romance of King Aneurin's life, so I appear to be immune to the curse."

For some reason, the words riled her. "All right, let's say I fall desperately in love with him. What harm will befall me here? No one dares challenge him, his troops are young and hale thanks to the magic of Della Ros, and I certainly hope none of your staff is planning on gutting me in my sleep. Tell him to stop being dramatic and promise he won't abandon me again or *I won't come down.*"

With a shake of his head and a sneer, Godfrey said, "Very well, Miss Renaud. But you risk much by being difficult. The staff doesn't hate you now, but by upsetting him, you upset *us.*"

Regret was like ice-cold water flooding her veins as her heart sank. "I'm sorry. But you have all been under this spell for hundreds of years. I am only twenty-two. I am not used to such isolation. At least my father spoke to me every day. I...I *need* the lord of the house to acknowledge me. Otherwise I'm nothing more than a ghost."

Godfrey's eyes softened. "I wish you would be more kind to him. Consider *his* feelings. You're so worried about your isolation, you don't consider that he *is* fond of you and it pains him to be so distant from one he would call a friend were he free to do so. You do not consider that it would hurt him even worse if you too considered him a friend and your affection cost you your life."

Shame billowed in her head and mind like ink spilled into water. She *hadn't* considered that.

"I—" she took a deep shuddering breath "—I'm sorry. But while I am *not* in love with him, my heart will still break if he lures me out with bait like I'm a bear to be trapped only for him to leave me in the pit when he feels guilty for condemning me. But tell him..."

Godfrey raised his eyebrows.

Calla sighed. "Tell him I will keep my distance from him so long as he doesn't disappear again."

The tension in Godfrey's shoulders melted away. "I will do so. It is safe enough to like him, but build a cage around your affection, Miss Renaud. Do not let it grow."

Calla picked up the dress and held it to her body in front of the mirror. "Unless I grow feathers of my own, I dare say I am in no danger of falling in love with a bird."

Chapter Eleven

The unmistakable aroma of pancakes met Calla's nose as she drew near to the dining room. And bacon. And cinnamon.

She quickened her pace and slipped through the double doors leading to the expansive room. From end to end of the long mahogany table were platters and platters of food. Cinnamon loaves sliced and smeared with whipped cream, cinnamon rolls dripping with glaze, pancakes, eggs, bacon, fruit, butter, and pitchers and pitchers of grape juice.

And seated around the table was most of the staff, even a few of the soldiers from the small army Della Ros also enchanted to help Lord Aneurin protect the Vale.

Lord Aneurin stood by one of the tall windows near the enormous fireplace, gazing out on the garden. When he heard her enter, he turned to face her. His jaw tightened as he saw she was wearing the dress and her waist-long brown hair was brushed and loose over her shoulders. He lifted his chin and nodded to her, but she didn't look at him for long.

Before, they ate simple fare—porridge, sausage, sometimes fruit and toast. Eggs, if she was lucky. And it was always only the two of them, or her alone.

"Why—" she began.

An owlish trill whistled out from Lord Aneurin and Mary Milkes, the head housekeeper, stood up from her place at the table. Everyone shushed each other, eventually falling silent. The woman patted her red hair and smiled at Calla. "We're here to celebrate your birthday with you. You will receive five gifts today: four from Lord Aneurin, and one from us. The first gift is this breakfast."

A wide smile spread across Calla's face while Mary spoke, and she took a step toward the table. "I suppose this is the gift from you," she said.

Mary laughed. "Oh no, Miss Renaud. You will receive our gift last. Lord Aneurin created the menu for the breakfast. All we had to do was make it, but, well, that's our job."

As Calla approached the table, Lord Aneurin quickly beckoned her to the seat nearest him. She diverted her course immediately to go to the chair he selected. With a flourish, he pulled the chair out for her, easily pushing her in once she was seated.

She watched him as he settled into his own dining chair, carefully avoiding sitting on his wings. He reached for a steaming teapot and gestured at the teacup at her place setting.

She nodded and he poured her a cup of green tea from somewhere far away. Exotic tea was never something she'd been fortunate enough to have tasted, and she didn't know they'd had it.

The cup in her hands was delicate and lightweight, and she

worried she was going to crack it just by holding it. She sniffed at the tea, recoiling a bit from the raw, herbal scent.

Lord Aneurin smiled so briefly, she might have missed it had she not been looking at him over the rim. He plucked up a tiny pair of tongs in his elegant pale hand, the only part of him except the pit of his throat and his cheeks that she knew was unfeathered. With the tongs he picked up a sugar cube and brought it near her tea.

"If you've never had it, you might want some sugar to make it more palatable," he said softly.

"Thank you," replied Calla. "I used to take my tea sweet but Cresedan never brings milk or honey or sugar when she serves us."

Lord Aneurin's eyes snapped up to her face. The owlish trill sounded again, and Cresedan and Godfrey rose to come to him. Into Godfrey's ear, he whispered something too quiet for Calla to hear.

Godfrey nodded and stood. "My apologies, my lord. To you too, Miss Renaud. We should have thought to ask. It is our shame that our inconsideration has lasted this long."

Lord Aneurin scowled at both of his servants before settling into his meal, selecting a healthy portion of bacon and eggs which he placed on toast and ate that way.

Not two minutes later, Cresedan appeared at her side again, a hot cup of black tea lightened with cream and honey in her hand. "Forgive us, Miss Renaud. We won't forget."

"It's not that big of a deal," Calla mumbled, still holding her green tea. She looked between it and the cup of black tea. "I want both but I'm not sure in which order to drink them."

Lord Aneurin watched her as she considered. Then he reached up and tapped the far rim of the cup she held. "This one first, lest the sweetness of the other ruin your taste for less decadent pleasures." He turned back to his food.

Calla's throat went suddenly dry as she looked at the cup of green tea in her hands. For some reason, all she wanted was the *decadent pleasure* of her sweetened tea. But she took a deep breath and followed his advice.

It was good. She imagined drinking it while greeting the dawn in the garden. She knew just the spot—a small stone bench at the highest point of the property, where Lord Aneurin had taken her that first day. Where the horizon stretched into the east. The place she could pretend she could see the ocean, the place she'd always wanted to go.

When she finished her green tea, she picked up the cup of black tea.

"Hm," grunted Lord Aneurin. But he fell silent.

"What is it?" Calla asked, surprised at how much he was speaking to her. It was more than he had in the first two years combined. And her heart was *racing* with the thrill of it, drinking in the attention and conversation as if it were the last water she'd ever drink.

Lord Aneurin swallowed his sip of tea. "It is only..." His voice was low and quiet, and Calla leaned in to hear him better. His eyes darted up to her face and he leaned away. "I think before you drink your tea you should eat something. Otherwise you will fill up on *tea* and this magnificent meal will go to waste."

Calla laughed, setting her teacup down. "I don't mean for your gift to go unappreciated, my lord."

He said nothing, only watched her until she heaped her plate with pancakes and cinnamon rolls. Still he watched as she drowned the confections in syrup and whipped cream. Without a word he reached over and placed a strip of bacon on her plate.

She ignored it, choosing instead to focus on how good it felt to eat in a noisy room full of people enjoying the same bounty as her. As a poor carpenter's daughter, she'd never enjoyed a finer meal, and as an Ambrosius, she'd never had company. Her heart swelled with the sense of companionship it brought her to share it all with so many.

Calla ate quickly, eating until her stomach was full to bursting. But she left a little room for her tea, which was still *just* warm enough to drink when she finally lifted it to her lips.

It had been so long since she drank it sweet. She scarcely remembered how it tasted. The *decadent pleasure* of it coated her tongue and she sighed when she realized she was too full to drink it all.

Lord Aneurin dabbed at the corner of his mouth with a napkin before standing. He looked down at her, his wings tensing as he waited for her. To say something, to stand, she didn't know. So she did both.

"Are you sure it won't rain? It poured all night," she said as she pushed herself to her feet.

Lord Aneurin merely stepped away, heading toward the door that led down the stairs to the kitchens.

"Thank you, everyone," Calla said to the table.

"Happy birthday!" they replied, laughing as they kept eating.

She looked around, but the Strix Lord was already gone. Gathering her skirts in her hands, she ran to the stairs to follow him.

Petrichor and rose, a wall of it almost as strong as the wall of damp air, greeted her as she burst into the garden. The landscape was a sunrise of orange and yellow and pink bursts of color—roses, carnations, tulips, and marigolds. Above, the sky was blue but dark clouds blotted out the freshly risen sun.

Down the white path, Lord Aneurin waited by the moss-covered stone wall, his hands clasped behind his back. His tall, dappled wings flared and relaxed as he watched her approach. Just as she stepped beside him, he began walking.

"Godfrey said I may speak to you, but I should not expect you to answer. I don't suppose he was wrong and now that we are alone with no one to overhear, you might talk about something more substantial than food," said Calla.

To no surprise, Lord Aneurin said nothing.

Before long, he led her down the path toward the wooded area that made up the eastern border of his property, far away from the manor. She followed in silence, not knowing what she could possibly say that wouldn't require an answer. Making dull-witted observations about the likelihood of rain or the carefully tended planters of marigolds and tulips even so far from the palace, well. They weren't options worth considering.

"What's your favorite color, my Lord Aneurin? 'Naturally it is black like my heart for I deny my houseguests the least pleasure by withholding polite conversation.'" When she spoke the imagined answer from the lord of the house, she made her voice gravelly and low.

Lord Aneurin glanced at her sideways, his lips pressing together.

"No, my lord, for black isn't a color. It is either all the colors together or the absence of color. What is your favorite color? 'I am the lord here and I say it is black like my heart and like the fearful dead who have haunted me for five hundred years.'"

He gave her another glance.

"It's probably white because I imagine if you weren't too afraid to speak, you'd reveal yourself to be terribly contrary just out of boredom."

She fell silent as Lord Aneurin came to an abrupt halt. When he didn't say anything, she growled more mockery. "'My tantrums are as legendary as I am. Once, because a woman asked me a question, I cried in my bedroom *for four months*. Her audacity had to be punished.'"

Suddenly, a melodic trill sounded from Lord Aneurin as he laughed. He turned to the planter beside them and twisted the stem of a yellow marigold. He turned back to Calla and offered it to her. "Your answer, Miss Renaud."

Calla reached for the flower, but as if enchanted she noticed how his sleeve pulled up as he stretched his arm. Black feathers tapered to a cuff just after his wrist. As she took the flower from him with one hand, her other came up to stroke the feathers.

Never had she felt something quite so soft.

Her eyes flickered up to Lord Aneurin's face which remained imperious and guarded as he looked back at her, but his wings flared out, remaining extended for a long moment before they slowly began their descent back down to their resting position.

Calla's lips parted and she took a step closer to him, reaching for him, but what she'd do when she obtained whatever it was she was seeking, she didn't know.

With a feline grace, he stepped away and resumed his walk down the path.

With her cheeks burning, Calla kept her eyes on the ground and the flower in her hand as she followed behind him. Yellow. His favorite color was *yellow*. So strange for a lord whose house was shrouded in his misery.

Along the border wall, the Strix Lord continued to lead his

guest. A few times there was a rustling in the bushes just beyond. When those leaves hissed, Lord Aneurin instinctively stepped in front of her, shielding her from whatever lurked in the woods.

It was always just a critter. Squirrels, raccoons, rabbits.

"I doubt anyone suspects I'm here," Calla said after the fifth time. "Papa was going to tell everyone I was kidnapped by brigands. He practiced all night before we came here to ask you to hide me, wailing and sobbing in front of the fire until even I was almost convinced I had been taken." She laughed. "Ah, I know I'm ridiculous. But you shouldn't worry. Even if someone knew I was here, everyone in the village fears you. They wouldn't dare come."

As if summoning Della Petricha the god of rain, the sky released a torrent of silver showers.

Calla smiled and stepped into the rain, lifting her arms up to the sky. It felt so good to touch something perhaps not unexpected, but unplanned for.

A hand wrapped around her wrist and Lord Aneurin pulled her to his chest. His mighty wings extended up and folded over them, shielding them from the downpour.

"I wish *you* feared me," Lord Aneurin said quietly as his hand pressed into the small of her back. "Do not think of me, Miss Renaud."

"Fear you? You're the one who is afraid of *me*," she retorted as the hand that wasn't clenching the marigold pressed into his chest.

"Do not think of me. The reason you're here is so you don't suffer man's weakness and deep down, underneath all these hideous feathers, I am nothing but a man, Calla. Stay away."

Panic rose in her chest even as she delighted that he spoke

so many words to her at once. To Calla, his voice was like ambrosia, heady and intoxicating, even though it was rough with disuse. "Will you disappear again? Another four months hiding away from me because you think I'll die of love for you? I promise I will forget you at the stroke of midnight on my twenty-fifth birthday if you will just keep me company while I am trapped here."

Something close to rage but closer still to regret washed over his features as he held her, the corners of his mouth turned down. But Calla thought he must think he'd said too much, for he said nothing at all as he stared down at her.

As suddenly as it started, the rain ceased, and just as suddenly, Lord Aneurin released her, turning back the way they'd come.

Reeling from the wash of dizziness that overcame her when she no longer felt his arms around her, Calla held her flower to her chest as she followed.

Chapter Twelve

To Calla's surprise, Lord Aneurin did not lead her back through the kitchens. Instead, he led her to the front of the house. Taking a deep breath before her, he straightened his shoulders and folded his wings. He cleared his throat. "Close your eyes," he quietly said.

After giving him an odd look, she did.

Then came the unmistakable click of the double doors opening. Calla stepped toward them.

"Careful," he whispered. She felt him put his hands over her eyes. "Go forward. Mind the steps."

Whispers and giggles greeted her as she stepped inside the house. The intricate rug she knew was in the entry dried the soles of her shoes as the king led her inside. He guided her down the corridors, corridors she knew but couldn't quite remember with her eyes shut. Another door opened, and the familiar echo of footsteps on marble resounded all around her as she was ushered into the center of what could only be the ballroom.

"Godfrey's idea, but as Mary said, you'll receive it last. But for now, look," Lord Aneurin said, taking his hands away.

Calla's eyes flew open and she gasped. Everywhere around the room were tables covered in festive tablecloths in cornflower blue and goldenrod. Blue streamers hung from the ceiling and there were crystals in the potted fig trees around the border of the room reflecting all the light, sparkling. Tall vases of yellow lilies and blue roses stood at the ends of every table. Sofas and chaises were around the room. And there in the back, a stage for musicians.

"What?" she whispered.

The king stepped around her to stand at her side, saying nothing.

Godfrey moved forward. "His Grace has agreed to throw you a party. One which he will likely not attend himself for fear of dampening the festive mood with his presence, but he hopes you enjoy it."

Calla shot a sharp look at Lord Aneurin. "That goes against everything you've said to me. Who will attend this party?"

He frowned.

Godfrey cleared his throat. "Perhaps Miss Renaud could be grateful. His Grace has a brooch blessed by Della Ros that he would have you wear to disguise your face and enchanted perfume to disguise the scent of your ambrosia. You may borrow these things so you may enjoy the party freely, and none of the guests will recognize you."

Heat flushed Calla's cheeks. "Guests? People other than all of you? Not that I don't love your company, I am so fond of every one of you."

"They will arrive in five hours. Please follow Lord Aneurin so you may collect the brooch and the perfume, then meet Delilah in your chamber so she can get those wrinkles out of your dress and fix your hair." Godfrey smiled benevolently, but she could tell he was on edge.

Lord Aneurin turned on his heel and headed for the door. Calla stared at Godfrey who nodded his head, encouraging her to follow. She mouthed the words *thank you* and hurried after the king.

He led her up the stairs to the fourth floor, and her eyes widened with shock as he turned toward his own chamber. The racing of her heart was like a charging cavalry as he unlocked the door and opened it, guiding her inside.

The sitting room was elegant and finely furnished in gray cushioned furniture with yellow embroidered marigolds on them. A sofa, two armchairs. A low mahogany table set between them. In front of the massive fireplace, a plush black rug. On the wall hung portraits of a beautiful man with raven hair and an equally beautiful woman who was golden blond.

In a daze, Calla lurched toward the portraits hanging side by side on the far wall. Lady Eugenia's hair was piled and pinned elegantly on top of her head. The red sash she wore brought out the color in her cheeks, and Calla wondered how such a hale woman wasted away and died. But it was easy to see why Lord Aneurin had loved her. She was gorgeous—in a rigid, commanding sort of way.

Even if Calla could fall in love with a bird, now that she'd seen them, she knew that curse or no curse, she'd never live up to the standard set by such a stunning couple. If Lord Aneurin were free, any love she allowed to grow would be doomed. People who looked like *that* didn't fall in love with peasants like *her*, regardless of what prettiness she may have possessed.

As she turned to study the portrait of Aneurin Roran, she realized Godfrey was right. His beauty bathed her in grief for the loss of it to the world. It must have been obvious since he was young that he was destined for greatness. A champion of Della Ros, clearly, what with his eyes so green they seemed to glow and the line of his jaw, which was the only overtly masculine thing about him. The man in the portrait seemed to be soft and gentle, which must have come to the great surprise of his enemies as he defeated them.

The beauty of Della Ros. Undefeatable in battle.

Calla turned sharply to Lord Aneurin who studied the portraits beside her. "You were an Ambrosius. Like me."

He turned to face her, laughing softly. "Yes, but unlike you, I was a prince and kept quite safe. I never had anything to fear, and indeed I feared nothing until Ginny got sick."

There was an edge in his voice. His love for her must still burn, even after five hundred years. A love like that was destiny. It had to be.

"Was Her Ladyship an Ambrosius too?" she whispered, melancholic but she didn't know why.

Lord Aneurin tilted his head, studying the painted face of his wife. "No. She was a wealthy second daughter who dabbled in witchcraft out of boredom and to spite her parents." His voice took on that steel again. "It was her audacity that claimed my heart."

Calla nodded.

He trilled as he sighed, then offered his hand. "We will miss the reveal of your fourth gift if we don't hurry."

She stared at his fingers for a moment, then grasped them. He led her out to his private veranda that overlooked the front of his property.

Up the road, a fine carriage approached the house. Another lord? There were no more earls or dukes in the Vale. They'd abandoned it when Lord Aneurin did.

"I had the most estimable of my guests arrive early so you may practice speaking. It has been so long since you've done much of it," he said.

Calla stepped forward to the stone railing, peering over it so she could watch the carriage approach. Up the road it came, agonizingly slow until it came to a stop just below the balcony.

And out of it stepped Peter Renaud.

"*Papa!*" Calla cried.

Peter looked up, his face collapsing as he saw his daughter. "Oh, my girl!" he shouted. He disappeared past the gold columns toward the door.

Calla whirled around to face Lord Aneurin. "You said he was forbidden to come here."

He said nothing.

"You said I couldn't even write to him," she pressed.

Again, he said nothing. He kept his eyes on the far horizon.

"You said—"

"—You need to see Delilah before you go downstairs. The brooch and the perfume are on the wine cart."

Calla lunged, wrapping her arms around his shoulders even as she avoided touching his wings. "You say you're just a man, Lord Aneurin, but you are a *good* man."

He froze, his arms at his sides. But she felt him shiver. Tears stung her eyes and she stepped back from him and smiled. "Thank you."

Once again, he said nothing as he grimaced.

Shaking her head, Calla ran into his chamber, searching for the wine cart. *There.* She rushed to it, found a white lily brooch and a bottle of perfume. She pressed the nozzle to spray the air to detect the scent: jasmine, with notes of the sandalwood that seemed to permeate Lord Aneurin's rooms.

Her eyes fell on the tapestry behind the cart just as she turned to leave. She paused as she saw it was the same as the one in her room. She tilted her head and stepped around the wine cart, pressing a hand to it. When she did, the pressure of her hand made something underneath the tapestry click. Looking over her shoulder, she made sure Lord Aneurin was still outside before she pulled the tapestry back to reveal a door.

That a house as large as this one would have secret passages came as no surprise to her, but as much as she wanted to see where this one led, she had to get to her father.

Delilah worked quickly to smooth out the wrinkles in her dress. Calla asked her to style her hair the way she'd seen Lady Eugenia's hair, remembering how elegant it had looked. Delilah nodded. When she was done, she fastened the brooch to Calla's breast, gasping as she stepped away. "Miss Renaud, you're blond."

Calla turned to the mirror, but she only saw herself the way she always looked. The same brown hair, the same honey-colored eyes, the same pert nose, the same full lips. "Am I?"

"Yes, and very beautiful. You were already quite pretty, but you look like a grand lady now. No one will know it's you," Delilah said.

Calla laughed and took off the brooch. "My father will probably want to see my real face. I'll keep it with me and put it on before the other guests arrive." She spritzed herself with the perfume and tucked the brooch between her breasts, careful it wouldn't prick her.

"Calla lily!" Peter cried as she entered the drawing room.

She flew into his arms. "Papa, you're all right! I tried to get him to let me write to you, but he refused."

Peter shook with his tears. "Oh, this is worth it, muffin. This is worth it. Mr. Fontaine has kept me apprised of everything. He says you have plans to become a florist and are an accomplished harpist now."

"Or...maybe he will let me write if I sign my name as something else."

"That might be acceptable," Godfrey said from behind her. "But His Lordship has been very generous today. If you promise to wait to ask him, I will lend my voice to your cause, provided you adhere to some *strict rules.*"

She smiled and looked behind her at the handsome steward. "Papa, Godfrey has been so good to me while I've been here. He's the only person I've had a full conversation with other than you."

Godfrey bowed. "You're too kind."

Calla shook her head. "You've kept my spirits up this long. I'm sure you'll continue to do so."

He bowed again. "Unfortunately, Miss Renaud, if you say your spirits have been 'up' at all during your time here, I have not done my job well at all. I must do better."

Calla rolled her eyes. Her melancholy was born of years of poverty and isolation. Despite the way she cried herself to sleep most nights, she had felt better since coming to the palace.

She led her father to one of the sofas where they sat beside each other, grasping hands.

"Tell me all about your stay here. Is Lord Aneurin a kind man? He hasn't hurt you, has he? He's been...honorable?" Peter murmured, drinking in the sight of her face.

"Nothing but honorable, I assure you," Calla said. "Today he has gifted me with more words than he's given me the entire time I've been here. I have no complaints."

Peter nodded. "Good. Tell me more. Tell me everything."

Calla did—the only things she left out were the details of the curses that plagued Lord Aneurin, knowing that the tragedy of the Roran household should be locked away from the ravages of rumor and gossip.

Before the ballroom, Calla stood fastening the brooch to her breast once again. Jaunty music played from beyond the double doors. "Well," she said to Godfrey. "I guess I…"

She squared her shoulders and put her hand on one of the doors.

"What is it, Miss Renaud?" Godfrey inquired kindly.

She sighed. "It's been a long time since I spoke to strangers or anyone other than you, Mary, Delilah, and Cresedan."

"And Lord Aneurin."

She rolled her eyes. "That hardly counts. We've never had a meaningful conversation."

"That's for the best," he said, frowning.

She knew he was right. She exhaled, blowing out her breath as if she could shed her nervousness. She pushed into the ballroom.

Night had fallen, and the chamber was illuminated by the two chandeliers dripping with crystals. The room was washed in golden light. Hundreds of people stood by the tables, lounged on the sofas, drank wine. All laughing or speaking, *existing* as if they were real and not specters of longing from her lonely heart. As she entered, they all turned to look at her.

"Who are you?" asked a merchant in his forties. He had a mess of mouse brown hair and a shadow of a beard across his chin and jaw. Quite handsome, even for a man so much older than she was. He didn't wait for an answer as he walked around her, sizing her up. "When I heard Lord Aneurin was throwing a party after all this time, I suppose I should have assumed it was because he had a noble guest."

Calla laughed nervously. "I am Lady... Briar Beauregard. From Soliza."

Lady Briar Beauregard was the name of a character from one of the books in Lord Aneurin's library. Soliza, as far as Calla knew, didn't exist.

The man smiled, utterly delighted. "An exotic beauty then, to have come from so far. I wonder what business you have with the king. You must tell me while we dance."

Calla searched the crowd for her father, but he couldn't know who she was, or he might reveal her identity. She spotted him near the cask of wine, refilling his glass.

"I'd be happy to dance with you," said Calla, "but Soliza is a poor country and I don't know the steps to the dances of the Vale."

The man laughed. "They're quite simple and I'll show you. I'm Loewen, a merchant from the city of Dawnwood. Come, my lady."

Loewen took her hand and led her to the center of the floor where dozens of couples were already spinning.

So strange that I wanted this, and yet now I have it I am afraid.

Making up a story was easy, although Calla had no knowledge of the affairs of nobility. Being poor her whole life left her ill-equipped to create too detailed of an illusion, so she altered the events of the book she read about Lady Briar. "I brought the king ill tidings from Soliza. My uncle, Duke Reginald, had hoped the Strix Lord would marry me despite his affliction, but Lord Aneurin is not interested in a bride."

Loewen laughed, spinning her around. "That's good for you, my lady. He is a violent man. If you're unlucky enough to still be here the next time someone crosses him, you'll see. Be grateful for his apathy."

Knowing the details of the curse, Calla had to admit that she should regard his apathy toward her as a blessing. *If* it was real, and those members of his staff hadn't merely been unlucky, the way her heart raced when Lord Aneurin entered the room was a spark in a hayloft.

Why should I long for him? I don't even know him. And he is a bird!

Hours passed and the party maintained its joviality deep into the night. Several full glasses of wine later, she collapsed against Loewen as she tripped over her own feet, giggling. "Thank you for your company, sir. It is a quiet house, but the memory of your companionship will sustain me until I can go home."

"You have captivated me like a flame draws a moth," Loewen said. "May I write to you?" He pressed her fingertips to his lips as they twirled yet again across the floor.

Calla hesitated. There was no way Lord Aneurin would allow her to correspond with anyone except her father. And probably not him either.

"You may, but I do not promise I will reply," she said, hoping to sound elegantly vague and distant.

Loewen opened his mouth to speak, but the doors to the ballroom slammed open with a clamor that shook the whole palace. Even the musicians fell silent. Everyone turned to look, and Calla's eyes widened.

Lord Aneurin stood in the doorway, swaying slightly. Quiet whispers hissed as the guests began murmuring to each other.

"Music," he said softly. Without hesitation, a melody began to play.

Slowly the dancers on the floor resumed their gaiety, though their furtive glances at the Lord of Lorana Vale could not be avoided. Calla watched him as he strode into the ballroom, his wings tense and high, his posture straight. As he passed, everyone bowed to him, but he paid no attention to them. His gaze washed over the room until it landed on Calla.

She wondered if he knew who she was, remembering the brooch changed her appearance. The imperious face of Lady Eugenia surfaced in her mind.

He crossed the room with deliberate steps, cutting through the crowd until he stood before her. "I would dance with the lady," he said.

Loewen released her and stepped back. "Of course, Your Majesty. Lady Briar, I will write to you."

Lord Aneurin took her into his arms and waited for Loewen to retreat to a chaise across the room. "Lady Briar Beauregard?"

Calla nodded.

The Strix Lord trilled and began to move, but not before she smelled the wine on his breath. He was *drunk*.

The music was loud and festive, and he was a capable dancer, but between them, silence reigned.

"Are you well, my lord?" Calla asked after the fourth tune.

"The dress suits your natural beauty better," he said, slurring slightly. "I chose it with the…the hue of your hair and your… golden eyes in mind. I will be glad to see you return the brooch to me."

Calla shivered. "Yes, my lord."

She watched his face as they danced, and he stared right back, just as intently.

One by one, the couples on the floor retreated, bowing to their king. Calla watched her father approach him and say, "Thank you, my lord. For everything." And then he too was gone.

A glance out of the tall windows, and she knew dawn was coming. But still the musicians played for still the king danced.

"I'm tired," Calla whispered, her voice tinged with regret.

He spun her so her back was against his chest. "I'll escort you to your room," he said quietly into her ear. "After you rise, I will no longer speak to you. For your sake, I cannot. But I will bid you goodnight."

Dizziness overwhelmed her as he took her hand and led her out of the ballroom. She looked over her shoulder and saw the musicians lower their instruments.

Although she knew where they were going, he didn't release her hand. She wished he would. She wished he never would.

Just shrivel up and die, she commanded her heart.

Her birthday had been magical, as magical as the brooch at her breast. Calla realized she wouldn't be afraid if she didn't believe in the curse. But believe she did, and she knew she was in danger.

Was it love? She doubted that. But it was a longing, born out of her isolation. Despite his voiced preferences for her dark hair, she knew she was no beautiful calamity like Lady Eugenia had been. He couldn't love her back, even if there was no curse. That reasoning hadn't been diminished. And Calla was too practical for unrequited love. She had a destiny before her, which meant she had no time for futile hopes.

At her door, Lord Aneurin finally released her hand. "Two more birthdays," he said, slurring even more. He must have drank right up until the moment he crashed through the doors. "Two more, for on the third you are free."

This time, Calla said nothing.

"You may write to that merchant as Lady Briar Beauregard. Perhaps if he falls in love with you, he will forgive your lie when you reveal the truth in three years."

Calla was drunk too. Drunk on wine, and the sound of his voice.

Lord Aneurin sniffed, his eyes opening and shutting as he tried to see straight. His fingertips came to her breast, but he was only unfastening the brooch.

When he held it in his hands, his gaze swept over her. "Much better," he crooned. "Goodni—"

Calla closed the distance between them, cupping his feathered face in her hands. "I forgive you for not speaking to me tomorrow," she said. "Do not worry about me. But I would hear your voice again. Someday."

He blinked slowly as he put the brooch in his pocket. He reached up to cover her hands with his own. "On your next birthday. You have my word."

"Lord Aneurin," she breathed.

"Do not speak my name, Miss Renaud. Do not think of me."

"How could I not? You are so beautiful, my lord."

An odd look contorted his features. "Beautiful…" he repeated. Then his eyes widened. He stepped back out of her reach, stumbling away as he turned and fled, disappearing around the corner.

Calla collapsed against her door, burying her face in her hands. The scent of jasmine was too much; it choked her, suffocated her.

"You reckless fool," Godfrey growled as he appeared before her. "You have doomed him. For five hundred years he prevented another loss, and now you have assured he will see it happen again."

Red, tear-filled eyes flickered to him. "I didn't mean to," she said. "I didn't."

"You are not permitted to bathe alone. You are not permitted to dine alone. You are not permitted out of the house without an escort. I will *not* allow you to die while you are under his care. Stay here and don't move. I'm going to fetch Delilah to help you get ready for bed."

Calla had no choice but to slide to the ground where she wept.

Chapter Thirteen

Fearful that Lord Aneurin would not show at breakfast, Calla chose to stay in bed all of the next day, and the day after, taking a tray in her room. Godfrey was enormously pleased at her avoidance of him, but when she inquired about the king, he remained vague. "He is well, Miss Renaud. Do not worry yourself."

On the third day, she rose just before dawn. Delilah wasn't waiting for her to wake, and Calla jumped at the chance. She slipped her shoes on and wrapped herself in her fur-lined robe. She padded to the kitchen where Mary and Cresedan were already at work. Their jaws dropped when they saw her in the entry arch.

"Miss Renaud!" Cresedan exclaimed. "You're up early. I'll prepare something for you right quick. Please have a seat at the table. Someone will sit with you shortly."

Calla shifted on her feet. "I know Godfrey doesn't want me to eat alone, but he's worrying for nothing. I will not attempt to seduce Lord Aneurin, nor do I have any desire to do so. I am grateful for his company, but as much as I have grown to love all of you, I am eager to be free of this place."

Mary and Cresedan exchanged a glance. "Until Mr. Fontaine says so, we cannot allow you to eat alone."

Calla sighed. "Then I won't eat at all. I'd like a cup of that green tea, if you please. Without any sugar. Bring it to the bench that looks out to the east, on the hill with the camellias."

Mary stepped forward. "You cannot go outside."

"I will, and by doing so I will prove that there is nothing to fear. Bring the tea."

Despite looking like she had more to say, Mary nodded. "Yes, Miss Renaud."

Calla gave her a tight-lipped smile and exited into the garden.

The path was dark, even though the sky was lightening. The sun had not yet broken the horizon, and the sky cast everything in a gray hue as she stayed on the stone, winding her way up the terraces to her favorite spot. When she got there, she settled on the bench, folding her legs underneath her.

If she squinted her eyes, she could almost pretend to see the swathe of blue that was the ocean. She inhaled the crisp air, flexing her toes and imagining sand between them. Dawn would break any moment now, but she imagined it already had over the sea, the golden sun reflecting off the waves.

It was cold, but a glance up at the sky told her it would not rain. She rubbed her hands together, breathing onto them.

A steaming mug appeared in front of her eyes, held by a pale hand with a feathered wrist. Raising her eyebrows, Calla looked up at Lord Aneurin as she took it. He didn't sit beside her, nor did he say anything. He turned to face the east along with her.

"I knew you were the type to wake up early," she said. "They always say that to become a legend, you have to seize your destiny. Got to wake up to do that."

Silence answered her.

"You're going to stick with it, are you?" She sipped her tea. He had been right to sweeten it for her on her birthday, but she liked it without almost as well.

Lord Aneurin, as usual, said nothing.

"That's all right. I assume you're here because I proclaimed to the staff my utter disinterest in seducing you. Fear not, Lord Legend, you are safe from me. You won't find *me* begging for one night with you. After all, you already gave me one."

Alarmed birdsong echoed through the garden as Lord Aneurin snapped his head to look at her, utterly affronted.

Calla choked on her tea, then laughed so hard she had to unfold her legs to steady herself. "It was three days ago, and you don't remember? I'd make a dismal courtier if you can't remember dancing with me *all night long*."

Lord Aneurin trilled again, but this time it was different—this time, it was very obviously a sound of frustration. In the blink of an eye, he launched himself into the sky and left her alone, just as the dawn broke.

Calla slept in late the next morning. Sometime around noon, she opened her eyes, but the gentle light streaming through her window pierced her vision and she winced. Pain roared in her head; her body was coated in a thin, sweaty film.

"Delilah," she whispered coarsely, her throat swollen so

much she could barely breathe.

Her servant, who had been cross-stitching an image of Della Ros, stood up. "Yes, Miss Renaud? Would you like some tea?"

"Yes, I—" Calla's vision swam as she shivered, and her eyes rolled back in her head. She collapsed against the pillows, convulsing.

She floated between consciousness and unconsciousness. When her fever spiked, her body rebelled and locked up, her shoulders tightening and her legs rigid.

"What is this?" she heard Lord Aneurin's voice from far away, and then delicate fingertips against her collarbone.

"The rash is a good sign, my lord. It means her body is fighting the disease. But if it spreads to her face, she must be bled at once."

A low trill. "She *cannot* be bled. The smell of her ambrosia would attract every hunter within twenty miles."

Godfrey—she thought it was Godfrey—sighed. "Then she will die."

Lord Aneurin trilled again, low and regretful. "How did she get druver pox? None of the staff have it."

Godfrey said nothing.

"How, *Mister* Fontaine," Lord Aneurin demanded, his voice like a blade.

Calla mourned how she could feel his tension though he sounded like he was on the other side of the room.

The steward sighed. "Her father has it. He is on his way to recovery, but you know it affects women more than men. It gets in the womb and festers there."

She tried to open her eyes, to reach out her hand for Lord

Aneurin, but she couldn't move. But her Papa was sick; she had to get to him.

"Every ten feet in a ring around the palace, I want a bonfire. We will burn a thousand pounds of sage and rosemary to disguise her scent. She will be moved to my room, where she will be bled." Lord Aneurin's tone was final. With a flutter of feathers, she heard him tear the door open and leave.

Godfrey settled on the bed next to her. "I told you," he whispered to her. "If you survive this, you..." He stopped. Then he took a deep, shuddering breath. "I don't know if you will, Miss Renaud. The curse is come upon you." His voice broke on the last word. "I'm so sorry, Calla."

She couldn't hold on any longer. She sank into oblivion.

Chapter Fourteen

Smoke filled her lungs as she breathed. Her eyes opened but immediately shut as they burned. Sage, rosemary, wood. They were burning it in the room too, not just outside.

"Aneurin," she croaked. Her arm ached from where she'd been bled, and she sought the comfort of a touch, any touch. Or even just a presence. "Annie."

A ruffle of feathers answered her, but she heard Godfrey protest. "No, my lord. You mustn't. The rash isn't gone yet. There is still danger."

"She is dying because I was too soft to be cruel," Lord Aneurin replied.

Calla opened her eyes again, squinting through the smoke to watch him as he sat beside her on his bed. His hand caressed her face. Though her eyes burned, she fought with all her might to keep them open, to meet his gaze.

"I'd rather die bleeding here than murdered for this same

blood," whispered Calla, whose heart broke as Lord Aneurin's grief-stricken face fell even further. "Even if I die, you saved me from a lifetime of loneliness. When you remember me, remember…" She took a wheezing breath. "Remember *that*."

"Calla." He slipped off the bed and knelt beside it, clutching her hand in both of his and putting his feathered brow to it. Her name fell out of his lips like water poured into a cup that was already full. "Calla, Calla, Calla."

Everything good that had ever happened to her had happened in his palace. If it was Aneurin Roran's kindness that was cursed, she was doomed from the moment her father concocted the idea to beg him for his help.

But she wasn't strong enough to voice her gratitude. Another feverish seizure wracked her body and she succumbed to the darkness.

Light penetrated through her eyelids and she shielded her face with her arm. But then her eyes snapped wide open. She had the strength to move.

Hesitantly, she looked around the room. Still in Lord Aneurin's bedroom. The four-poster bed was hung with thick goldenrod drapes. The dark wood of the frame was engraved with beautiful floral designs—lilies, camellias, marigolds. Even after being confined to it for who knows how long, the bed was luxurious and comfortable. She supposed it had to be to accommodate those wings. She could tell the linens had been changed recently, for they were still crisp.

There was a large desk with a high backed, black-cushioned chair behind it. End tables on either side of the bed and an armchair right beside where she rested. And in it was Lord Aneurin. His arms were crossed over his chest, his wings adjusted to a comfortable angle, and he slept, his head drooped to his shoulder.

Calla didn't have the heart to rouse him. She was still too

tired to speak much anyway.

Rolling onto her side, she clutched one of his indulgent pillows to her chest and watched him breathe. She needed a bath. She needed water. But for now, she was content to drink in his beauty.

Della Ros didn't curse him with ugliness, like he asked for. All the god did was make his beauty invisible to those disinclined to see it.

The idea spurred something in her chest. In every story she'd ever read about gods and curses, a loophole meant a way out.

The curse could be broken. Why not? The curse Lord Aneurin put on himself didn't work on her, and her heart still beat so Lady Eugenia's curse didn't work either. She was either immune or...

Her heart beat faster. Lord Aneurin was a legendary warrior. Lord Protector of Lorana Vale. He was meant to keep it safe. And if he didn't, it was because he feared something worse than his own disregard would befall it.

A great destiny awaited her if she made it to twenty-five. Three years was a hell of a long time but as she gazed upon his face in repose, the span of *five hundred years* weighed on her. He'd been alone for so, so long.

If she were a lesser woman, she'd hate him for not being cruel. Why shouldn't he carry the blame? He was the one who was cursed. But she remembered Godfrey's story about the code of honor and virtue he'd instilled in poor Aluard. It hurt to think Lord Aneurin was *incapable* of cruelty to those who did not deserve it, which made his fate as twice-cursed even more tragic.

"Three years," she whispered to his sleeping form. "Protect me for that long, and then I will free you. I swear it."

Chapter Fifteen

For three months, Lord Aneurin indulged Calla's every whim. When she wanted to walk, he would follow behind her in silence. If she wanted to dance, he'd send for minstrels, ones he subjected to Godfrey's intense questioning about their health and past exposure to ambrosia. Then he would dance with her until she grew bored of it.

When she read, he did too; over her shoulder in silence.

When she dined, he did too.

When she slept, he did too, unless she happened to doze while reading or sitting by the fire. When that happened, he'd just watch her. Sometimes, if he knew she was sleeping deeply, he'd brush her hair back from her face.

Calla knew he didn't want to speak, so she didn't either. She *couldn't*, because her thoughts were only ever about two things—how much she longed to touch him and how she was going to free him.

As they played chess or arranged flowers, her mind was elsewhere. Planning.

Could she hire a priestess of Della Ros to exorcise the curse from him? Surely they'd have already tried that. Or could she ask Della Petricha if he could bathe in his pool of holy rainwater? That might work, and it was foolish enough of an idea that she doubted anyone had thought of it.

Wickedly she thought she'd like to try to break the curse by destroying Lady Eugenia's tombstone. Her corpse too. But before Lord Aneurin permitted her to get up from bed after her illness, she'd watch him as she tried to fall asleep or over the pages of her book. The room was always dark, the only illumination from the oil lamp on the bedside table and the two sconces mounted to the wall that illuminated a portrait of Lord Aneurin and Lady Eugenia side by side, his hand on her shoulder while they gazed lovingly at each other. And Lord Aneurin watched that portrait, heat in his gaze. He'd stare at it whenever he wasn't watching Calla. And while he stared at his wife, his hand massaged his chest above his heart as if it pained him.

There was no chance he would permit her to desecrate Eugenia's grave. His love had been so holy it moved her to curse him for fear of losing it. Love like that would take longer than five hundred years to dissipate. Despite how abhorrently wretched and horrid and *evil* Lady Eugenia had been to curse him, Calla knew Lord Aneurin loved her still.

And although Calla's blood heated to think of them together, the image reminded her that for his sake, she wished they'd have died together centuries before she was born. Not because she wasn't glad to have met him, but because if he'd had the chance to die happy in her arms, it was the death he deserved. That was what Calla wanted. For him to greet his death with no regrets. Not accept his death with relief that his long isolation was over.

But one cannot change the past. As an Ambrosius, Calla's life purpose was to herald the future.

The harp lessons Lord Aneurin had paid for during the first half of her time with him revealed that Calla had a natural affinity for music. He stood by the window when Bruvean Salvalle—the instructor—said, "My lord, as usual you have exquisite taste. My pupil has such a natural gift, I must beg you to allow me to teach her piano as well."

Calla hadn't heard Lord Aneurin's voice in twenty-seven days, so she was surprised when he turned from the window, clasped his hands behind his back, and said, "Find the finest piano in Lorana Vale and tell whoever owns it that I have claimed it. If they send me a statement of their claim with the value of the instrument, I will pay them for it. You may leave."

Bruvean clapped his hands. "Oh splendid, my lord. I will be here the day it is delivered for her first lesson."

When the rotund, red-haired man left, Lord Aneurin turned back to the window.

Calla watched him in the light. On the floor, his shadow stretched out behind him. A ghastly, demonic shape. But in the shower of sun, his white feathers seemed to glow golden while his black feathers swallowed the light. She was used to seeing him like this, in profile. It gave her the opportunity to study the lines of his face. The shape of his head was like an owls, with the tufts of feathers on top. He had the ears of a man, but feathers made them appear tipped like a creature of legend, which she supposed he was that. Below the ridges above his eyes, his high cheekbones were sharp even when washed out by the sunlight. Gentle lips for his gentle words.

When she thought about how terrified she'd been when her father first suggested asking for his help, she was unbearably frustrated. It took her eighteen months to truly see just how beautiful he was.

"Shall I play for you, my lord?" she asked softly.

Without looking at her, he raised his hand and gestured. *Carry on, then.*

Placing her fingers, Calla began to strum the harp.

She watched him when she could, her eyes darting over to him. But the longer she played, the happier he seemed, and eventually, she was rewarded with a gentle smile on his face.

She played until her fingers couldn't take it anymore, past the point of bleeding. Then she slipped from her stool and slowly approached the Strix Lord.

It was impossible for a warrior like him not to sense her coming, and that is why she *knew* as she reached for the mottled feathers on his wing that he was fully aware of how close she was. Closer than she had any right to be.

"I'm alive," she said the moment he whipped around to face her.

"It's impossible."

"*I'm still here,*" she insisted.

"*You don't allow me to forget it,*" he breathed before grasping her in his arms, one hand on the back of her head as he pressed her face into his silk-clad chest.

Torrents of emotion washed over her, unrelentless. Shock came first, then elation, then hope, and finally, desperation.

The chaos of her heart forbade her to resist, and she reached for his face, cupping it and feeling the feathers that spread from his neck just over his jawline. She stood on her toes, stretching to bring her lips to his cheek. "I won't die," she murmured into his skin. "I can't. Whether I broke the curse by surviving or if my ambrosia makes me immune, she can't kill me. She can't take me away."

"Do not allow me hope, cruel Calla," he said, his voice barely more than a low grumble.

"It's true. The only threat to me is my blood. Not *you*."

"No," he groaned as he pulled away. "Never again, Miss Renaud." He pointed at her accusingly as he fled the music room. "Never again."

That evening, as Delilah combed out Calla's hair until it shone, Godfrey knocked on her door.

"Come in," she called.

Godfrey crossed the room to stand before her at her vanity. He leveled a glare upon her that would melt steel. "*Miss Renaud*, have you lost your goddamned mind?"

Calla looked at the floor. She knew Godfrey would be disappointed if he found out about the embrace, but she had hoped Lord Aneurin wouldn't say anything.

"I didn't know he would tell you," she said. "It won't happen again."

Godfrey threw up his hands with a groan. "Tell me? He didn't have to *tell* me. After he left you and your bewilderingly foolish behavior, he went straight to his room and tore every portrait down. Of himself, of Eugenia. When I asked what happened, he said, 'Even now I will not break my word to her, but you must tell her I want to be alone.' As I am not an *idiot*, I knew you either touched him or confessed something you shouldn't have. If you dare so much as *think* of forcing him to keep that reckless promise to you, I will...I will..." He reached for her shaking hands as he shouted. "How could you be so stupid? You almost *died*, Miss Renaud!"

Calla waved Delilah away. "But I *didn't*. I'm still here,

Mister Fontaine! Perhaps I broke the curse. Maybe by saving a life with his kindness, he took from it the power to kill anyone else."

Godfrey scoffed. "We can't prove whether or not it's broken. Stay the hell away from him. I will not tell you again."

Calla groaned, a high-pitched cry of frustration as she jumped to her feet and climbed into bed. "I can prove it by *not* staying away. I want nothing from him, Godfrey. Don't mistake me. Even after I prove the curse is broken, I will not ask him for anything he doesn't want to give. I won't try to win his love. On the morning of my twenty-fifth birthday, I will leave."

The steward's voice lowered dangerously. "Do you understand how much *irrevocable* harm you will do if you test this theory and you are wrong?"

Calla rolled over and pulled the covers to her ears. "I'm not wrong. And if I am, I will repeat what I told him before. I would rather die trying to make him happy than be murdered in the woods for my blood."

"He doesn't want to be happy, Miss Renaud. His isolation and despair keep immortality simple. Fewer friends to watch grow old and die. Fewer regrets. Don't force him to face the ugliness of death more often than he already has."

Calla flipped to her other side to face him. "I have only two and a half years here at most. I will spend them in service to Lord Aneurin, whether he wants my help or not. But don't worry—I won't touch him again. Tell him he can take as much time as he needs."

Godfrey seemed to deflate a little. "At least you're starting to see reason. I hope you know what you're doing."

"I don't. But that doesn't mean I'm not going to try."

Chapter Sixteen

*A*s *much time as he needs* turned out to be a little under two months. Calla spent the entire time plotting how to break the curse and what it would mean for her when she did. She was starting to think the only way to end Lord Aneurin's suffering was to confront a god directly and ask them to break it. But Calla had been one step above destitution her entire life. That someone as lowborn and base as her could ask a boon of a god...it was unthinkable. But if she did it and succeeded, then she was right. Her destiny was to free Lord Aneurin.

To her mind, that connection was to blame for the reason she craved his company. She was born to free him. And she intended to do it as soon as she could. And when it was done, she would ask Lord Aneurin for a horse and venture east—to the sea.

April gave way to May, but a couple weeks into June, Lord Aneurin was seated at the breakfast table, reading a newsletter from the village's one-man publication.

Calla froze in the doorway, then began to rub her arm nervously.

Lord Aneurin said nothing, merely watched her over his paper for a moment before raising it higher so she couldn't see him.

After breakfast, he followed her to the library. She perused the classic literature shelf while he climbed the iron spiral staircase on the far side, by the window, that led up to his stranger books—the mythology books, the heretical manifestos, the books written by once-great heroes who history later condemned. He paced along the little balcony, searching for something.

Calla selected the last book on the fifth row from the bottom. She was making her way up the bookcase. With her choice, she moved to the sofa, grateful for how cold the leather was on her arms. It was *quite* hot for June.

A triumphant trill sounded as Lord Aneurin jumped down from the balustrade, his wings spread magnificently as he coasted to the ground. Book in hand, he approached the sofa, proffering it to Calla.

"You want me to read this?" she inquired, taking it from him.

He said nothing.

The cover read *Black Curses, White Hexes.*

"What do you want me to do with this?" she pressed. Did Godfrey tell him she wanted to break the curse? Was he…encouraging her?

The tufts of feathers on his head twitched as he turned away. "I'm proving a point," he said. Then he left the room without looking back.

The book must have been hundreds of years old. Calla was prepared to read all sorts of esoteric secrets, but she could barely see the script underneath all the scribbling in the margins. Two contributors based on the different handwriting. As she flipped through the pages, her heart sank.

Sarah was fertile. She would have fallen pregnant had I given in, said one scribble next to a curse for scorned women to cast on their husbands' mistresses.

Aluard will be safe. He survived the raid on the bandit camp despite being ran through the shoulder, see white hex 33, said script in a different hand.

Calla flipped to the hex mentioned.

Love will endure, romance may not

Destiny is purer than a racing heart

Twist three times stripped bark of the yew-wood knot

Around the arm of the one I would take with me

Into the decimation of time.

Scribbled in the margin was *YOU WERE WRONG*.

Calla lowered the book to her lap. Aluard had survived Eugenia's curse, but eventually he was taken anyway. That was Lord Aneurin's point—she was not safe. She'd never be safe.

But he'd proven something else too. By showing her the frantic, desperate notes he and Godfrey had taken as they pored over the book of curses, he'd revealed that he'd sought to end the curse. That he knew he didn't deserve it. That Lady Eugenia had *wronged* him.

Mind unchanged, Calla snapped the book closed. Once she was twenty-five and the risk was as low as it would get, she'd break the curse or she would die.

With ragged determination, Calla spent hours poring over every book of mythology and curses and witchcraft she could find. Just as before, Lord Aneurin spent the time watching her, though he did not leave after twenty minutes like he usually did. Instead, he stood behind her, reading over her shoulder.

She opened *Twelve Destinies That Shaped Lorana Vale*, and Lord Aneurin trilled. She snapped her head to look at him, but he shrugged and moved to the bookshelves. He ran his finger over the spines of dozens of books before plucking one out.

"You're only twenty-two," he said simply, handing her the medium-thick tome. The pages were heavy with ink for almost every one had a detailed illustration upon it.

Horticulture and Why It's a Hobby seemed to be the most boring book Calla had ever read, but she assumed he chose it because of her little corner of the garden. Perhaps he was giving her ideas for how to cultivate it.

A distraction away from her obsessive quest to find a way to free him.

She turned to a section of the book that described the symbolic meanings of different flowers.

"'Blue roses,'" she read aloud, "'signify love at first sight or unattainable love.' Remember that first morning I was here?"

Aneurin said nothing.

"Well, you probably don't know the meanings of flowers. You're a king, what would you know about it?"

Again, Aneurin said nothing.

Calla flipped through more pages of the book reading some sections aloud while others she skimmed in her head.

"'Despite its sunny countenance, yellow marigold is not a very pleasant bloom to receive. It signifies a major loss and is an acknowledgement of cruel behavior either on the part of the giver or the receiver.'" Calla looked up at Aneurin to gauge his response. His lips turned down. "Is that why you gave it to me? Because you mourn your wife and know you're being cruel by denying me conversation?"

He moved toward the door.

"No, you're not leaving," she snapped.

Aneurin stopped, looked at her, then stepped again toward the exit.

"*No*," Calla insisted.

He took another step.

Calla slammed the book shut and threw it on the sofa. "You better not go through that door, *Your Majesty*," she hissed.

"Or what?" Lord Aneurin inquired smoothly.

Calla's eyes went wide as she ground her teeth together. "Or I will no longer speak to you. See how long you enjoy my *silent company* when that's all you get."

The King of the Vale stared at her, his lip curling in derision. Then he trilled in resignation and returned to the bookshelf, taking a random novel and finding a seat in the corner.

Calla knew he was pretending to read because his breathing was still uneven. Far too distracted to comprehend the words on the pages. But she smiled and opened her book again. After a while, a little chuckle sounded from her mouth. A victorious bubble that she kept him with her, that he didn't deny her the small pleasure of his company just because he was uncomfortable. She chuckled again, and again, until she was giggling into the pages of her book. She brought the tome up to her face to breathe in the smell of the pages to try to calm herself down, but she kept remembering the stubborn stare Lord Aneurin had given her from the doorway.

A low rumble sounded from the corner of the room, and Calla's laughter came to an abrupt halt. She looked over her shoulder at the Strix Lord, but he just stared at the pages of his novel. Utterly stone-faced and unmoved, like the laughter she'd heard had been imaginary.

Unwilling to push him any further, Calla read her book quietly, indulging in his royal presence until Godfrey came to escort them to dinner.

Chapter Seventeen

A week before her twenty-third birthday, Calla confronted Lord Aneurin at breakfast. "I imagine after what happened last year, I will not be getting a birthday party *this* year," she said, sipping her orange juice.

He shot her a look over his newsletter. *Definitely not.*

"That's fine. Will Papa be invited back? You can't get druver pox twice."

Lord Aneurin sighed, folding up his newsletter. Clearly he didn't want to talk about it.

"No, then." Calla sighed. "What about Loewen? I can wear the brooch and perfume again."

He glared at her. "No," he said, rising to his feet.

She couldn't let him leave. "Wait."

He stopped, his fingertips grazing the table. Even though his patience was frayed, it seemed to be unending.

She lifted her hands in a placating gesture. "I don't even want a big party. But I'd like to do *something*. Could we…" She hesitated. It was a silly request. "I know you don't want to speak to me, but could you read to me? Any book you'd like, and just for fifteen minutes. That would be a good gift for me this year. It would be enough."

Lord Aneurin eyed her suspiciously. "You make this request of a king?"

She nodded. "I do, Your Majesty."

He pursed his lips. "Fine." He swept from the room without giving her a chance to thank him.

A week later, she woke to Godfrey delivering another dress.

"Does our gracious master forget that once I leave this place, I will have no occasion to wear such finery? My father is one of the poorest men in the village because of me." Calla sighed as she tossed her legs over the side of the bed so she could rise and dress.

"No, he isn't," Godfrey said. "The first time Lord Aneurin withdrew from you, he spent his time thinking about how to improve your circumstances once your time here is done. Giving money to your father was out of the question—the sudden wealth would make your father a target. Instead, he purchased better tools for him and sent *me* to politely request the other carpenter in Senden's Branch leave and never come back." He smiled a bit. "I was very persuasive. Your father has had enough business to make his own way, and he is thriving." He eyed her shrewdly as she combed her hair. "I dare say you will have plenty of genuine suitors once you return home, Miss Renaud. And it is our hope that these dresses help you find the right man for you. A man who encourages that spark in your mind, who gives you the life you deserve. A man who will reward your kind heart and take you to the sea."

A hot flush rose in her cheeks. Men and marriage seemed abstract concepts she couldn't grasp. It had been so long since she'd been in the presence of a man who desired her. A year to be precise, since her last birthday. And the letters from Loewen proved every week that desire still lingered.

But her heart didn't beat for him. As much as Godfrey and Lord Aneurin wanted her to be safe and provided for, she wouldn't settle for the first uncursed man to look at her without being tainted by her ambrosia.

The dress was black with yellow lilies embroidered on the sleeves and over her breast. Calla knew the repeating theme of lilies was because of her name. A little on the nose, but she didn't mind. Perhaps Della Ros would bless her with exaggerated beauty when she wore it—lilies were his symbol.

"What's for breakfast?" she asked before Godfrey left.

He smiled. "Pancakes and cinnamons rolls, Miss Renaud. His Grace said that's what you ate last year."

A closed-mouth laugh sounded from her. "What will he eat? I think he's allergic to sugar."

The steward chuckled too. "He will eat the same. It isn't that he dislikes sweet things. It is that he has spent centuries restricting himself from indulging in many aspects of his life. Naturally, his sweet tooth diminished as well."

Calla pouted. "Poor man."

"Indeed."

When she entered the dining room wearing her new dress with her hair in curls that fell around her shoulders and a glittering opal necklace at her throat, Lord Aneurin dropped his newsletter right on top of his food.

Calla blushed under his scrutiny as she took her seat beside him, reaching for a cinnamon roll. "Thank you for indulging my sweet tooth," she said.

Still he stared.

As awkward as it was to chew with him watching her, she did it anyway. She sipped her tea sweetened with cream and sugar to wash down every rich bite. It wasn't until she was halfway through her roll that Lord Aneurin shook his head and began to eat his pancakes.

"Will we go for another walk this year?" she asked after a long silence.

He cleared his throat. "I thought I was to read to you."

Delight lit up her face. "Yes, my lord. If you're still willing, but I won't hold you to it. I could read to *you*. I just want to spend time with you."

His wings twitched as the corners of his mouth turned down, but he turned back to his newsletter, grimacing at the syrup soaked into it.

After breakfast, he led her to the library. He went to the shelf and carefully deliberated his options. Finally he plucked three volumes from the shelf and brought them to her.

A romance novel about a servant in love with a princess.

A book of poetry with no author listed.

And an adventure-romance novel about the god of liberty Della Victus and how he avenged the violation of his human lover.

Calla discarded the novel about the servant. "I'll read the one about Della Victus and you can read the poetry. We can read to each other."

Lord Aneurin grunted his assent.

Calla moved toward the sofa, but instead of following her, he looked over his shoulder at her from the doorway.

"Oh," she murmured, stepping toward him.

The king led her up the stairs and through his chambers to his veranda, where an enormous round cushion was newly set up. The cushion was elevated on a wicker base. Pillows and blankets covered it, and over it, a white canopy. The rest of the veranda was transformed by pots of white and yellow lilies and a multitude of tall oil lamps at intervals. Calla thought it was wonderful and much better than the unadorned stone the veranda had been before.

Lord Aneurin arranged the pillows to form a sort of seat, then gestured at it. Calla nestled on the cushion, folding her legs under the billowing skirt of her dress and leaning against the piled pillows, book in her hands. The king sat cross legged at the edge of the cushion toward her feet, the bottom tips of his wings brushing against the ground behind him.

He waited.

"Ah, me first," she murmured, opening the book. "'The love of Della Victus is forged in steel, for liberty cannot be granted, only claimed. Whether by those who would be free or those who work for them, liberty is taken and fought for, for the nature of man is to restrict it in others while exalting it for themselves. So it is, and how it has always been.' How pretentious."

Lord Aneurin trilled, urging her to keep reading.

"'When a god bestows his blessing on a mortal, sweetening their blood with the magic of destiny, Della Victus claims his sovereignty over the rest of the gods. His gift is taken away as the Destined fights for survival, but after a quarter of a century, the Destined's steel rings true and their freedom is claimed.'"

Heart racing, Calla searched ahead in the book for when the plot of the story would begin. The more she read, the more the story seemed meant for her. Della Victus was who she should ask to free Lord Aneurin, even if she had to challenge him to a duel so her steel offering was accepted.

Lord Aneurin would never consent to her training with real weapons, even wooden weapons. Unless they were wrapped in wool, perhaps.

He trilled again, waving his hand in frustration. Calla murmured her apology. When he smiled tightly at her, a strange warmth bloomed between her legs.

"'The lover of Della Victus was destined to die from the moment she was born. Not a grand destiny that made her blood melodious with magic, but a poorer kind of fate—the destiny of the Forsaken. And forsaken she was, for she was beautiful, blessed by Della Ros only to spite Della Victus, who'd wagered that the god of beauty could not create a mortal so lovely she tempted him to grant liberty to someone who did not pay the steel price.'"

Calla read to the king until her voice was hoarse, but she couldn't stop. She had to know what happened to Miriam Bells, the lover of Della Victus. When she got to the end, when the god of liberty wept over Miriam's body after learning she'd never loved him; only the man she'd persuaded him to free, the man who killed her; the book fell from Calla's hands.

And she *wept.*

The futility of it all. If she survived until twenty-five, was her destiny to serve as the muse for a book like this one? A tragic tale of hopelessness, a warning against loving those who do not love you.

Lord Aneurin offered her a white handkerchief, which she took. But she narrowed her eyes at him as she wiped her tears away. "Did you know it would make me cry?"

The owl lord breathed heavily. "It was a risk I had to take."

Screwing up her face, Calla pushed herself to her knees. She couldn't bear to look at him, but she must. "It is unlike you to be cruel."

He said nothing for a long while. He looked out over the balustrade, over his property. Then he said, "It's been a long time since you've cried. Since you've done anything that made you feel alive. The risk was not whether you'd cry, it was whether you'd forgive me for allowing it."

She laughed and cried at the same time while fresh tears cascaded down her face. She tried to catch them with the handkerchief, but there were too many. When she finally looked at him, there was a softness to his gaze that she had never seen. As soft as his feathers, as soft as silk. And like silk, the way his gaze slipped over her body made her shiver.

"Thank you," she said, sniffling. "That's quite the gift, Your Grace."

He said nothing.

"This is my third birthday with you, and yet I don't know when yours is," she said, adjusting her legs to better hold her weight.

Lord Aneurin licked his lips, sighing. "It's a matter of record in any history book," he said quietly.

"I'll find out then. Whenever it is, I already know what you'll want for a gift."

He glanced at her just for a moment, his eyebrow ridges raised. Then he turned back to the horizon. "Then you're an oracle. I don't even know what I'd want. I don't *want* much anymore."

Blood pounded in Calla's ears. The urge to test her immunity once again raged in her soul. An undeniable longing to see just how far she could go without triggering the wrath of

Lady Eugenia.

Back and forth her mind traversed her reasoning. She should, she shouldn't. Her destiny wasn't assured for two more years. She could fall down the stairs and break her neck and her destiny would be unfulfilled. For most people, nothing would change. But Lord Aneurin would never be free.

What troubled her the most was how sure she was that she had been right. In the past few months, doubt was a frequent but temporary failure. Most of the time, she was absolutely certain. And that certainty rushed through her brain like wine, and she was drunk off it.

"An oracle?" she said, her breath hitching. "I just know you, my Lord Aneurin, although you've tried to hide yourself away from me. I know the only reason you deliberately chose a book that would hurt me was because you knew I would savor the pain of it. But I also know it hurt *you* to see me cry. I know that what you want for your birthday is my forgiveness."

His wings tensed as if he sensed danger. "Yes."

Precariously poised, Calla shivered but kept her hands folded in her lap. "What price would you pay for it?"

Subtly, his head shook. "I'd pay a fine commensurate to my crime, Miss Renaud. I do think you benefited from your tears as much as I did."

She whispered, "Then shall I deliver your sentence?"

Lord Aneurin sighed and straightened his legs, swinging them off the cushion so his feet were on the stone. "Deliver away, Judge Renaud. But do not be unjust. I am the king, and lord here."

Calla held her breath and leaned forward, crawling to him.

He looked away.

With her hand on his shoulder, she straightened her legs too, so that she sat beside him. "Very well, my lord. I sentence you to one minute holding my hand. You may not pull away."

Lord Aneurin laughed, keeping his eyes on the sundrenched stone of the veranda. "We both know I will not do that."

"I have said so, my lord."

"Why? Is my heart so disposable that you can toy with it to test your theories?"

"Hold my hand and I won't ask you to speak to me for the rest of the day. You don't even have to read to me," she retorted.

He rolled his eyes, and the expression was chilling with his magnificent owlish eyes. He proffered his hand, palm up. "I'm counting."

Calla slowly interlocked her fingers with his. She didn't want to waste a single second. *Star's despair*, she swore in her mind, *my heart is a constant spring of misery.*

Within fifteen seconds, it wasn't enough for her. Her longing compounded upon itself, her veins suffocating from the rush of blood. She reached over with her other hand and rested it on his arm, her fingers slipping up his sleeve to feel his feathers.

He inhaled sharply.

Thirty seconds left. She scooted closer and raised her hand to his face, urging him to look at her. He resisted at first, turning his face away, but she grasped his chin between her thumb and forefinger. She *insisted*.

With a strangled sigh, he turned sharply to face her, his eyes wet and glimmering. "Why are you doing this?"

"Because I know you need me to. How long has it been since someone touched you for more than a few seconds?"

"You're going to *die*, Miss Renaud.".

"I'm not. And I'm going to prove it to you."

Ten seconds left.

"I won't let you prove anything," he growled. "I won't."

"Then pull away."

"I gave my word."

"I'd rather die freeing you than live knowing you're in this prison. That wouldn't be a life at all."

"Damn you!" he shouted, releasing her hand and grabbing her face, kissing her as if it was the only logical thing to do.

If Calla were quite honest with herself, she wasn't sure until that moment that she'd been in love with the king for more than two years, despite all her denials of it to everyone. Including herself.

Her eyes fluttered closed as the knowledge that his kiss was born of five hundred years of isolation, not love. As if she was pressed between them, Calla breathed in the spirit of Lady Eugenia.

But Calla was lonely too, so she slid her arms around Lord Aneurin's neck and let him pull her to the cushion as he propped himself on his arm over her, his mouth not leaving hers for a moment. The longer he touched her, the more she thought she was dreaming.

Calla's fingertips gently stroked the feathers on his neck and jaw, fully conscious that Lord Aneurin was going to wake up from whatever dream he had that compelled him to do this, not allowing herself to fully enjoy it so she would mourn it less when it was gone. Just waiting, waiting, that's all her life was: waiting.

But the king did not stop. His hand slid from her face to her breast, but it didn't linger. Down her body until it rested on her hip and his mouth moved to her jaw.

Her heart was going to break. She'd thought she'd been desperate for his touch, but it wasn't enough to quell her loneliness because she knew it wouldn't last.

"What are you doing?" she asked softly, sure her voice would break whatever spell he was under.

"You say you're immune," he murmured into her neck. "And I am the king, so I will do what I want."

Calla wanted to believe that. And while she didn't fear for her life, she knew he wasn't telling the truth. Maybe the truth as he understood it as his blood burned, but hers was burning too and it wasn't fair.

It was intimacy she craved, but intimacy is not touch, it's the emotion behind the touch. And Lady Eugenia's regal face haunted her mind. Lord Aneurin would never love her.

"I'm sorry," Calla said.

The king froze. Slowly he pulled his mouth away from where he nibbled on her neck. Tragedy bloomed in his eyes when they met hers.

"I shouldn't have taken advantage of your loneliness. Please don't be angry with yourself. I'm the one to blame," she said, sitting up when he did.

He panted, regret pulling his mouth into a grimace. "Godfrey must never know," he said blankly.

Calla nodded and moved to recline on the pillows once again. "We've been doing nothing but reading. Open your book of poetry, my lord, lest the game be given away."

"It's not a game, Miss Renaud. It's your life."

She had an answer for that. She should have said, "It's not

my life I'm worried about, but my heart."

But she didn't open her mouth again. She rested her head on the pillows and listened to Lord Aneurin's soothing, raspy voice until she fell asleep, knowing that come tomorrow, he would shutter himself in his rooms and she'd be lucky if she saw him at all before her next birthday.

Chapter Eighteen

Only one month. That's all he stole from her as the world came to a halt in his absence. In that time, she sent him only one note: *I would like to learn how to defend myself. I am willing to use wool-wrapped wooden swords to practice until I possess some modicum of swordsmanship.*

Lord Aneurin hadn't replied, but when he came out of his room thirty-two days later, he had two practice swords wrapped in wool and gauze and cotton.

"I will teach you myself. There is no better teacher and I am the only one I trust not to harm you," he said.

Calla nodded, avoiding his gaze.

Dressed in cotton pants and a loose white shirt, she followed Lord Aneurin out to a meadow in a wooded area of the property. He tossed one of the swords to her and she clasped it in both hands.

"Hold it up," he demanded.

She did.

"Keep it up until you can't anymore."

She nodded and hefted the sword. She lasted around a minute and a half before her arms shook, and five seconds after that, she lowered the sword to the ground.

"Do it again," said Lord Aneurin. Calla nodded and lifted the sword. This time, she didn't lift it quite as high. "Higher," he said.

She raised it. Her arms carried the weight for twenty seconds before they collapsed at her sides.

Lord Aneurin crossed his arms and looked at her while she panted heavily, her arms quivering. "Again."

She whimpered but tried to lift the sword. It was heavy to her untrained hand and wouldn't come up more than to her waist. He stepped behind her and slid his hands over her arms until they were under her elbows. He lifted them up, carrying most of the weight before grasping her forearms to improve her form.

Then he stepped around her and said, "Hold, Miss Renaud."

A keening whimper spilled out of her mouth as she commanded her body to obey. Her arms shook, her abdominals clenched.

A dip in her form; the king's eyes flashed. "I said *hold*."

Gritting her teeth, her elbows lifted. But she couldn't hold it for long. After less than a minute, the sword toppled out of her hands and her arms fell to her sides. "How?" asked Calla.

Lord Aneurin tilted his head at her.

"You're a legendary warrior. Fought many battles. And

those battles, according to the King Aneurin Roran stories I've read, lasted sometimes for *days*. How did you do it?"

He chuckled, clasping his hands behind his back. "Training and practice until I was twenty-five. And then I had no choice. The Vale was falling apart after the death of my father, and I tried to clean it up. I *did* clean it up, until Ginny died."

She shook her head.

He swallowed, then cleared his throat. "Miss Renaud, a month ago I had the nectar of battle-frenzy in my veins when you said you'd rather die freeing me than leave me to my curse. I cannot tell you how badly I want you to be right. I was overwhelmed by that desire, and it was not fair to you."

Calla's eyes watered as he spoke. She'd tried not to think of it, but she did sometimes, late at night after Delilah was gone. When she was free to slip her hand between her thighs.

She massaged the back of one arm, then the other, already feeling sore. It only added to her discomfort. "It was my first kiss," she said at last.

An unreadable expression crossed his face.

"But I'm glad it was you," she added. "You're a good man, and if I do die freeing you, I'm glad I won't die unkissed."

He looked at her as if she'd grown a second head. She could practically see the wheels turning in his head. Finally, he said, "I am happy to have given you that little peace, at least."

No peace, my darling Aneurin, she thought. *No peace, only purpose. I will free you.*

Chapter Nineteen

Calla's twenty-third year passed more quickly than the others as she learned to defend herself. Her entire life, she'd admired the women who passed through Senden's Branch. She'd watch them through the bars on her window. Swords on their hips and a swagger to their steps. While Calla had some spirit in her, she knew she'd never pull off the swaggering. A life lived in fear didn't lend well to confidence, and she knew herself well enough to know that even if she made it to true adulthood, after the magic in her blood was fully absorbed, she would always cower a little when anyone drew too close.

By the third month, she'd improved so much that Lord Aneurin started landing blows on her in retaliation for blows she'd successfully landed too many times. Soft, never enough to truly damage her, only to bruise.

"Are you blind?" he hissed at her as he brought his wooden sword to the side of her neck.

She shoved it aside. "You've had five hundred years of practice and I've had three months."

He said nothing, circling her. She spun, one foot behind the other, ready to parry. Hopefully he wouldn't do another feint.

When he lunged she brought up her weapon to block it. "Was that so hard?" he murmured.

Calla used his distraction to shove him back, swinging her sword at his chest. "Keep mocking me, Strix Lord."

He smiled, saying nothing. Around and around he went.

When he lunged next, she blocked the blow just in time. Both huffing, their faces inches apart, they glared at each other.

The only thought that ran through Calla's mind was that he must not have faith in her ability to free him. That it was a fool's errand. That she'd forget it. If he believed she was going to take her new skill and seek out the gods to free him, he wouldn't have agreed to teach her. By instructing her, he was calling her bluff.

With a grunt, she jammed her knees between his legs. He swore and backed away, doubled over.

"So you do have the parts of a man," Calla said. "I'd wondered if you had a cloaca like all the other birds."

He gasped and dropped his sword. It wasn't until he didn't stop gasping that she realized he was *laughing*.

"Do I amuse you?" she spit at him. "Heartless, ignorant pigeon."

That seemed to sober him a little, but he chuckled again as he straightened. "If only I were heartless, Miss Renaud. Lives could have been spared."

She hefted her sword. "Yes, what a tragic destiny. That so many people would *like* you too much."

Their eyes met and he tilted his head. "Would you strike a defenseless beast?"

She gritted her teeth. "You want me to hate you."

He said nothing.

"I'm going to free you," she said, lifting her sword higher. "It's been months since you kissed me and I'm still alive. I'm not sick, I'm not weak, I'm *stronger* because of it."

Lord Aneurin's lips twitched as if he would smile. "And yet you haven't tried to touch me since. Perhaps you are still alive because you did not want me to kiss you. It would be your heart that doomed you, not the act that inspired it."

With a roar ripe with frustration, she rushed at him, lunging for his stomach. The blow knocked the wind out of him, and he fell to his knees, his mouth open as he tried to reclaim the air she denied him.

"You don't know anything," she shouted as she stood over him. "You don't believe I will save you. It *must* be my destiny because I am certain I will never do anything else. Until you are free, I'm not either!"

"Your...loneliness...will end," he said between gasps. "Less than two years from now. It'll be...over."

She shrieked as she swung the sword at the ground over and over. "Damn! Foolish! Canary!"

Lord Aneurin watched, wide-eyed, as she unleashed her assault on the innocent earth. With one final roar, she flung the sword into the bushes and stormed off.

She didn't get far. The landscape was still wooded when she collapsed against a gnarled oak and wept. Both of her hands scraped over the rough bark as she bowed her head, letting her tears fall to the ground. Each one an apology for her violence.

She growled as a hand gripped her shoulder and turned her around.

"I do not want you to grieve," the king said.

She leaned away from him, her back to the tree. "As long as you are forced by your nature to deny everything that makes you a person, I *will* grieve," she said, wiping her tears away with the back of her hand.

He pressed his lips together, emerald eyes darting from side to side as if searching for something. "Denying myself my humanity is how I keep everyone safe. Everyone I care about."

"I *am* safe," she whispered. "From you, at least."

He sighed, shaking his head. "I don't know what you want from me, Miss Renaud."

She scoffed. "I know what you want from *me*. That's why you kissed me. Your strength is failing you. Loneliness is winning."

A warning trill answered her as he stepped forward. "How little you think of me."

His narrow hips pressed against her own, and between her legs, she felt a desperate heat. "That's what you want, isn't it? For me to think little of you if I think of you at all."

"I do not grant you permission to speak about what I want," he said softly. "I will reign for another five hundred years, Miss Renaud. My authority within the Vale is absolute."

"And yet you are too afraid to wield it," she hissed. The defiance in her eyes would wound a lesser man, but it just made the king daring.

Calloused hands rested on her hips as he blocked her escape, pinning her to the tree.

"You confound me," Calla breathed, furrowing her brow.

"What you want changes from day to day. How conflicted you must be."

"Do not speak," he commanded quietly.

When he kissed her, his teeth caught her bottom lip. Another kiss, more heated blood. Part of Calla wanted to rejoice that he believed her theory. A second part of her was dizzy with the hope she could be kissed like this and not die because of it. And a third piece despised how deeply it wounded her that while he had no faith in her ability to free him, he was willing to touch her so intimately.

But this time, as one hand cupped her face and the other cupped her rear, she didn't want him to stop. If her love were doomed, she'd take whatever she could get.

Calla whimpered as his mouth moved to her jawline, whispering across her skin. One of her ankles hooked around his, pulling him closer.

"Do you feel alive, Calla?"

Her hands fell to her sides and she froze. Was he kissing her to bandage *her* loneliness? He was too kind and honorable to outright lie to her, but this kiss was just as false.

Enraged, Calla shoved him away. "I don't need your pity."

Lord Aneurin didn't speak to Calla. While he did not isolate himself, he instructed her swordsmanship in silence. When he wanted her to stretch, he stretched. When he wanted her to do her endurance exercises, he did them also. She followed his lead, and then together they walked back to the manor—he to bathe in his room, her to do the same in hers. She stopped dining with him in the evenings, but after she ate in her room, he would often join her in the library or the sunroom. Everything returned to the way it was during the first two years—back when they didn't talk, didn't touch. No interaction save a mere acknowledgment of the other's presence.

Eventually, she slid a note underneath his door.

I do not want your pity, not even in the form of the torture you put me through when you kiss me. But I would like to hear your voice on my birthday.

When she woke the next morning, a note sat folded on her vanity.

Does a hummingbird pity the blossom as he drinks its nectar, or does he kiss the bloom because if he doesn't, he will die?

I have never pitied you.

Calla scoffed, crumpling the note in her hand. Lord Aneurin misunderstood what kindness was if he thought flattery was anything but mockery. She reached to the waste bin, her hand clenching the note as it hovered over the rest of the trash.

She hesitated.

Hating her forsaken love, she peeled apart the paper, smoothing out the wrinkles as best she could.

Calla sat with her hands folded in her lap as Godfrey told her the king was eagerly awaiting her downstairs and had even requested cinnamon toast for breakfast. "We have a new hot drink, similar to tea, but made from ground roasted beans, not leaves," he said. "It's called coffee. His Lordship heard about it from correspondence with a descendant of one of his childhood friends, and he insisted the Duke of Lower Zretia send him some before he agreed to import it into the Vale. He wants you to try it."

His gaze flickered to the note, but Calla missed it. She asked, "Does he like it?"

Godfrey looked back at the note, then back at her. "He hasn't tried it yet. He is waiting for you." He looked again at the note.

This time Calla noticed, and she reached for it, but the steward moved faster. He paced the room as he read it.

"Does a hummingbird…" he read, trailing off. Then he stopped, gawking at the paper. His eyes snapped to focus on Calla. "Does he kiss the flower? *What have you done?*"

Calla stood and ripped the note out of his hands. "*I* didn't do anything. Ask His Majesty what *he* did."

Godfrey reached for the note, but Calla held it away from him.

"Do you love him?" he demanded. "Is that why you haven't thrown that away? The creases in the paper tell me you were going to dispose of it."

"Leave me alone."

"*Do you love him?*"

"I don't know," she cried. "I know that both times he kissed me I wanted to die because I wanted it so badly, but I hated it because he was only doing it so he could pretend we are not both utterly alone. But we are."

Godfrey stared. "Both times?"

"It wasn't my fault. I didn't ask him to do it. He did it himself, and then he punished *me* as if I were to blame for his foolishness. But I'm not dead, Godfrey, so don't you dare lecture me."

His jaw opened and shut. He stumbled to her bed, perching on the edge of it, his hands on his knees.

A look of confusion lifted the corner of Calla's lip. When she spoke, the words fell out of her mouth, and she couldn't stop them. "Why are you so shocked? He's been alone for five hundred years and now he has a woman living with him who thinks he's the most beautiful creature she has ever seen, so he took an opportunity to snatch up some affection. I don't blame him for that. What makes me want to tear out his feathers is how he abandons me afterward." She seethed, breathing through her teeth. Her next words were barely more than a whisper. "Well, he got his wish. I fear his kindness, just like he wanted. A piece of me dies every time he touches me because I know he will leave me alone, and I'll be in hell once again."

But all the pain that roiled in Calla's heart couldn't block the wretchedness she felt when Godfrey began to cry. He doubled over, his elbows on his knees and his face buried in his hands and he *wept* as if he were reliving every little hurt he'd experienced over the past five hundred years.

At first, Calla just stood there, her mouth open as she watched the beautiful, ornery servant cry like a baby. She looked at Delilah and found *she* was crying too.

Godfrey groaned as he sobbed, then cleared his throat. Sniffling, he raised his head, wiping at his eyes and nose with a handkerchief pulled from his waistcoat. "Delilah," he croaked.

She stepped forward. "Yes, Mister Fontaine."

He pushed himself to his feet and stood before the woman. "You will not repeat what you heard in here. Not to anyone. I would not have to comfort hundreds of broken hearts rather than four if this isn't what we hope. Do you understand? I will lock you in a cell if you tell even *one* soul."

Delilah nodded. "Yes, Mr. Fontaine. I won't tell anyone. I wouldn't dare."

He patted her cheek. "Good girl. Run along now. I did Her Ladyship's hair once or twice back in the day. I can take care of Miss Renaud from here."

She embraced him as if she couldn't help it, then left, shutting the door behind her.

Godfrey turned back to Calla, folding his hands in front of

his waist. "May I ask one more question?" He cleared his throat.

Calla eyed him suspiciously but nodded.

He took a deep breath, his eyes welling with tears again. "How long ago was the last time he kissed you?"

She straightened her back. "The first time was on the veranda on my twenty-third birthday. The second was a few months ago after sparring practice. He…" She looked at the floor. "Both times, he had the chance to stop but didn't. He forced himself to kiss me because he thought I wanted him to."

An incredulous laugh bubbled out of Godfrey's mouth, but he quickly regained his composure. "Did you not?"

She frowned. "It was my first kiss. I'm glad he did it, I'm glad it was him. But I had hoped that my first kiss would *mean* something."

He nodded but to Calla's astonishment, he threw his arms around her. "Well, it's best you don't entertain fanciful thoughts of romance. But you have proven that he can have a genuine friend in the world, at least while you live. Perhaps you have done it, my girl. Perhaps he is free."

Calla jumped, eyes wide. "Are his feathers gone?"

Godfrey sighed. "No. But they wouldn't be. The curse that feathers him is separate from the one that kills those who loved him."

Her mouth turned down as she tried not to cry. Her arms came up and she embraced him back, burying her face in his shoulder.

"That's right, Miss Renaud. You've done this old man a world of good." He sighed and put his hands on her shoulders. "Let's get your hair done up so you can go to him." As she settled onto the vanity bench, he leaned down to whisper in her ear. "I'll tell you a secret: the coffee is very good. I bet you ten shillings you will prefer to take it with cream and sugar, and he will grimace but insist on drinking it straight."

Calla chuckled. "Is it very bitter, Mr. Fontaine?"

He brushed her hair. "Incredibly so, but it is quite decadent with the accoutrements. We can punish him for his wicked stubbornness by pretending you've had it before. When offered the coffee, immediately ask for the cream and the sugar. When His Majesty asks you why, tell him you know from experience that it is satisfying and rich when taken that way."

She snorted. "And he won't question it because that would require he speak."

He pulled the top third portion of her hair back as he grinned. "Quite right, Miss Renaud. He will drink the rest of his cup and then ask for another with cream and sugar. His intention will be to make you think he also took it that way, but we'll both know the truth, won't we?"

He braided the gathered hair and spooled it into a bun. He picked up a yellow lily hairpin and stuck it in to keep the bun together.

Calla grinned.

Chapter Twenty

At the table, Lord Aneurin sat moving his eggs aroundhis plate. Upon Calla's entry, he looked up and watched her cross to her seat beside him. His wings shuddered. After licking his lips, he took a sip from his mug. He grimaced, then took a deeper sip.

Godfrey picked up a dark kettle. "This is the drink His Grace would like you to try, Miss Renaud. We would be interested in hearing your thoughts."

Calla placed some cinnamon toast on her plate, then sniffed the cup he poured for her. "Oh, this smells familiar. I'll need cream and sugar, please." Her gaze darted to Lord Aneurin, who stiffened.

Godfrey nodded vigorously. "Of *course*, Miss Renaud. You have a sophisticated palate indeed!"

Silence took over the room, a tangible presence, as the

steward finished fixing her coffee. She began to get nervous, but Lord Aneurin watched her hungrily as she brought the mug to her lips.

It was *good*. She had an idea of how much sugar Godfrey must have put into it, but she quite liked it. Satisfying and rich, just like he'd said.

"Why?" Lord Aneurin rasped.

It took every ounce of willpower Calla had to resist the urge to look at Godfrey. She focused her gaze on the Strix Lord, took another sip, then fluttered her eyes closed. She conjured the heat between her legs the first time Lord Aneurin had kissed her, then opened her eyes. She licked her lips, never removing her eyes from his.

The king's expression never changed, but his wings flared out one, two, three times.

Calla exhaled. To seal the deal, she took another deep sip of the drink, then licked her lips again.

I won't let you near me, she thought. *I want you to want me until you mean it when you kiss me.*

His wings flared again and again until he cleared his throat and drained his cup. He breathed heavily through his nose for a minute, then growled, "Mary."

Mary Milkes stepped forward. "Yes, my lord."

"Another cup."

Godfrey cleared his throat and stepped back from the table as Mary bustled forward to pour. The sound was almost Calla's undoing, but she bit down hard on her tongue.

Mary stepped away after pouring the coffee, and Lord Aneurin trilled his displeasure. "Do not forget the cream and sugar."

She cast him a worried look but poured a splash of cream and a spoonful of sugar into his cup. He waved her away. He stirred his coffee himself, staring at Calla while he did.

She bit her tongue again as he took a sip, looked at the mug in surprise, then took another sip.

When he set his cup back on the table and looked at her again, Godfrey wheezed, and Calla lost all control. She burst out laughing, grasping her napkin from the table and dabbing her eyes.

"Oh *god*," she gasped, unable to catch her breath. "My poor pigeon."

Lord Aneurin tilted his head this way, then that. His mouth spread in a grimace. He looked between Godfrey; who had fallen to the floor unable to breathe; and Calla who was fanning her face with the napkin.

He trilled inquisitively, then again louder. Calla sensed his alarm and reached her hand over to pat his, which was gripping the table. She brushed past his feathers, meeting his gaze while her brow creased.

"Bad form, Bird Prince," she said.

"You dare." He said it like a statement, not a question.

She scooted her chair closer to him, then reached over and patted his cheek. "Godfrey is a very wicked man, my lord. He tempted me most grievously to play a trick on you."

"Oh, yes?"

She couldn't help herself. Before she answered, she took in his posture. One forearm rested on the table and his other extended out from him, his hand still gripping the edge of the table, his broad, rigid shoulders hunched. Like he was getting ready to launch himself away from the table at any second.

"Only that…" Her mouth went dry. The intensity of his stare was unimaginably hot. Like holy fire, consuming the sins of her soul.

I'd face any fate just for a chance to accompany you into eternity.

"Only that you would chain yourself to bitterness just to pretend that it is impossible for you to indulge in more *decadent pleasures*."

Lord Aneurin's wings flared again. "Leave," he said in a low voice.

Godfrey, whose face was slack with surprise, bowed and followed Mary out of the room.

The second they were gone, the king rose from the table and went to the window. His wings still flared.

"You—" He paused. He peered out of the curtains, then snapped them shut. "You laughed at me." He turned to face her.

"We were laughing at—" Calla began.

"I know what Godfrey was laughing at. He's known me my entire life. It was he who cut the cord linking me to my dead mother the night I was born. Why was it him and not my father, you ask?"

He shoved his hands in his pockets.

"Because he was the only one who was not afraid to be in the room with me. An oracle told my mother her first and only child would be an Ambrosius, and she was afraid. My father was thrilled but threatened to execute anyone whose gaze lingered too long on me. Childbirth is a messy business, and the placenta would have been a mighty tempting snack for any ambrosia runner within miles. Godfrey delivered me alone. When he couldn't save my mother, he cut my cord, cleaned me, and dressed me in a white silk shroud. He massaged sweet orange oil into my black-tufted scalp. And he brought me to Lord Octavian, then-king of Lorana Vale. But the only thing Octavian ever gave me was the most overwhelming determination to be *better* than he was. And when I was twenty-four and he *died*, I was glad. For you see, Calla, Godfrey was my mother's physician, and he loved her very well." He scoffed. "I didn't learn of that until Octavian died and I inherited the crown, and I wanted to promote the only member of the staff who wasn't afraid to talk to me. I wanted him to be my steward. The uproar that caused confused me for weeks until finally someone was brave enough to tell me why everyone was so concerned about who served as steward."

It was more than he'd said to her at once. Ever. But Calla didn't care. "Are you saying Godfrey is your—"

"—No. He has never confirmed nor denied it. All he said was that I was lord now and the tragedies of the past are better learned from and forgotten. I made him steward and got rid of everyone who'd tried to stop it. So, Miss Renaud, I know quite well what *he* was laughing at. After all, he knows me better than I know myself, for it is only he who knows the truth."

Calla pushed herself to her feet, pacing until she was at the little serving cart in which a bottle of white wine chilled. "It's good he didn't answer you, my lord. If it were true, if history learned it was true, he would no longer be immune to the curse. If it were written that he was your father, and the Roran line ended and the Fontaine line began…"

Lord Aneurin moved toward her. "Indeed." He reached for the bottle of white wine, then a corkscrew. When the bottle was open, he knelt and reached past her skirts for two glasses in the cabinet below the tray. When he stood and poured a glass, she took it and eyed him warily, not daring to sip.

"What I want to know, Calla lily mine, is what exactly I

have done to make you think I'm bitter. Lonely, certainly, but as I recall, it is *you* who throws around accusations of pity and pretension."

To avoid answering, she sipped her wine. He sipped his and watched her, and when she'd finished her glass, he set his own down and pried her fingers from the stem and took it from her, setting it aside as well.

"The king demands an answer."

She lifted her chin. "You deny it, but you do pity me. Why else would you kiss me? If you forget your wife, everyone you know will become susceptible to the curse."

He looked like he wanted to say something, but he hesitated. Then he said, "I don't know if I believe that anymore."

"What?" she stammered, looking at where one of his hands still held her own against his chest.

"I want to kiss you, Miss Renaud. And I want to keep doing it until you *believe* me that pity has nothing to do with it."

"My lord," she began, shaking her head. "I—"

"Just say my name, *rosara*. And then don't say anything again. Put your mouth to better use."

At the term of endearment, her enchanted blood surged in her veins. It was a word used only by the most holy scions of Della Ros. A sanctified word, a magical spell in six letters. To call something or someone *rosara* was to declare them the most beautiful thing in existence. And it could only be used to name one thing. Once it was used, it could never be used to refer to anything or anyone else ever again. Not by the same person.

Breathing was impossible. "Why?"

"Because you are immune, and I can."

Her heart sank, hope deflated. "That's not good enough."

She pushed past him and headed for the door, her steps quick.

Lord Aneurin grabbed her wrist and spun her around. "Do not flee from me. I know what game you're playing, Calla, and it delights me, but you do not get to lie to me about what you want. You wouldn't start a fire with your gaze every time you look at me if you didn't want me." He brought his hands to her face.

It took all she had not to turn her head and kiss his palms.

"Tell me true," he whispered. His voice had long since grown hoarse as he stretched cords that hadn't been used so much in centuries. "*What do you want?*"

"I don't know," she whispered back. "Every day I wake up and all I can think about is you. About freeing you. There's no room for anything else. I want to free you and I want you to be happy, and then I want to go to the sea and dive into the waves. And after I've soaked up the essence of the ocean, I want to return to Senden's Branch and help my father with his business. I want to grow old watching the good you do when you're not afraid to speak to your people. I want to prove I'm not walking toward my death, that every day is not just borrowed time."

Aching, her heart roiling like a river after a heavy rain, she silently begged for him to tell her that he needed her as much as she needed him. That even though their time together was temporary, it *mattered*.

"If you freed me, you would not live in the village. You, and your father, would live here. Publicly and openly. And I would kiss you, publicly and openly, if you allowed it."

She peeled his hands from her face. "I would not, my lord. Even without the curse, I couldn't dishonor your lady wife." But she couldn't hide from her voice the disdain she felt for the dead queen.

He raised his hands again and clutched her to him. "Why not?" he whispered dangerously. "Lick your lips again, *rosara*. You thirst for water, but when I offer it to you, you will not drink."

"It isn't water I want, my lord. What I want might as well be ambrosia."

He looked at her strangely, then took a step back. "If you are immune, why are you afraid? Have I truly misunderstood your desires? Do I not know the rules of the game?"

What Calla should have said was that she wasn't playing a game, and she would see him later. What she would never have said was that she was hopelessly in love with him and it broke her heart that he thought it was a game at all.

What she *did* say was, "I'm afraid I've not been a good sport, my lord. I *was* playing a game, but I stopped following the rules long ago."

He titled his head. "Do you want me to kiss you?"

She could not lie to him. Not outright. "Yes."

"*May* I kiss you?"

"Only if you make me believe that you want to."

"Oh, Calla," he murmured before capturing her mouth with his. As his tongue tasted hers, he pushed her back, step by step, until she bumped into the table. His arms came around her and he gripped her as if she belonged to him.

Her fingertips explored every exposed feather of his neck and jaw. She delighted in the feel of them. "I love the taste of you," she murmured when he licked her bottom lip.

He groaned into her mouth. "Do not tease me."

"Why not?"

"Because you are immune, and I would beg you to allow me to prove how immune you are."

Her breath caught in her throat, and he took it as a sign to continue. Gripping her hips, he picked her up and set her on the solid wood table. His hands roamed over her breasts, back down to her hips, then back up again as if he couldn't decide where to put them.

There was something to the kiss, certainly, but Calla knew it was her immunity he loved. He loved it because it gave him the freedom to satisfy those urgings he'd neglected since his wife died.

But what Calla regretted most was how grateful she was that he was willing to use her. It was not cruelty: legends didn't fall in love with carpenter's daughters, and she'd always known that.

And yet she let him kiss her until Godfrey knocked on the door.

Lord Aneurin didn't allow her to pull away as he said, "Enter." He kept his arm around her clutching her to him. Calla wanted to hide her face as she watched Godfrey take in the state of her hair and flushed face.

The steward coughed. "There is a visitor for you," he said nervously. "He demanded to see a Lady Briar Beauregard. I told him there was no Lady Briar Beauregard here, but he said he didn't believe it. He demanded an audience with you, my lord."

Calla's eyes widened. She hadn't written back to Loewen after the king had kissed her in the woods.

Lord Aneurin glanced at her out of the corner of his eye. "He appears to be fond of you."

"You read my letters. I did not encourage him. He is far too old for me."

He glanced at her again, a bemused twist to his mouth. "Is he? Well, we cannot have *that*."

Untangling himself from her, he straightened the lapels of his jacket. "By the stairs, I presume?" But he left without hearing an answer.

Godfrey snapped to attention, his focus on Calla. "Why do you look so unhappy? I thought you wanted this."

She looked everywhere but at him. "I want...I want his love. Or at least I want him to mean it when he kisses me."

Godfrey scoffed. "I'm looking at you, girl. He does mean it. I'm surprised you didn't start sleeping in his room the moment he realized you were immune."

She blushed, feeling the ache of awkwardness in her shoulders. "I've never been with a man, Godfrey. And I want my first time to be for love. But if I don't break the curse, no matter how much I love him, he will watch me grow old and ugly, and then he'll have to bury me. I cannot have him see me like that. If I can't free him, even though I am immune, or the curse is broken...I cannot stay here with him. There is no future for us."

The steward shook his head. "So free him."

Her eyes gleamed. "He does not love me. He cares for me, desires me, but he does not *love* me. What use would he have for me?"

Godfrey ran a hand through his hair as he said, "Miss Renaud." He crossed his arms and spoke with a deadly skepticism. "*Miss Renaud.* Are—are you fucking blind?"

She jumped off the table. "No. And you'll see. In a year if and when I break the curse and he opens his doors to all the courtiers and courtesans of Lorana Vale and beyond, he will find a woman worthy of his exalted attention. You'll come to me to collect that debt and with you will come news of a royal wedding. Do not humiliate me further. I will kiss him until our lips turn blue because that's all I'll ever allow myself to have. I already may give my life for him, curse or not."

He took a step forward as if he meant to comfort her. "You cannot mean that. You're in love with him. What if your great destiny were to spit on the grave of the witch Eugenia? To defy the curse, not break it?"

Chapter Twenty-One

T he temptation was too great. Calla wanted desperately to see her friend Loewen again. She hadn't seen him in almost two years.

Hoping her scent wasn't too strong, she lightly navigated to the hallway she knew opened up behind a door under the stairs in the enormous entry to the palace.

The king stood on the first-floor landing. She could not see him from her position, but she could hear him.

"What business have you with my betrothed?" he asked.

Calla's eyes widened, and she pressed herself against the door to listen.

She heard Loewen scoff. "Your betrothed? You're a *bird*."

"I am a man where it matters," Lord Aneurin replied coolly.

If her heart raced any faster, she'd die. Is this what Lady

Eugenia cursed him for? Did she too succumb to the consuming heat of his power and consideration?

He was kind. He was honorable. But he was *Lord Protector of the Vale*, and he did not shy away from proving it.

"That's…that's disgusting," Loewen said. "You're an animal, regardless of what parts you have. You cannot hold her hostage here. She does not *love* you."

"She is here because she wants to be. And it is my hope that by the time she leaves, she loves every part of me. My feathers, my fingers, and everything else. She has been a great comfort to me."

Why would he want her to love him when he knew someday she'd leave? That was not like him at all. It was too cruel.

The thought occurred to Calla that perhaps Godfrey was wrong. It was not his kindness that was cursed. Maybe it was his influence. Those that altered the course of their fates to accommodate his greatness were the ones who died.

"Let her go," Loewen said. "She does not belong in these haunted halls, Your Grace. And you know it."

She heard the ruffling of wings as he must have flared them. "Leave, merchant. You are not welcome in Lorana Vale anymore."

Loewen made a strangled, sputtering sound. "You cannot do that. I was born and raised in the Vale. Everything I have, everything I've built is here. She would not want you to do this. I am her friend."

The king trilled. "As am I, merchant. And yet you will leave and never come back. You will not write to her. I know she has not written to you, for I have read every letter. To you, she is nothing but the Lady of the Vale, and when you think of her, you will remember it."

Calla clapped her hands over her mouth.

"Please, my king, set her free. Send her *home*, if you must, but don't keep her here."

"She *is* home. If you are willing to defy *me*, you would be willing to defy *her*, but I tell you, she does not desire your company."

"I don't mean to defy anyone, my lord, but she is a rare beauty and it is an affront to Della Ros himself to lock her away."

"Leave before I kill you," the Strix Lord said, and Calla's blood froze at the malice she heard in his words.

Footsteps moved toward the door, but then halted. "You know, they say your tale is a tragic one. That you were cursed for loving too well. But your heart is as ugly as your visage," Loewen said.

Again, the Strix Lord trilled. A warning. "The only reasons you are still standing after your impudence are you made her smile on her birthday and, of course, I don't feel like making my servants mop up your remains after I tear you to pieces. Take advantage of my mercy, merchant."

Silence took over the hall, but Calla knew Loewen hadn't left.

After a while, he said, "Did you murder your wife, Strix? Is that why you're cursed?"

The king was quiet for a moment. "If I did, that would make me a rather dangerous creature, wouldn't it? A wifeslayer, and yet powerful enough to conquer death and time."

"Let her go."

"*Never.*"

A cacophony erupted in Calla's mind and as it overwhelmed her, she fled to the safety of her room,

Chapter Twenty-Two

The next day, Calla met Lord Aneurin on the sparring field. She looked him right in the eye and took off her shirt.

His wings flared. But he didn't move. He switched which of his hands held his practice sword and said, "Why?"

She threw the shirt on the ground. "So you can see where I'm bruised. Though the worst wound is deeper than you can see."

Slowly he lowered his gaze from her face to her collarbone. The skin there was creamy and unmarred.

Down to her stomach, around to her sides, where there were three bruises on her left and one on her right. Black and spreading like mold. He winced a little when he saw them.

Despite the cold and damp, when his eyes fell on her belt, she began to remove it. She kicked off her boots and wriggled out of her pants, standing before him only in white underthings.

"Get dressed," Lord Aneurin demanded.

"Look," she commanded.

Gritting his teeth, he looked over her legs, legs so pale except where purple smeared over her thighs and knees. "Battle is dangerous," he said. "Learning how to avoid these bruises will save your life."

Calla dropped the practice sword, still standing before him. Bare and cold and shivering. "Do you have any idea of what I mean to do? How far I am willing to go to save you?"

The corners of his mouth turned down. "I know you care, Miss Renaud. But I was an Ambrosius like you. I know what it means to face your destiny. This is mine."

"And *mine* is to free you. Do you understand that?" she cried, stepping forward, her feet making almost no sound on the rain-drenched leaves. "Even if we're right and *her* curse cannot kill me, I will probably die doing this and I am *glad* of it because I don't want…"

She shook her head.

"This…feeling has been growing within me since the day I walked in your door and met you on the stairs. You stood there, at the top of that grand, sweeping staircase, and peered down at me and I felt *safe*. For the first time in my life, I was *safe*. But I know now that my intuition comes from whatever god blessed me with this destiny. If I make it to twenty-five, I *will* free you. You and I both need to accept that the day I step beyond the wall is the last day you will ever see me. You must stop kissing me. For my sake as well as yours."

He took a step toward her, shaking his head. "I did not intend to hurt you," he breathed. "I did not know my affection was a burden on you. I thought you wanted it."

Calla said nothing. She wordlessly got dressed. After she

pulled on her boots, she picked up her sword.

As she swung her sword, Aneurin parried her blows, then swung his own. Parry, block, counterattack. Being shorter than he was, Calla found it easier to dodge than to block. He was just too strong.

More time passed on the field than any other practice, and they said nothing at all. Sweat matted Calla's hair, and she felt it dripping down her back. Lord Aneurin breathed heavily, his arms awkwardly dangling as if they were incredibly sore.

Eventually, he landed a blow to her shoulder that made her cry out and drop her sword. He trilled as she whimpered, and he rushed to pull the collar of her loose shirt aside so he could see.

"I'm fine," she insisted, pushing him away. She bent and picked up her sword. "I'm fine."

All he could do was follow her back to the manor.

In silence they ascended the stairs. At the fourth-floor landing where she would go left and he would go right, he hesitated.

But Calla did not.

As soon as she was out of sight of him, the arm holding her sword fell to her side and the woolen-tip dragged along the carpet as she trudged to her room, her heart heavy.

An enormous weight collided into her, pushing her up against the wall. "I can't," Lord Aneurin said. "If destiny denies me, so be it, but I would have this."

This time, *she* pulled him down to bring their lips together. Hers parted to allow his tongue entrance and she whimpered as his hands roamed her body. It was like the fatigue of hours spent sparring completely evaporated like the sweat from her skin. "Annie," she whispered as his mouth moved to her neck.

"Calla lily, lily mine," he murmured into her skin. "Tell me to go and I will. I'll not make you ask a third time."

But she knew she would accept everything he offered her. Little more than a year left until she would look upon him no more, and she would take every sweet memory, every gasp and whimper. She would take them all with her, beyond the wall, beyond the Vale. When she met her fate, she would cling to them, praying the sheer beauty of each one would guide her safely to Arronet, the celestial valley where the Destined went when they died.

Her hands grasped desperately at the loose shirt he wore. It would be so easy to tear it right off. The only things keeping it on as she tugged and pulled were the two buttons on the back, fastened below his wings for ease of dressing.

Calla mewled again when he caught her earlobe between his teeth. "Calla," he breathed, warmth soothing her frost-bitten ear.

"My lord, we're in the hallway," she gasped as his hand slipped between her legs.

"Aneurin," he murmured. "Or Annie. Only ever use my name. Use it for the rest of your life."

She panted as he stroked her. "Aneurin, someone will see."

"Let them dare question the king."

Calla whimpered as his hand withdrew, but then it found hers. He pulled her toward her room, and her blood roared in her ears as she let him.

Godfrey turned the corner. He stopped in his tracks when he saw them, peering oddly at their joined hands. Calla's face turned red, but Lord Aneurin snapped, "See we're not disturbed."

"Yes, Your Grace," Godfrey said, watching them pass.

Lord Aneurin locked the door to her room behind them before putting his mouth back on hers, pushing her toward the bed.

"My Lord," she protested.

"*Aneurin*," he corrected.

She collapsed onto her bedspread, propping herself up on her elbows, but he stretched out beside her almost immediately, his hand slipping up her shirt as he tasted her mouth again.

"Aneurin," she whispered. "I'm not...I don't know how far you're trying to go."

He hummed in response. "Not too far, Miss Renaud. Just a little more. Is that all right?"

Calla gasped as his hand brushed past her breast. She collapsed against the mattress. "That's fine," she said.

"Fine?" He laughed, low and deep and rasping. "I'd hope for more than *fine*."

Calla didn't say anything, only hooked her arm around his feathered neck and pulled him down to kiss her again.

That's what he did for a long time, his hands whispering over her skin under her shirt until she began to shake. A glint appeared in his eyes as he moved to continue his ministrations between her legs until she cried out, so close, so close.

Then he stopped.

Her eyes snapped open as she protested the loss of his fingers, and then the loss of the rest of him as he pushed himself to his feet.

"You're stopping?" She rose to be sitting.

The Strix Lord smiled, smoothing his shirt. "Yes, Miss Renaud. It is my hope that the next time I kiss you, you tease *me* just as viciously. Worse, even." His tall frame seemed to take up the entire room as he looked down on her with heavy-lidded eyes. He bent at the waist to bring his face near to hers. "When you're ready, make me beg for it."

Then he was gone, swept from the room with a majesty only a king could command. And Calla thought the room was a duller place than any she'd ever known, because while he'd been there, she'd never been surrounded by more beauty.

Chapter Twenty-Three

A loud thump woke Calla from a deep sleep. After how long she'd sparred, and the hours she'd spent with her hand between her legs before finally succumbing to slumber, she was dead to the world. Yet the noise was like thunder.

Someone was trying to open her door.

Calla's eyes snapped open and she rolled out of her bed, crouching behind it as someone tried the knob. Anyone with permission to enter her room possessed a key to it. Godfrey, Delilah, and the king himself.

She looked around the room. Silver moonlight flooded through her window, making her gauzy curtains glow. That someone would invade *here*, the home of a fearsome creature like Lord Aneurin...she was almost too surprised to be afraid.

A candlestick stood on her bedside table. She reached for it, brandishing it as she peered over the edge of the bed.

Such noise. Surely someone was coming to help. But then she remembered that she and Aneurin were the only ones on this floor. The staff had quarters in a rowhouse on the southern edge of the property. Godfrey's room was on the second floor, on the opposite side of the house. The army barracks was nowhere close to the palace.

Calla swallowed hard as she heard a clicking sound, metal on metal. Someone was picking the lock.

Screaming was out of the question. It would be better to pretend she wasn't there, wouldn't it? If she screamed, if she confirmed her presence...Perhaps the intruder would give up if he thought no one was in there. Calla prayed to Della Sorvis for protection. If any god heard the pleas of innocent victims, it was the god of justice.

The door creaked open as the lock was picked. She ducked as a shadow entered the room, then shut the door behind itself.

The sweat of her palms made her grip on the candlestick tenuous. She held her breath, squeezing her eyes shut.

"So it's you," said a familiar voice.

Calla turned her face, wide-eyed, to stare at Loewen.

"Sir, you are not permitted to be in my room. You must leave before Lord Aneurin knows you're here," she said.

Loewen crouched beside her. He was dressed in leather garb, a jacket over a jerkin, leather trousers, leather boots. His hair was slicked back. "Are you one of the Strix's pets? A pet Ambrosius for him to taste to get him in the mood? I smelled you when last I was here."

His tone was not unkind, and Calla realized he must have come to rescue Lady Briar Beauregard from the clutches of the Strix Lord who held her captive. But she didn't want to be rescued.

"Do you know where Lady Briar is?" Loewen said. He seemed to notice how violently Calla was shaking because he added, "I will not hurt you, Ambrosius. Just tell me where her room is and I will retrieve her. You'll never see me again."

Calla shook her head. "She's not here, sir," she lied. "Lord Aneurin wanted her to see her family one more time before they are wed." Expanding on Aneurin's lie seemed easiest.

Loewen snorted. "She will not marry him. She clung to me two years ago and I watched how she stared in fright as he claimed her the night of the party. I will free her. I have wealth and means to. I can protect her. Where is she?"

She shook her head again. "She's not here. She's gone."

Loewen sighed and stood up. He moved to the window and peeked around the gauze to check outside.

Calla stood too, slowly moving toward the door while his back was turned.

The merchant sniffed, then sighed. "Not here, you say. And yet I cannot believe you. I'm not sure what it is, but *something* rings false." He looked around the room. He bent and sniffed at Calla's bed, shuddering when he stood. "You've almost fully absorbed your ambrosia."

His gaze fell on her wardrobe. A shaft of moonlight shone directly on it, illuminating the embroidered lilies of the dress Lord Aneurin had given her for her twenty-second birthday. She wanted to wear it tomorrow. It had been her hope seeing her in it would excite him.

Loewen whirled on her, and Calla's blood turned to ice. With a cry, she ran for the door, but he'd locked it. She fumbled with the lock, but she wasn't fast enough. Loewen grabbed her shoulder and twisted her around, a dagger pressed to her throat. "Where is Lady Briar? Did he kill her? Did *you*? Whore. Bestial slut."

Calla whimpered as the blade cut her and a drop of blood was exposed to the air. Loewen's eyes widened as the scent of her ambrosia filled the room.

"Arronet preserve my soul," he whispered. He dug the blade deeper into her skin. Blood dripped down her neck, coating the breast of her white nightgown. Loewen didn't seem to care that she cried out. He lowered his mouth to her neck and lapped at the blood like a wolf might lap at the viscera of the deer it had hunted.

Calla whimpered as Loewen's eyes glowed pink as the high took him. He brandished the weapon again, slicing her shoulder and the strap keeping her nightgown up. Then he licked her there.

Crying and shaking, Calla balled up her fists and beat at Loewen's chest, trying to shove him away, but the ambrosia had taken him, and he was too strong. She might as well have been a mouse.

"I will have every drop," Loewen whispered. With a flourish of his hand, he sliced at her breast, then her stomach. "Bleed, girl. Bleed for me."

Calla fell to her knees, her hands pressing into her stomach.

This cannot be the way I die. I was safe here.

The merchant grabbed her arm and pulled her away from the door. She tried to stand, but she was losing blood fast, and her vision swam.

He threw her to the carpet beside her bed, kneeling beside her. He coated his hands in her blood, then licked his fingers. Moaning at the taste.

"No," she cried. "Please. *Please.*" Calla wept as the moonlight dimmed as if a cloud passed over the moon, but she knew it was a clear night. "Please," she whispered.

Loewen coated his hands again. "The Strix took the one I'd call wife. He took her from me. So I'll take his slave from *him*."

Calla kicked her feet, trying to find purchase on the carpet, but it was soaked in her blood and her bare feet slipped.

The grief Lord Aneurin would feel when he found her. It was the last thing she thought about as Loewen began fumbling with his belt, the lust stage of ambrosia intoxication overwhelming him.

"No," Calla whispered, wishing she had the strength to scream. "No, no, please."

Just as Loewen pulled himself free of his trousers, a roaring shriek exploded from the corner of the room. Loewen jumped, looking over his shoulder and trying to shove himself back into his trousers, but Aneurin was too fast. He flew over Calla's bed and put the curved blade of his own dagger through Loewen's throat. "You *dare*," he hissed at the merchant as he pinned him to the ground. The would-be rapist gurgled on his blood as the King of the Vale punched him in the face again and again, then thrust his dagger into his face. "You dare take her from *me*."

Aneurin unleashed his rage until there wasn't anything left of Loewen's head.

Then he tumbled to Calla's side, his wings drooping with his grief. "No, *rosara*," he whispered. His hands pressed into her stomach, trying to stop the bleeding, but it spurted around his hands. "No, no, Calla. Don't." He tore the covers from her bed and balled them up, pressing the linen into her wound. "GODFREY," he screamed. "For god's sake, Godfrey. Please."

He brushed her hair back from her face, kissing her brow. "I'm sorry, my darling. I'm so sorry. I was selfish, and I thought I could have you. Please don't."

She coughed, blood coating her lips.

"No, Calla," he said. "*GODFREY!*"

Calla's heartbeat slowed as her legs went numb. She reached up and caressed Aneurin's face, smearing her blood over his cheek as she slipped away.

Chapter Twenty-Four

Aneurin

Aneurin paced his bedroom, wings flared. "Do something, Godfrey!" he shouted as Calla grew even paler. Sweat coated her brow and her mouth hung open, her eyes shut. Not even fluttering. Even behind them, her eyes did not move.

"Does her heart still beat?" Aneurin asked nervously, turning around to pace in the other direction again.

Godfrey bent over Calla, his hands coated in her blood. Blood was everywhere, on the carpet, saturating the sheets of Aneurin's bed, staining Godfrey and Aneurin's clothing. The sweet tang of the magic in her blood nauseated Aneurin. He'd been an Ambrosius. It just smelled like the blood of a diabetic to him.

At least he wouldn't have to worry about Godfrey being tempted by Calla's blood. He'd raised Aneurin from when he was a boy and had never so much as kissed his cuts.

"Weakly, sire, and I don't know for how much longer," Godfrey said. He pulled one of her wounds open a little further, assessing the damage to her intestines and other organs. "He didn't hit anything important. She just won't stop bleeding."

"Make her stop," Aneurin wept. "I'll follow whatever you say, I'll stay away from her, I promise, but please save her."

Godfrey kept his gaze on Calla as he wiped the stab wounds with saline and iodine. Aneurin turned his gaze away from her navel. It was going to scar so horrendously.

Aneurin thought he was going to be crushed under the weight of his guilt. If he hadn't fallen so hard for Calla, if he'd only stayed away like Godfrey had insisted...

He looked again at Calla's dying body and wished for the millionth time that he never made that stupid bargain with Della Ros. That he'd abdicated the throne in favor of Godfrey and hung himself from the highest rafter in the ballroom. That was what he deserved. He'd been so selfish, so arrogant to think he could tempt fate.

He hated Eugenia for cursing him. He wished his father had never invited hers to the palace. He wished, again for the millionth time, that he'd never met her. That he'd been free to be a good king, a wise king, a compassionate king. But he was none of those things. Eugenia had stolen his destiny from him, and even after she mercifully died she'd stolen any chance of him finding it after she was gone.

Groaning, he knelt on the opposite side of the bed from Godfrey and took her hand in both of his and held it to his face. He kissed it, gagging on the blood that coated it but needed to feel her skin against his mouth. "I needed to tell you," he wept.

"I needed to tell you how I feel before you went into the world to find the sea."

"Tell her now, boy," Godfrey huffed as he dug in his bag. "It may be your last chance. Perhaps she can hear you somehow."

A sob wrenched from Aneurin's throat as he said, "I love you, Calla. You gave me the only happiness I've ever felt. You made this horrid immortality worth it, if only so I could meet you. And if you die now, you're going to take with you everything good in me. Everything redeemable. What will be left is nothing but the husk of the son of Octavian Roran.

Godfrey inhaled deeply through his nose, then sighed. "She's lost too much blood, Annie."

Aneurin sobbed again and kissed Calla's hand. "Please don't," he pleaded. "Please. Not this way. Don't be another one of my failures. I swore to protect you, Calla. Please don't let me fail in this. I cannot bear it."

Godfrey huffed, and Aneurin glanced up at him. His steward's green eyes were wet with tears. He huffed again as if refusing to cry, then shook his head. "Annie," he said.

Aneurin grunted.

Godfrey sniffed. "I'm going to give her my blood. But she needs more than I can give and survive, so you will have to learn to make do when I'm gone. Do you hear me? Delilah can carry on for me. Trust her the way you trust me."

Aneurin shook his head. "I cannot lose you, Godfrey."

The steward—and the best man Aneurin had ever known—smiled weakly and pulled a thick needle out of his bag with some sort of implement and a thick rope of tubing in which he fastened another thick needle. He pierced Calla's arm, and then his own, then turned a lever on the implement. Blood began to drain from his arm and into Calla's.

"Will that work?" Aneurin asked. "She's an Ambrosius. You are not."

Godfrey shrugged. "It's her best chance."

"Godfrey," the king said. "I don't know how to thank you. For everything."

Emerald eyes met emerald eyes, all gleaming like jewels in the sunlight. "I served you as well as I could because it was the right thing to do," Godfrey said. "I do not regret any of it, except for not protecting you against that witch."

Aneurin's heart fell out of his body and his soul compressed into a lump of coal. He turned his face down and wept into Calla's hand. "What have I done?" he muttered over and over. "What have I done?"

Chapter Twenty-Five

Calla

The moment Calla knew she was alive, she regretted it. Pain wracked her body. Her head swam with dizziness, likely from the yarrow and feverfew tincture she could taste on her tongue. She grimaced, struggling to open her eyes, but she was so, so weak.

So she groaned instead, just as an image came to her mind of a tortured Aneurin awaiting her return to consciousness.

"Calla," he said immediately. She felt him touch her hand.

She groaned again, straining to open her eyes.

"Don't try to speak, just rest," he said.

But Calla did not want to rest. She was alive. His apology in her room was unnecessary. Surely those targeted by fate should know that the winding roads are treacherous—a coincidence is not fate, but it may cause even the most dedicated traveler to stray from the path anyway.

With a sigh, she forced her eyes open. It was dark, but she could see the moon was a waning three quarters. She must have been out for days.

Godfrey sat on the side of Aneurin's bed, a massive bandage wrapped around his arm. A hollow needle and a long, narrow tube covered in blood lay in his lap. He watched her, his sweat-covered face slack with relief. "You are not well enough to sit up or move. I did what I could, but you may well miss your birthday."

"I—" she started, but Aneurin trilled a warning. She glared at him. "I'm thirsty."

Godfrey stood but Aneurin voiced his warning again. The Strix Lord rose from his seat and went to the table, pouring a glass of water and bringing it to her. He slid his arm behind her head, lifting her just enough so she could drink.

Even that small act was too much for her. She winced, her hand drifting over her stomach. Aneurin offered her a dropper, and Calla could smell the concoction from where she lay. She shook her head. "I just want to sleep. Don't…take away my senses…"

The next time she woke, she was alone with Aneurin. He watched her, chewing on his nail with an anxiety she'd never seen from him. As her eyes opened, he leaned forward. "What do you need?"

Her eyes widened and closed, then opened again as she struggled to sit up. "The toilet. I need you to take me to the toilet and then I want you to leave."

He chuckled with relief. "Can you stand?"

"I will stand whether I can or not." She tried to move but couldn't. She groaned, her cheeks flushing. "Fine. Carry me."

He nodded, rising to pull the covers back. He bent at the knees and scooped her into his arms. She winced as pain surged in her aching body, but she noticed with relief that she was in a clean nightgown. Whoever changed her, she didn't care to know.

Aneurin took her into his sitting room and then into his private bathroom. He sank to one knee to make it easier for her to wobble to the toilet. She swayed next to it. "Leave," she insisted.

He trilled his amusement and left, closing the door behind him.

When she was done, she took hesitant steps to the door; her knees threatened to give out at any moment. She opened the door, but the movement was too much for her. She toppled over.

Aneurin caught her as she fell. "Careful," he murmured, carrying her to the bed.

When she was tucked in again, he said, "I'll get you something to eat."

"Wait," she said. "Where is Godfrey? What happened to his arm?"

A look of pure tenderness washed over his owl face, the lines around his mouth softening. "He fought so hard to keep you alive. So hard. He almost failed, and we were going to lose you, but he bled himself for hours to replace the blood you'd lost." He grimaced to hide a trembling lower lip. "We didn't know if replacing your ambrosia with unenchanted blood would kill you, or if it would work to save you. He didn't let me help him until he collapsed. When you woke before, I had just finished wrapping his arm." His breath caught in his throat and he stared at the ceiling, blinking rapidly to banish his tears. A soft, sad smile turned the corners of his mouth. "He almost gave his own life to save yours, Calla lily. And I will *never* be able to repay that debt."

He slipped through the bedroom door, leaving Calla to close her eyes and think of Godfrey until she fell asleep.

When she woke, the steward sat with her. She smiled at him and he smiled back. "I am relieved to see you smile, Miss Renaud. You must be feeling better," he said.

She reached for him, and he stared at her outstretched hand with a softness she didn't know he was capable of. "Thank you, Godfrey. He told me what you did."

He sighed and took it. Then he shrugged. "I did what needed to be done. Nothing more, nothing less."

She squeezed his fingers. "You're a silly old man if you think anyone else feels that way. You saved me. And him. Because you know he would have blamed himself for the rest of his thousand years."

Godfrey nodded and looked at the floor, releasing her hand. "Yes, I know. That was half the reason I did it. The other half, of course, was because you are a dear girl to me and after everything you've done for him, I couldn't let you die. Not *that* way." He was quiet for a moment. "I watched his mother die. And I would gladly give my life to spare him from such a fate."

She knew that. And she was sure Aneurin did, too.

"Where is he now?"

His face darkened. "We did our best to remove all traces of your blood from the manor, but it was everywhere. We burned the carpet and the linen. Everything we couldn't scrub clean. But he has had to dispatch six ambrosia hunters since that night. He is out hunting any others that may be in the area."

Calla's face paled. "Even if they aren't coming here?"

Godfrey's mouth tightened into a firm line. "Anyone found

who has tasted ambrosia will be put to the sword. He is not willing to take the risk, nor is he going to be merciful to those who only tasted it once. No Ambrosius is safe while they are around. You know that."

That was the worst part. He was right. But it still made her sick to think that she was the cause of so much bloodshed, even if it was the blood of the guilty that was spilt.

Calla read a book after she bathed. She was starting to doze off when Aneurin swept into the room. His chain armor was covered in blood, as were his plate pauldrons.

"Aneurin," she murmured, setting her book aside.

He tore the clasp of his cloak, ripping it off of him. "You will return to your own room tonight. Everything has been replaced. If the memories are too much for you, choose any other chamber."

Calla froze. "Annie, what happened?"

He pulled off his pauldrons and let them thunk on the floor. "Do not speak my name, please. I cannot bear to hear it. There are too many of them. If I... if there is not some distance between us, they will come for you again. Ginny will see to it."

She nodded, her eyes cast down. With significant effort, she swung her legs over the side of the bed. "I wasn't wrong, Annie. I'm alive."

He shook his head. "I will not allow you to take the blame for my mistakes."

Mistakes. The sting of the word was worse than the ache in her belly.

She put her hand on the doorknob. "Don't do this, Aneurin. I could stay. The bed is certainly big enough for the both of us."

"You will go, Miss Renaud. I will see you on your birthday."

Three days without seeing him. But Calla knew his pain was great, and the minute she closed the door, he'd collapse under the weight of it. "Sleep well," she said.

He didn't watch her go.

Chapter Twenty-Six

The light of dawn refracted rainbows on the walls of Calla's bedroom as it filtered through the crystal box on her windowsill, which contained all the jewelry Aneurin had given her over the years. He never gave them to her himself. Just sent a box with Godfrey, who told her the jewelry was obtained and might as well go to her.

It didn't make sense that Aneurin would push her away. She'd survived. It was just coincidence after coincidence that kept them apart. Destiny was the only thing she believed in anymore. Not curses. Not now.

As she watched the sun rise, not directly but by watching the rays shift over the wall, she spied the tapestry was askew. She rose, padding on bare feet across the room.

She'd never asked how Aneurin appeared in her room the night he saved her from Loewen, but as she ran her hand over the tapestry, suspicion raised the hair on the back of her neck.

With a flourish, Calla threw the tapestry aside, revealing a wooden door. She wasted no time, popping the door open and studying the hallway behind it. No one. Thinking she'd not like it if she got trapped within the innards of the house, she propped the door open with the bench from the vanity, wincing as she bent to lift it.

Before she ventured into the tunnel, she wrapped herself in her robe. Who knew how cold it would be where the fireplace could not warm her?

The passage was a living, breathing dark. The deeper she went, the more oppressive it got. Haunted by the ghosts lingering within the walls of the palace. With her hand against the wall to keep track of where she was going, she kept moving forward.

Fear clenched her heart as she missed a step down. She prodded with her toes to see if there was another step, but there wasn't. She moved more slowly after that.

Down a flight of steps, she reached a corner, and she followed the path as it turned right. Here there were windows— white light streamed through little boxes of glass set high on the wall. The light illuminated the wall of the corridor. Someone had taken the time to paint it—while the floor was wood, the walls were goldenrod yellow.

The hall had a dead end. But Calla's heart surged, and she pushed lightly on the wall in front of her. A satisfied exhalation, and she pressed her way beyond the shadowed gold of the corridor.

Coming out behind the tapestry of the door illuminated by light from beyond, Calla stepped into Aneurin's sitting room. He was probably already awake. She knew he usually rose with the dawn to soar in the virgin light, casting his gaze on his realm.

A benevolent lord, if an absent one. It was not just for his sake that Calla wanted to free him. Until he dared pay attention to the villages, he couldn't know how terrible things were for those without means. Especially those with Ambrosius children. When food got scarce, the blood of children was sold. And most of those children didn't live long enough to see their destiny. Calla could have been one of them, but she was lucky. Peter Renaud usually made enough for both of them to eat, and when he didn't, he gladly went without to provide her with food.

She knew he'd wanted her to keep up her strength. If she ever had to run, to hide, as her father he'd needed to believe her body was strong enough to do it.

The sudden urge to flee twanged in her wounded stomach. Invading Aneurin's rooms when he told her he didn't want to see her was rude and inconsiderate at best. But she had to see him. He'd saved her life, and the way he'd screamed for the man who was a father to him would haunt her for the rest of what time he'd given to her.

The carpet under her bare feet was plush and new. She must have bled all over what was there before. Guilt at how expensive a guest she'd proven to be elevated her pulse even more. She should have turned around and pretended she was never there.

But she missed him. Even one day without him was too painful.

The bedroom door was open, and she could see the tip of one of his wings. He was still there, still in bed.

Silently she entered his room, but she stopped when her eyes fell upon him. Sprawled across the bed, he lay on his back, his wings extended to either side of him. All he wore was a pair of white silk pajama pants, the waistline of which hung low on his hips. He was shirtless, so Calla could see the feathers along his sides, a smattering across his chest, but the rest of him was creamy bare skin. His form was beautiful, muscled and firm, radiant in the morning light. One arm reached out toward the edge of the bed; his long fingers curled. The other hand rested on his stomach. In repose, he looked peaceful. And she noticed, stepping closer to the bed, how full his lips were as his mouth hung slightly open.

A lump rose in her throat as she gently perched on the edge of her bed and watched. Watched his chest rise and fall with his steady breathing. Watched how the feathers on his arms gleamed all the way to where they tapered at his wrists. Watched his fingers twitch as he dreamed.

She breathed in the sandalwood air, telling herself that no matter how badly she wanted to, she could not touch. He did not want her to. All she could do was watch him from afar. She'd always known that would be her fate. From the moment she met the fearsome Strix Lord, she knew she'd always watch his majesty from a distance.

The heat of his mouth was not meant for her. But it made her feel so *alive*. Regret washed over her as she realized she would die ignorant of so many things that would have made her feel alive—love and being loved. Freedom. Pleasure.

Aneurin's eyes fluttered open. "You shouldn't be here," he rasped when she met his gaze.

"That's all I am. Here. I cannot replace your wife just by being here," she said quietly, looking away.

Aneurin's breath caught. "Yes, you can," he said just as quietly. "You already have."

She looked at him sharply. "You love your wife."

He all but rolled his eyes and looked at the ceiling. "Not for a long time. And what begrudging respect I had for her died when Aluard did. He was my brother. I'd have made his children my heirs had he lived long enough to sire them."

Calla's hands itched. His slender, calloused fingers were inches from her thigh, and she wanted to scoop them up and kiss them. To comfort his ancient hurts as best she could. "Godfrey told me about him. He said you forged him into a noble man."

Aneurin scoffed. He was silent for a while before speaking again. "What virtues I passed on were given to me by Godfrey himself. Octavian never taught me anything, not how a king should behave, not what he should stand for. In fact, he did the opposite. And every day until he died I wondered how someone could be so heartless. Why did the people not riot in the streets in opposition to his rule? How could they not see him for what he was?" He pursed his lips. "But then I met Ginny, and I didn't see *her* for what she was until she was dying." He gestured at his bed. "Right here. She died here in my bed, or rather the bed that was here before you bled all over it. Godfrey doesn't know she'd bewitched me at a party when I was nineteen. I found the evidence later, in that book of curses I showed you. I tore the pages out and burned them, of course, refusing to believe. She'd loved me, but my love for her was all a fabrication. And like a fool, I asked her about it as she died, begging her to release me from her spell. 'You're my wife,' I said. 'Let me love another once you're gone. Set me free.' And she did. She released me with the same breath that cursed me so that the moment fate set love of any kind before me, it was taken away. I did not love Sarah, but I would have loved the child she would have borne had I given in to her seduction. I loved Aluard like a brother, and he was taken. I love Godfrey like a father, and it doesn't matter whether he is my father in truth, because I keep him at a distance. He is my servant, and I am his master. And I…"

He stopped, and Calla watched a single teardrop fall from the corner of his eyes to the pillow beneath his head.

"I'd learned to live with it. After Aluard, I closed my heart.

But when you touched my face, it was the first time I'd felt alive in five hundred years. And I took from you, and took from you, and took from you, and you've almost died twice because of it. I wish... I wish I'd never let you in my home because when you're gone, I will no longer be satisfied with my silent, isolated house. The rest of my reign will be hell. Utter hell. Because, Calla, you replaced her the second you pounded on my door and demanded I speak to you."

His eyes met hers again. Glistening emerald and fresh, wet honey.

"I tell you this so you don't spend a single moment of the next year wondering if you matter to me or if I meant it when I touched you. I hope each one of those embraces made you feel as alive as I felt. I will always remember them. For the next five hundred years I will remember them. And when my reign is over, I will die thinking of them."

A sob wrenched from Calla's throat as she clenched her fists, digging her nails into her palm to quash the urge to fall into his arms. What he said was enough for her. It was enough.

"I—"

"Don't say anything, Miss Renaud."

She swallowed her sobs and put her hand on the bed, leaning over. "No. I will speak," she said, sniffling. "I will speak. I am going to die saving you, Annie. I know it as surely as I know the sun will rise tomorrow."

He grimaced, shaking his head.

"*Yes*. And it will be worth it. I hope you find real love someday, once you're free to chase it. I don't ask you not to forget me, I ask only that if you do remember me, you remember me fondly when you embrace your wife, when you hold your child. When you make the Vale a place worth living in. Remember that you are so, so loved and carry that love with you wherever you go."

He grimaced again, but this time his hand moved the few inches to her thigh. She shivered at the touch.

"How can I find what will be lost?" he breathed. "When you go, you will take it with you."

Her head tilted as she began to cry again.

"I'm sorry," he said, his hand gripping her thigh, beckoning her to come closer. "Calla lily, come here."

She fell to the bed. Her head rested on his arm as she lay with her back turned to him. She realized she had lain on his wing, but he didn't seem to mind. His other arm came around her and he held her as she wept. His lips brushed against her temple, her ear. "Stay with me. I'd rather live eighty years with you and then watch you die happy in old age after a lifetime of genuine love. Better that than live all but five of a thousand years without you."

She shook her head. "I can't. I was born to free you."

"Calla." He kissed her hair again. "Please. *Please.*"

The ache to give in was overpowering most of her rationality, but she couldn't. She *loved* him, and her destiny was intrinsically tied to that love. Fate would not allow her to make that choice. And it terrified her that her life was not her own. It never had been, but now she felt the bars of that prison enclose around her.

"I'm afraid," she whispered. "I feel like I'm already dead. What if I'm a ghost like Eugenia but don't know it yet?"

Aneurin said nothing. He stopped kissing her hair, stopped stroking her cheek. She heard him swallow, his breath coming in more shallowly.

"I would show you how alive you are, Calla lily mine," he

whispered. "Before it's too late."

Heart racing, she gripped his hand to her chest. "All right," she whispered.

His breath caught as he slid his hand to her waist where her robe was tied. With agonizing slowness, he untied it.

Calla barely blinked as he helped her out of it and discarded it at the foot of the massive bed. As he did so, he adjusted his wings, pulling them out from underneath her so he could lie better on his side.

She curled up into a ball. To be nervous when this was what she'd been longing for was ridiculous, but she couldn't help it. This was the beginning of their goodbye.

Aneurin's lips brushed across her shoulder and his fingertips whispered over her arm, hooking around the strap of her nightgown, pulling it down. "You're trembling."

She couldn't say anything, not at first. But he kept touching her, kept kissing her. She gasped as he reached around her hip and slipped his hand between her legs. Inch by inch, her nightgown was gathered up, the silk brushing against her thighs. Through her undergarments, he stroked her, gently, slowly.

Unable to stand it, she rolled over just enough to be able to turn her face so he could kiss her. She whimpered her gratitude to Della Ros for his beauty as he took his time touching her.

The thought that nothing could be more beautiful than how he was making her feel flashed through her mind, but she changed her mind when she saw the tender set to his feathered jaw as he watched her face as his fingers worked faster.

"I—" she started.

"Declare your heart when you come back to me," he said softly. "Whether you succeed or not, even if you fail, tell me when you come home."

She gasped as a sweet sort of sensation ached in her core. "But I need to…" Her hand flew down to slow his fingers as her hips bucked. "I need to hear you declare yours. Maybe not today, but before I go—ah!"

He kissed her brow as she was rocked with pleasure. "Did that please you?" he whispered, kissing her again.

"Yes," she said softly. "Though I wish I knew what to do with my hands."

Aneurin smiled. "Well," he said, his voice impossibly gentle, "I would think you'd touch me with them."

Heat flooded her face as she rolled over to face him. She dragged her fingertips over his chest, her breath catching as she delighted in the feel of his soft skin. The black feathers along his sides contrasted gloriously, hauntingly, with his pale abdomen and she traced the line where feather met flesh.

Aneurin shivered, and Calla furrowed her brow. "Did that hurt? I'm sorry."

She pulled her hand away, but he held her wrist, returning her hand where it was. "Quite the opposite, Miss Renaud. You're just the first person to touch me there since Ginny got sick. Before my deal with Della Ros, I was quite ticklish but with the feathers…"

Calla held her breath, and he swooped in to kiss her.

"It is *quite* pleasurable. Please don't stop." His smile was as soft as ever, but she could tell he was teasing her.

She thought her heart was going to beat until it fell out of her mouth as she kissed him again, pushing him away so she could sit up.

He straightened too, unfurling his wings, and settled back

against the pillows. The intensity of his stare as he watched her straddle him set her blood on fire. "I wish you had a better view," he said wryly, his hands sliding up her thighs to rest on her hips.

"I'd tell you what I think of the view," she said, running her hands over his chest, focusing on wherever there were feathers, "but you told me to wait to declare my heart."

The corners of his mouth turned down, but then he smiled, and she knew that he was grateful for the implied compliment. But the nature of his smile changed as he lunged forward and flipped them around. As Calla's back hit the bed, he nuzzled her neck.

"That tickles," she laughed.

"That's an advantage," he said.

Aneurin moved down her body, grazing his teeth over her clavicle. As he moved down, his hands slid up, up, underneath her nightgown, until he exposed her undergarments and belly.

Her face flushed. With regret she wished she'd persuaded him to do this before she was so scarred, before her body was aching and sore and weary and broken. She tried to pull the nightgown back down.

"No, *rosara*," Aneurin said, nibbling on her knuckles. "I'd see all of you."

She looked at the ceiling. "But the scars...they're not healed."

"They'll fade," he said tenderly. "Look, beautiful one, and do not despair." With a kiss to her brow, he pushed himself to his feet and turned around.

His back was covered in scars. Faded white lines crisscrossed the flesh of his back, but even the feathers were not unmarred. The scars within the black and white were still red, newer than the white. Some of the feathers near the ligament where the wings sprouted from his body were torn and ragged. She'd never known. He'd always been dressed.

He looked over his shoulder. "Most of mine are faded. And no, *rosara*, they did not take five hundred years to heal." He turned back around and crawled toward her, the sinew of his shoulders rippling as he drew closer.

"What about the ones near your wings? They're new," she said, fretting.

Aneurin hesitated for a moment. "I no longer have someone to protect me. I have no champion."

Yes, he did. And he knew it, though he would not say it. Destiny was all but assured if an Ambrosius made it to twenty-five, but they still had to claim it for themselves. He knew what that call felt like. The yearning in his blood to fulfill his purpose.

If Calla was so certain that hers revolved around *his* happiness, then he had no choice but to support her as she pursued it. He'd pursued his to become the Lord of the Vale his people needed— and Ginny had taken that from him. He wouldn't take that glory from Calla, no matter how much the thought of losing her made him want to scream.

"You have me," she said, cupping his face in her hands.

"That's all I need. But I do think we have other things to do. After all, tomorrow is your birthday. The most exciting time of year since you came into my life. And we should leave this room eventually."

"Must we?" she sighed.

Aneurin considered the flush to her cheeks and the dampness between her thighs and made a decision. "We're leaving it now." He clutched her to his body and when her arms came around his neck, he flapped his wings, flying backward to his feet. Calla's legs wrapped around him even as she yelped in surprise.

Smirking, he carried her through his sitting room to his veranda, out into the sunshine. He didn't let go of her until he deposited her on the wicker-supported cushion.

Calla's face burned even brighter as she covered her chest. "I'm not dressed."

"No one will see," he murmured as he kissed her.

She tore her mouth away. "How do you know? What if Godfrey—"

He sighed, rearing back just a little. "Calla lily, I mean to make love to you, and I cannot do that if you keep getting distracted. If I'm half the man history thinks I am, you won't be able to say anything but my name for the next hour at least." He put his fingers to her lips. "You're hesitating. If you don't want me to do this, say so and I will take you back inside. But if you do, lie back and enjoy it."

She opened her mouth and he covered it with his palm. She tore his hand away. "You're not begging yet," she said, and her gaze took on a more focused quality.

Eyebrows raised in surprise, he sat back. "I did tell you to make me beg, didn't I?"

She smiled, shy again. "I don't want to disappoint you."

He smirked and pushed her back. "You've already been declared *rosara* by a king, but now you want one to beg."

"So beg," she said. Then she sat up and took off her nightgown.

A deep groan sounded from the back of Aneurin's throat at the sight of her. Five hundred years of celibacy down the drain. He hoped he'd last long enough to please her, but he couldn't make any promises.

By the time they both were completely undressed, she could see between his legs how his body ached to be inside of her. And although Calla's body was sore, she wanted nothing more. But still she waited.

He stretched prone beside her, kissing her, and nibbling on her neck. The sun rose in the sky and the veranda grew warmer, but she waited. His hand stroked her again, but before she achieved anything close to climax, she stroked him. At the first brush of her fingertips against him, he'd whimpered and put his face to her shoulder and bit down. She smiled and stroked him again.

"Calla," he murmured. "You're going to be twenty-five before you let me prove anything to you."

She laughed, taking him fully in her hand. "That's up to you. I'm still nervous." She hesitated, and her hand fell away. She buried her face in her hands. "I'm nobody. A carpenter's daughter. The only thing that makes me special is that I'm here with you. Hundreds of Ambrosius die every year. I was just lucky enough to have a father brave enough to ask you for help. I think..."

She pursed her lips as regret washed over her. "I don't think I deserve this. Just four years ago, I hadn't ever seen the moon except through my window because it was too dangerous for me to be outside, especially at night. And now I'm here, outside in the sun with the *king*, and..." She covered her chest with her arms as insecurity made her shoulders tense. "I am nobody. Just nobody. If I don't succeed, I'll die a nobody. You're King Aneurin Roran. I—"

She reached for her nightgown and pulled it on. Aneurin didn't try to stop her. He watched her until she was dressed and then he sat up and sat cross-legged in front of her, their knees pressed together. "That's ridiculous," he said.

She looked at him in surprise.

He swallowed and licked his lips. "I've lived a long time, Calla lily, and what wisdom I've garnered in that time makes me think that your hesitation now, when we were both undressed, is rooted in your fear that once we do that, there's no going back. For either of us. You will be forever changed, your heart will be forever claimed, and all that will be left is the destiny that you still have to wait a year to claim. And it's that waiting that has you so afraid. You're trapped. My palace is still a prison, and you aren't free to make the name Calla Renaud as revered as the name Aneurin Roran."

She nodded, looking at the cushion.

"But we know that isn't my true name, don't we?" he said, lifting her chin with a finger so she met his gaze. "Destiny means nothing unless history recalls the truth of its claiming. The world doesn't know me. Your father never had anything to fear from asking me for help. But history remembers me as violent and deadly and callous and cruel, and I allowed the nuance of my violence to be lost to time. But if you fail, my love, my *rosara*, I will rewrite all of history. For the rest of my five hundred years, I will ensure that history remembers Calla Renaud as the Ambrosius who won the heart of a king with her silent, and sometimes rather verbose, company. Your life was not meaningless, even when you were hiding in your hovel. You will not be forgotten. Not by history, and not by me. Don't you see? You've already achieved a great destiny."

All at once, it became too much for her. The gentleness of his voice, the weight of how hard she had fought to survive, her relief at being here, the sucking emptiness of her insecurity, and the blinding hope he was offering her.

For all her twenty-four years, she'd assumed she'd die alone. And she knew when she met her fate and her death she might be alone, but not in spirit. Not anymore. He would follow her to the realm of Della Victus, and she would wait for him in Arronet when her soul got there.

No Ambrosius had a destiny of great love. Some found love, yes, after they succeeded. Most of the ones who survived to true adulthood, however, died as drunks or ambrosia hunters themselves, clinging to the glory they had tasted and swallowed and would never touch again.

Except Aneurin. He was cursed for love, and then he cursed *himself* to protect the love he had left. And Calla would die for love. Would sacrifice herself for it. And she was happy to do so, for true love is not selfish. She would die so he could finally, truly, joyfully *live*.

"Annie, I need you," she said.

Aneurin smiled at her and lifted her nightgown over her head. He kissed her as he lay her back down and poised himself between her legs. "Are you sure? I can wait."

She kissed him again, her eyes gleaming with tears of joy and relief and love. "You are beautiful, *rosara*, and I've never been more certain. I want this."

Some emotion between anguish and hope made his jaw slack and his mouth dry, but he cradled her to him, his arm under her head to bring her close.

"I love you," he whispered as he sheathed himself within her.

The only words said for the rest of the morning were their names, benedictions to whatever god heard and might have mercy on them.

Chapter Twenty-Seven

When Calla and Aneurin went down for afternoon tea—bathed and dressed and *together*—the king invited Godfrey to take tea with them.

Before, the steward would have likely declined, but Calla realized with a mortified flush that the entire palace probably heard them. After all, they'd issued their challenge to Eugenia and Della Mortis, the god of death, outside, where anyone could hear them from anywhere in the house if the windows were open.

Neither she nor Aneurin were surprised when Godfrey accepted the invitation. He told Mary and Cresedan that he'd serve the tea himself and that their presence was not required.

The Strix Lord and the Ambrosius exchanged a glance.

Godfrey took his time as he pleasantly poured the tea and fixed each up the way he knew everyone wanted them.

Calla tapped her feet as she watched him prepare his own cup and finally take a seat.

The steward was silent for a while. Then he took a deep breath and leveled his gaze at the two of them. "With all due respect, Your Majesty, Miss Renaud, you just tempted Della Mortis and Eugenia to rain chaos on this household. Did you perhaps forget that Calla is very obviously not immune to the curse? She just happened to survive. There *will* be a reckoning for what you've done."

Aneurin trilled angrily, but Calla reached over and stroked his wing. His agitated breathing slowed.

"I think you're right, Mister Fontaine," she said. Aneurin looked sharply at her. A sheepish expression crossed her face. "I'm sorry Aneurin, but I considered it before you said everything you said. I've known what I wanted for a long time, and I knew you wanted it too when you didn't insist I leave when you woke to find me in your room. I knew that I would take every risk, the bigger the better, to be able to face my destiny knowing exactly what I will be fighting for. I fully expect to come face to face with Della Mortis again before my next birthday."

Aneurin's heavy breathing started again, but she shook her head. "If I can survive it a third time, we will know for an absolute certainty that your imprisonment is going to come to an end."

He reached for her hand and clutched it to his chest. "I wish you would have stopped me."

She smiled. "No you don't. Would you rather I die not knowing what it means to be loved by a man? Even if I die, it is worth it to know what you feel like."

Godfrey's voice was raspy when he said, "You do love him."

With a scrape of table legs on the wood floor, Aneurin jumped up and left the room.

Calla peered into her teacup. "I have loved him for years."

The steward huffed, almost crying but not quite. "At least he will have that to hold onto. That you loved him knowing the danger of doing so. That you did it anyway."

"After today, I can be fearless because I know if I die, it will be because I have succeeded. I have everything I need to do this; I just have to get to my birthday. Your son will be free, Godfrey. Free. *Free.*"

When Godfrey wept, Calla knew it was the truth. Aneurin's true name was Aneurin *Fontaine*.

"You should be brave too. When the curse is lifted, tell him the truth."

Godfrey shook his head. "There is nothing to tell that matters now, Miss Renaud." He stood up. "But I did…"

The next words got caught in his throat; he choked on them. He took a breath to compose himself as his hand rested on the back of the chair he'd been sitting in.

"I did love her. Cordelia Roran. She would have liked you, for you are so much like her. She was brave like you. So fiercely courageous. That's why she dared—" He stopped and shook his head. "So long ago now but I still remember her face. I will never forget it. And I know Annie will never forget yours."

He left, leaving Calla to wonder why he bothered to deny the truth while calling Aneurin by his childhood name, not his title.

Aneurin

Listening by the door, the king stepped in front of Godfrey as he exited the dining room. "I want you to know that whatever happens, finding something real and not the product of some enchantment has brought me peace."

Godfrey bowed. "Then Miss Renaud will be at peace as well." He tried to step around, but a hand on his arm stopped him.

"I'm not just talking about Calla, Mr. Fontaine. There are many kinds of love."

The steward cleared his throat. Then he did it again as if he couldn't get rid of the lump that rose there. "Indeed, Your Majesty. And the ones that matter are eternal."

He wrenched his arm out of Aneurin's grasp and disappeared down the hall.

The Strix Lord leaned against the wall, folded his arms, and smiled.

Chapter Twenty-Eight

"That's not a valid move," Aneurin said. It was more of a complaint, but his even tone and the softness of his voice almost sounded like he was granting permission for Calla to cheat.

She scoffed and crossed her arms. "It is. This piece moves diagonally."

The king flared his wings. "That piece has never moved diagonally."

Calla leaned forward. "We've played three games today and we both have moved that piece diagonally."

Aneurin shook his head. "That isn't true, and if you're going to lie, I'm not going to play with you." He started to rise to his feet.

Her jaw went slack. "Lie? It's the truth! You're joking."

Aneurin smiled and sat back down. "I'll let you move that piece diagonally just this one time, since you insist."

With another scoff, she retorted, "You're a tyrant lord. Owl man. Canary."

His lips twitched as he moved his final piece, winning the game.

The Ambrosius stared at the board. "That's impossible."

Aneurin stood up. "I tried to warn you." He moved to the closest bookshelf and began to peruse the titles. "But I suppose you've only ever once asked for my protection. I shouldn't have bothered."

Still staring at the board trying to figure out where she went wrong, Calla huffed. "You're supposed to be honorable. I'm telling Godfrey."

Aneurin trilled as he laughed. "Godfrey taught me all my best tricks."

Orange light diffused the room, and through the windows Calla could see rosy clouds and citrus sky as the sun set. It was still hot—August always was, even well into the night. Aneurin moved to the window to stare out into the garden, his avian form casting a long dark shadow.

Calla approached him from behind and ran her hands gently over his wings. He shivered. "I should light the fire," he said. "I'll read to you before bed, if you'd like."

She smiled and came to his side. "Poetry? Or shall we read about Della Mortis and the priest who loved him?"

The Strix Lord chuckled breathlessly. "Immortality is not a gift, Calla lily. That story depresses me because those who read it always end up believing it is a great romance. But I don't believe you can curse somebody if you love them."

She rested her head on his arm and intertwined her fingers with his. "No, that is a sick corruption of love. Diseased and rotting."

He was quiet for a moment. "I hope you're not angry I have not made love to you again. I know you say you are prepared to fight for your life, but I am not ready to watch you do it. I would wait until your birthday in eight months."

She exhaled sharply through her nose, amused. "I'm not angry. But that doesn't mean I wouldn't prefer for you to do it again, and again, every day."

He gave a low melodic rumble. "I would prefer that too, but unfortunately I am not as brave as you are."

Calla stood on her toes and kissed his cheek, right where the feathers started. "This is enough for me. Let's take a walk, *rosara*."

As he always did, he flushed a little at the holy term. "Very well."

In the dark, Calla almost looked like a ghost. Aneurin supposed that was what she was. The year before he'd turned twenty-five, when he'd inherited his title but had been unable to show his face to his people, he'd wandered these gardens just as they were doing now, anxious to go beyond the wall and pursue his fate. But he'd been lucky. Within the palace, King Octavian had allowed him to attend parties and entertain guests because those guests were being watched by guards at every moment.

Except the moments when Ginny had pulled him into dark corners to tumble with him against the wall. He'd thought it was real. She'd never lied about her interest in witchcraft, but he'd thought it was the boredom of a spoiled, unimportant second daughter. Not her ambition. If he'd had any idea about her true nature, he would have sent her away when he met her at seventeen. But he hadn't. Her beauty had convinced him that she was incapable of cruelty or malice. She was not gentle, but she was fair with her servant and his whenever she visited, back when there were dukes and earls and other lords of the Vale.

Even after he'd learned that his love for her was false, and even after she released him from the enchantment and died, he'd still respected her audacity. After all, it was her audacity to practice magic at all that he'd found so intriguing. And he never did stop calling her Ginny, even after Sarah and Aluard died. She was Ginny to him. She always would be. He did like her before she'd enchanted him. Love might have grown. The Ginny who was the first and only woman to touch him for five hundred thirty-two years was the Ginny he chose to remember when his hate became too strong for the Ginny she'd turned into. That for two years, the urging in his heart for her had been real.

She could have been a great queen. She had the makings of a great queen in her blood. Not an Ambrosius, but that was precisely why she would have been great. She'd wanted everything and had done terrible things to attain it.

But even Aneurin, her most tragic victim, could appreciate the irony that her ambition had directly caused the loss of his. He'd become a legend, yes, but he never became the king Lorana Vale needed, and now it was a crime-infested, unholy place. And he could do nothing about it because of Eugenia Roran's ambition. Sourly, he took pleasure in the fact that she married the son of a physician, not the son of a king. Her ambition amounted to nothing.

And if his *rosara* succeeded, he would make sure to correct every historian in the world and tell them of his true lineage so she could be reduced to nothing but a villain for all time.

As he'd told Calla, he'd let the *nuance* of his violence be lost to time. But that violence was very real. If Ginny hadn't died from her illness, he would have imprisoned her for the rest of her life after she released him from her spell and declared their marriage void. He wouldn't have killed her, but she would have been nothing but a specter long before she died. Never would he tolerate *betrayal*.

Aneurin was tired of the waiting. He wanted the freedom to make love to the woman he would make his queen. He wanted to greet her when she came home. Because he had to believe that she would. Every time he looked at her, he ached with the desperation of hope.

Calla's pale skin seemed to glimmer in the glow from the oil lamps illuminating the path, her dark hair swallowing the light. Her golden eyes seemed dark like the sinful chocolate she pretended she didn't hide in her room.

He hadn't allowed her to sleep in his room. Every time he saw her he wanted to unwrap her like a present and worship at her feet until she took pity on him and allowed him to touch her. And Aneurin *knew* she wanted him to touch her. That's why he didn't give her a single night.

He couldn't allow himself to get used to the feel of her body beside him as he slept. He couldn't, because when she left to pursue destiny, he would miss it too much.

It was fucking agony, this waiting. For the first time in centuries he had a clear vision of the future he wanted, and he had to *wait* for it. He was powerless to seize it for himself.

Calla

Something was bothering Aneurin, but Calla didn't know what. He'd glance at her as they strolled along the paths, but he was silent, his mouth set in a grim line. The tension radiating off him warned her not to inquire about it, but she wondered if she'd done something wrong. He'd seemed all right before they'd left the palace.

"How will you do it?" His abrupt question floated between them, and the balmy evening air turned cold.

Calla shook her head. She didn't want to tell him, didn't want him to try to stop her. Death was inevitable and she didn't think she could survive him acting like every moment was her last. She knew he still had hope that she'd come home to him. But she never would.

For almost twenty-five years she'd lived moment to moment. Now it was time to snatch up every crumb of happiness she could before she departed for Arronet. "It doesn't matter. It will be done."

Aneurin frowned. Within the orb of illumination from the oil lamp, he stepped in front of her and put his hands on her elbows. He tried to look gentle, but Calla could see his rage. His fear. "I would know the truth. If you—" a quick exhalation through his nose "—if you don't make it, I would like to know where to...to retrieve you. So you can be buried here. With me."

Calla fretted with the skirt of her dress, looking at the ground. "I don't want you to worry about me."

An amused trill whistled from the king. "Too late for that, lily mine." He lifted her chin with two fingers. "Let me see your eyes when you tell me. I know you well—after all, for three years, all I did was watch you."

Eyes on the purple sky, she tried not to laugh. "You're going to tell me to reconsider my plans, and I won't."

The corners of his mouth turned upwards. "I won't try to dissuade you unless I have evidence proving how foolish of an idea it is." He folded his hands in front of him. "Tell me."

Calla chewed on the inside of her lip for a minute. Most of the promises he'd ever made to her he'd kept. Perhaps he'd realize that she was dead either way and he'd let her sleep in his room between now and her birthday.

Her defiant golden stare met his regal emerald gaze and held it as she broke his heart. "I'm going to challenge Della Victus to a duel. I just have to land one blow and he will grant my wish to lift both curses."

A deep anguish contorted Aneurin's features as he stumbled backward. One of his hands covered his mouth as if he were going to retch. "Why?" he demanded, turning back to her. "Because of the book I had you read? That was a warning, Calla. It wasn't to inspire your method of suicide."

A broken promise, and Calla wondered why she was surprised. "He's the god of liberty. It is the only choice. Della Ros can only remove your feathers and wings, otherwise I'd beseech him instead. Only Della Victus can lift both."

Aneurin began to pace, withdrawing beyond the light and then coming back. "I—"

She lunged for his hand, stopping him. "I read every note between you and Godfrey. I know you tried to break the curse yourself and I know that every solution failed you. This is what I must do."

Aneurin was almost hyperventilating as he fought back tears. "I thought—"

The soft-spoken king looked at the ground.

"I thought when you said you were sure you were going to die, you were just trying to keep your heart from breaking if you couldn't find a way to lift the curse. I thought you were protecting me."

Calla lifted her hands to stroke the feathers on his jaw, and he leaned into her touch. "That was my intention. I've accepted my fate. As long as you are free to chase whatever makes you happy, I will die without regret."

"It isn't right," he whispered. "You shouldn't have to pay for my mistakes. Marrying Ginny, my bargain with Della Ros, I shouldn't have done any of it. Oh, I've won *battles*, but my people are virtually unprotected because I'm too afraid to walk amongst them. Lord Protector of *what*? Nothing! I could have prevented all of this by isolating myself for fifty years instead of five hundred. Let someone else be king." He tore himself away, resuming his pacing. "What have I done? What have I done to all of you?"

Back and forth on the stone path, his hand riffling through the feathers on his head. Calla had never seen him so agitated; had never heard him sound so afraid. He was the Strix Lord Aneurin Roran, King of Lorana Vale. And yet she watched as he crumbled before her eyes.

"You said you wouldn't try to dissuade me. Don't make me feel *guilty* for dying. My death is righteous, and I won't let you take that away from me," she said quietly.

It was clearly the wrong thing to say. Aneurin halted midstep and turned to stare at her, his head twitching like an agitated owl, which was what Calla supposed he was. He pointed at himself. "Am I being unfair?" he asked, his voice dangerously low.

She opened her mouth to speak but he held up a hand. Then he pointed at *her*.

"Aren't *you*? Perhaps you think my heart has grown tough like aged leather. Centuries of isolation, right? And I suppose you think I can just—" he gestured wildly with his arms "just go back to that. That I can watch you ride out from my gates knowing I'll never see my *rosara* again. Knowing that even if I wake up without wings, without these putrid feathers, I will be miserable because I don't have *you*. I will not think of you when I hold my wife, when I hold my child. I will *have* no wife, no child. *Five hundred years*, Calla. I was alone for five hundred years and the only person I spoke to that entire time was Godfrey. *FIVE HUNDRED YEARS*. And you give me your heart and your body and your…"

He still couldn't say it.

"You gave it all to me and now you're going to take it away and you expect me to just *watch*? I said I won't stop you and I won't, but I need you to *think* about what it is going to do to me. Allow me to *fucking* grieve." His voice was tight, so distraught Calla though his vocal cords were going to snap. He took her hands in his for just a moment before groaning and clutching her to his chest. "Just allow me to grieve, *rosara*. I know I ask too much of you but have mercy on me and my broken heart."

Calla wrapped her arms around him, her fingertips stroking the base of one of his wings. He shivered as he rested his head on top of hers. Enveloped in his arms, Calla felt as if time could stop, as if she could stay. What had the world offered her? If she could stop time, she could have eternity with Aneurin and Godfrey. With Delilah and Mary and Cresedan.

What a juvenile thought. Almost twenty-five and still she possessed the selfishness of adolescence. Aneurin and Godfrey and all the rest—they'd already tasted eternity. And their misery was the black specter that roamed these halls right alongside Eugenia's wicked ghost. Eternity in service, even to a lord so grand as Aneurin, would be hell after more than fifty years. And for many, sooner than that.

And yet they smiled for him. They served him with every care. They did his bidding, ever obedient.

The man Calla held in her arms inspired six hundred people to courageously endure a thousand years of service without a single complaint. Two he lost out of love for him, but the rest watched as he built a wall around himself no one could breach. Cursed together, surviving apart.

He protected them, so they protected him.

"You are worthy of love," she said to his chest. "It is my wish that you let someone love you when this is over. I will not haunt you. I'll meet you when you join me in Arronet."

He kissed the top of her head. "I have every intention of letting someone love me when this is over. As long as that someone is you."

"Stubborn pigeon."

"Oh, Calla. I have a book of ornithology in the library. You may borrow it at any time to learn once and for all whether I am a pigeon, an owl, or a canary."

Calla lifted her face to his, and he bent to press his lips to hers with a tenderness they both needed.

But tenderness revealed a deeper need.

Not a pigeon, an owl, nor a canary. A man.

"Trust me," Calla said as she took Aneurin's hand and led him deep into the woods on the border of his property.

When they entered the palace a long time later, Aneurin was still pulling leaves from Calla's tangled hair. And even with Della Mortis breathing down their necks, they couldn't stop smiling.

Chapter Twenty-Nine

A hand covered Calla's mouth and her eyes snapped open. Godfrey stood over her making a shushing gesture. She nodded and he retreated. As she sat up and threw her legs over the side of the bed, Godfrey tossed her dark trousers, a black shirt, and a belt. "Quickly," he whispered. He turned his back so she could dress. As soon as she pulled on her boots, she tapped him on the shoulder. He beckoned her to follow. He carefully locked her bedroom door behind them as he led her down the halls to the stairs and out to the kitchens.

"Silence is of paramount importance," he said quietly as he led her to the stables.

"What's happening?" she whispered. Fear was pungent in her veins like over ripe, rotting fruit.

Godfrey saddled a brown horse. "His Majesty is not behaving in a way appropriate for a man to behave, therefore I am doing what he is too afraid to do."

Fearfully, Calla asked, "Is something wrong with him? Where is he?" She started back toward the manor.

Godfrey snatched her arm, pulling her back into the stable. "Your father is dying, Miss Renaud." At her horrified expression, he shook his head. "We have time. You can say your goodbyes."

She pulled herself into the saddle. "What about my ambrosia? I can't defend myself against all of Senden's Branch."

He gave her a disappointed glare. He reached into his pocket and pulled out the perfume and brooch she'd worn on her twenty-second birthday. "Use them now."

She spritzed herself with the perfume, gagging on the jasmine. As she affixed the brooch to her breast, she noticed he was saddling a second horse. "Who else is coming?"

"Me. His Grace refused to take you himself, so I have no choice. You cannot have any regrets if you mean to succeed at finding your destiny." He opened a chest in the corner and pulled out a belt and sword, fastening it around his waist. After climbing into the saddle, he said, "Stay close and ride fast. Don't look back or he will stop you."

As desperate as she was to disbelieve it, she knew he was right. Going into the village now, at the height of the potency of the magic in her blood, was reckless at best. That was the curse of destiny—it tainted those chosen, with the most danger being right before they would achieve safety when the magic was fully absorbed.

Hours before dawn, the sky was still an inky black above her, littered with stars. Calla had never spent much time gazing at the sky—it was too dangerous for her to be out at night. She'd never noticed the purple smear that painted the black, stars nestled into it like diamonds stitched into a fine sash.

So much sky. That was Aneurin and Godfrey's gift to her. Making the world seem endless even while she was trapped.

"Godfrey," Calla said, bringing her horse beside his as they made for the village.

"Yes, Miss Renaud."

"Thank you."

His mouth tightened into a line. "Don't thank me yet. Wait until we're home safe again."

A shriek tore into the night behind them, but they were already beyond the wall. Calla turned to look behind, but Godfrey hissed at her.

The shriek sounded again. And again.

"I'm sorry, *rosara,*" she whispered as she dug in her heels so the horse sped down the road.

The streets were deserted when Godfrey and Calla made it into the village proper. But as the Ambrosius turned down the street she'd lived on her whole life, Godfrey whistled at her, shaking his head. Puzzled, she followed him to a slightly cleaner part of town. They stopped in front of a large shop with a residence on the second floor. The olive-green sign above the door said RENAUD'S and on the window was gold lettering spelling out the words CARPENTRY AND UPHOLSTERY.

"He moved here a year and a half ago," Godfrey said. Calla looked above and saw one window was lit by flickering candlelight.

He led her around the back to a flight of rickety wood stairs. He gestured for her to go first. Her heart thundered in her chest as she climbed—she'd always thought once she was twenty-five, she'd travel with him. That their fortunes would reverse and they'd have more time to be a family instead of prisoners of fate. He wasn't old, was never infirm. There was no reason for her to have thought she'd have to say goodbye so soon.

The living space above the shop was spacious. Three fully furnished bedrooms, two washrooms, and a sizable sitting room and kitchen greeted her when she opened the door. She followed the candlelight to the largest bedroom and took off her brooch.

Peter Renaud lay on the bed, sweat glistening on his forehead. The wisps of his hair were greasy. Around him were two doctors and a woman around his age. She was weeping. Everyone but her father turned to look at her as she opened the door.

"Who are you?" the woman hissed. "This is a private residence. Get out."

Calla stepped further into the room. "Papa," she whimpered, coming to the bed on the opposite side from where the woman sat. "Papa, I'm here."

Peter reached for her with one hand. "It's not safe, Calla. You shouldn't have come. Hunters are…everywhere."

"Of course I came, silly bear," she said softly, kissing his hand. "Godfrey made sure of it."

He coughed and nodded; his breath was ragged. "You are safe?"

She nodded, tears welling up in her eyes. "Safer than ever, Papa."

Peter tried to smile, but the movement of his mouth made him cough again. "Calla, this is Brenna. She was to be my wife after your birthday. I wanted to wait so you could come."

Calla turned to the woman who lunged forward and grabbed his other hand. "I'm sorry this is how we meet, Brenna. If Papa loves you, you must be someone truly special."

Brenna's lip trembled. "He told me about you. I was happy

to wait. I'm sorry for being rude when you came in. I didn't know."

"It's okay. We're here now, together," Calla said. She kissed her father's hand again. "Papa, I know what my destiny is."

Peter wheezed. "Tell me, Calla lily…"

His breathing slowed.

"I'm going to free Lord Aneurin, Papa. I'm going to lift the curse. He will be a man again."

Her father tried to smile again, but again he coughed, more violently this time. Blood tinted the corner of his mouth. "You'll take your place…beside him as a legend. A grand… destiny…indeed. I am…so proud."

His eyes fluttered.

"Papa," she said, wishing she could tell her father about the love she'd found. For Aneurin, for Godfrey, for everyone. How she'd been blessed more than any other Ambrosius to find happiness before twenty-five. That he was responsible for that happiness for it was his idea to call on the aid of the Strix Lord in the first place.

Peter reached out his hands, one to touch Calla's face and one to clasp Brenna's delicate fingers. "A family at last," he whispered hoarsely. "It's all I wanted to give both of you."

Surrounded by the women he loved, Peter Renaud died.

Calla and Brenna wept together, each of them reaching one of their hands to the other's, so the family Peter always wanted was whole, at least for the moment.

There was so much she could have said. So much she wanted to say.

Godfrey let her grieve for as long as he could, but as dawn drew close, he put his hand on her shoulder. "He is waiting for us," he said.

Dread seeped into Calla's bones. Not that she was afraid of the king, but she knew his wrath would be world-ending. Even worse, she knew how guilty she'd feel when she saw his face. Already that emotion began to coil itself around her heart.

After helping Calla to her feet, Godfrey turned to Brenna. "The Strix Lord will pay all funeral expenses. Send every creditor either of you may have to the palace to collect, regardless of the sum."

Brenna nodded. "Please thank His Majesty for me." She looked at Calla, curiosity creasing her eyes even as much as grief dampened them. "Where will you go now?"

To die, Calla thought. *Now that Papa won't miss me, I have no reason to delay. After my birthday, I am gone.*

"To the sea," Calla said. "Sell the shop and use what you make to live for yourself. Live the life he would have given you if he could."

A pallor came over Brenna's face. "You are kind, like he said you were. I was afraid you'd hate me for taking him from you."

Calla smiled, even as fresh tears dripped down her cheeks. "You let him find love. He's never had anyone since Mama died. He could never risk it because I was in the way. But you held his hand as he died, and for that, I love you well. Live free, Brenna."

Godfrey pulled on her arm as sunlight infiltrated the curtains. "We must go *now.*"

She rushed around the bed and embraced the woman who would have been her stepmother. "If you need anything, write to Lord Aneurin. Sign the letter Brenna Renaud. He will see to it you are provided for," she whispered.

Brenna nodded. "Thank you," she said, weeping anew.

Calla could hear Godfrey's shallow breathing, and his eyes were wide. "*Now*, Miss Renaud."

With one final glance at her father, Calla fled.

A man walking by the alley dropped his bag as he sniffed the air, his neck swiveling to stare at Calla. Godfrey hurriedly helped her into the saddle. "Fly, Calla. Don't stop. That perfume shouldn't be wearing off so soon."

Before she could flee, the man began to run. Godfrey drew his sword and stood between her and the man. "Stay back," he called, but the man was lost to his bloodlust.

Godfrey cut him down like he was nothing. He pulled his blade free and climbed into the other saddle. "Go, Calla!" He kicked her horse to get him to move.

They flew into the street. People stared as they passed them, but they fled so fast, Calla didn't think anyone could have truly known what she was. She realized with an inky, consuming terror that she hadn't put the brooch back on. If any in Senden's Branch remembered her, they knew she was alive. And they knew she was close.

Neck and neck, Godfrey and Calla tore through the forest. If her heart raced any faster, she was going to vomit it up. Deeper and deeper—it was only a thirty-minute hard gallop to the gate. They could make it.

Stubbornly requiring proof of her getaway, she glanced over her shoulder. A desperate little sob slipped out of her mouth when she saw the four riders gaining on them. One had a bow and was standing in his stirrups, taking aim like some sort of circus performer.

Not that Calla had ever been to a circus.

"What do we do?" she cried to Godfrey.

He stared forward. "Keep going, Miss Renaud!"

She whimpered but crouched low, her face in the horse's mane. Through the trees in the distance, she could see the gate. Just one more curve in the road.

Five of Aneurin's guards pushed the gate open and Aneurin stepped through them, clad in his chain and plate, his wings completely outstretched and a sword in each hand. The glare he shot at her as she and Godfrey rushed past him seemed to slow down time. In her worst nightmares, she couldn't imagine such betrayal and wrath.

The guards pulled the gate shut behind them.

Calla flew off the steed, breathless and panting, and ran to the gate. She gripped the twisted iron bars and watched as the four riders crashed into the wall of violence Aneurin unleashed.

Moving like lightning flashing through thunderclouds, Aneurin sliced the legs of the first horse. As it stumbled, he flapped his wings and ran through the man on the second horse.

Calla whimpered as the man with the bow fired an arrow at the Strix Lord, but it glanced off his plate. It got his attention, though. Aneurin whirled on the man.

"Aren't you going to help?" Calla cried to the guards standing in front of the gate, watching.

"Begging your pardon, Miss Renaud, but he doesn't need our help," the guard closest to her said.

Calla sputtered but turned back to the gory scene in front of her. He'd dispatched the rider whose horse he'd slain and now faced the man with the bow who was to his right. The other man still astride his horse wheeled around and around, refusing to dismount and face the king like a man.

The archer nocked another arrow.

"Hunting ambrosia is against my laws," the Strix Lord snarled. "The penalty is death."

The man with the sword laughed. "Nobody has enforced your laws in centuries, Pigeon Lord. You'd know that if you ever left your nest."

Calla's jaw dropped. But...it was true. She wouldn't have spent her life cowering in fear of every bump in the night if any of his laws had been respected. If the people hadn't been left to govern themselves.

Aneurin waited. "How did you taste the first drop of ambrosia, peasant? What horror did you inflict on another person because you wanted a taste of their glory?"

The man snarled right back. "I'm not the horror. You are. That's all you've ever been. A tyrant who collects our taxes but doesn't rule. What are we paying for? Ambrosia is the only happiness left to us because you abandoned the Vale long ago."

Aneurin waited some more, and Calla realized he was waiting for them to charge or loose an arrow.

"Get back, Miss Renaud," the guard said. "Don't make him worry about you."

But Calla shook her head. If she could do it again, she would still go to her father, but she couldn't deny that her recklessness put her *rosara* in this position.

The archer loosed the arrow and it landed in Aneurin's chain. "Thank you," the king said. Then he unleashed his attack.

"*Godfrey!*" Delilah cried.

Calla tore her gaze away from the flurry of wings and steel. She turned just in time to see Godfrey fall from his horse. Nausea clenched her stomach when she saw the arrow protruding from his back.

"No," she whispered and rushed to his side. She knelt beside him. "Mr. Fontaine…"

Godfrey panted and winced as he lay on his side. "Not a mortal wound," he sighed. "But, fuck, it hurts."

Delilah glared at her. "What did you do?"

Calla shook her head. "I—he took me to Senden's Branch. My father is dead. I had to say goodbye, Godfrey wanted me to—"

Delilah growled and pushed Calla over onto the stone. She slapped her face. Calla stared at her in shock as she returned to fuss over Godfrey. "How many of us are you going to put at risk? You did this by giving voice to it! Stupid girl! I hope you had fun fucking the king, because you're going to die because of it and I *hope* you do."

Calla whimpered, her lower lip trembling. But she pushed herself to her feet, her face still stinging. "I'm sorry. I thought we were immune."

"We have rules for a *reason*, Miss Renaud. While I'm glad you made him happy by spreading your legs for him, you don't get to drag Godfrey down with you. You should be ashamed." Delilah spit at her.

For a full minute, Calla was too ashamed to wipe the saliva from her face.

"Del, I'll be fine. It was my choice to go." Godfrey reached for Calla, who offered her arm. He pulled himself to sitting. "Pull the arrow out, Miss Renaud. I—" he panted with the pain. "I'll feel much better if you do."

Still Delilah glared at her, but the Ambrosius looked away first. She lifted her hands to touch the arrow but hesitated.

"What if I hurt you?"

Godfrey groaned a little. "You *will* hurt me, but then I'll feel *better* so if you don't mind!"

Calla winced and put one hand on Godfrey's unwounded shoulder and wrapped the other around the shaft of the arrow near his flesh. With a gasp, she yanked it out.

Godfrey cried out and beat his fists on the ground. "Ah, *fuck*," he exclaimed as the arrow pulled free. He fell to the side again, but Calla caught him.

"What do you need me to do?" she murmured to the steward as he breathed heavily in her arms. "I'm sorry, Mister Fontaine. I should have left when you first commanded it. I'm sorry."

"Please shut up, Miss Renaud," Godfrey panted. "I would do it again if I had to. You deserved to say goodbye to your father. Del—" He reached for the servant. "Apologize to her. It was my idea. She was following my commands. Have you forgotten what it was like to be young?"

Del glowered, but she said, "You're lucky he's going to survive. None of us would forgive you if he didn't. But I'm sorry for speaking out of turn."

It wasn't a real apology, but Calla would rather die than defend herself. She couldn't honestly do so. "Godfrey—"

"Shut up, Miss Renaud," he said again. "Tend to the king."

Delilah climbed to her feet and bent to help Godfrey stand. She slung the arm on his unwounded side over her shoulder and carried him into the house.

Calla watched them go, on her knees on the stone. Guilt ate her alive. She'd do it again, she knew she'd do it again, but she wished she'd been more careful.

Calla looked down at her dress. It was covered in Godfrey's

blood. She was so distracted by her grief for her father and for Godfrey, she didn't notice the screaming had stopped.

With a force she'd never expected from him, Aneurin grabbed her arm and pulled her to her feet. His face was a tableau of wrath unlike anything she'd ever seen, and she couldn't speak as he slung her over his shoulder and took off into the air.

Calla was *flying*.

Frozen with fear, she tried to grip Aneurin's armor but she couldn't find purchase. Her hands slipped off the blood-coated chain.

The Strix Lord said nothing as she panicked, but his grip on her legs tightened. It comforted her but only for a moment. She knew what was coming.

He landed with a grunt on his veranda, but he didn't release her. He carried her into his quarters, depositing her on his bed. It wasn't until she looked up at him with wide eyes that he said anything at all.

And when he spoke, his words were as quiet as the first he'd ever spoken to her.

"How dare you?"

Calla shook her head, swallowing the saliva that pooled in her mouth. The stare he gave her was not amorous, was not hungry like the way he'd watched her for years. It was something other, something vicious. The intensity of his stare was matched by the tightness of his jaw. This was the Strix Lord the people of Lorana Vale feared. And she knew his tongue was between his teeth; a dam against the flood of rage that roared to be unleashed.

"My father is dead, Annie—"

"I know. And I would have let you attend the funeral, with me by your side."

"I needed to say goodbye. Godfrey—"

"Godfrey defied my orders and will be punished once I am certain he is safe from infection," Aneurin said. His voice was cold, as if his breath was a frost that would doom every crop as far as the eye could see.

She shook her head again. "He was trying to help me. Please, I just wanted to see my fath—"

"—You knew what you were doing when you fled from me. Give me the brooch."

Calla dug in her pocket for the brooch and offered it to him, holding it up. Aneurin stared down at her but did not take it. He removed his gauntlets and tossed them on the floor. Then his pauldrons. Then he reached behind himself and untied the leather fastenings for his chain tunic. It fell away, revealing a sweat-soaked white shirt that he tore off with a harsh *rip* and threw on the floor with the rest. Moving to his mirror, he splashed his face with water from the marble bowl on the vanity. Finally, he turned back to her.

As he plucked the brooch from her raised hand, she grabbed his wrist. "My father is *dead*, my lord. And I'm glad I said goodbye. I will not die with regrets. Mr. Fontaine did what he did so that I have the strength to succeed at finding my destiny which is linked with *yours*. He did what he did to protect *your* future. Do *not* punish him for the mercy he showed me."

Aneurin tore his hand away and moved to a cabinet. From it, he pulled out a small, gilded chest. He fiddled with the lock, putting in a sequence, and put the brooch inside. After the chest was put back and the cabinet closed, he stood and faced her. "I am the King of the Vale. I am the Strix Lord. And I forbade him from telling you about your father's illness for this very reason. In the light of day, when I would protect you, you could have gone. But he defied me. *You* defied me. You are both disloyal.

And I will not let it stand."

Calla whimpered and pushed herself to sitting on the edge of the bed. "How will you punish him? His love for you is what drove him to do it. You cannot punish someone for loving you!"

Aneurin's feathered head turned sharply to face her square-on. "In some ways, I can't. You're right. Sarah Hanover died because I punished her for loving me by sending her away. But I've learned to be smarter than that. There are other ways than banishment to teach a traitor a lesson."

"He loves you! I—"

Aneurin snarled. "He loves *you*. If I were really his son, he would have obeyed me. He would have understood that I *have* to keep you safe. He betrayed me, Miss Renaud. You—" he scoffed, an anguished grimace stretching his lips "*you* betrayed me. I will not stand for it. I will *not*."

He inhaled deeply through his nose as he pursed his lips into a tight line. "You are forbidden from being in the same room as him. You will not speak to him again. Ever, if you have your way and you commit suicide by abandoning me."

Tears fled down Calla's cheeks like she'd fled from Aneurin's last night. "He is my friend," she whispered. "Delilah is furious with me for what happened. I'd have no one left."

Aneurin's wings shrugged. "You should have thought of that before you committed treason against me. I am the king."

She jumped up and stood before him, her hands on his bare chest. "I'm sorry I worried you. I'm sorry Godfrey got hurt, but don't take him from me. He's the only friend I have."

Aneurin scoffed. "An Ambrosius with a friend that doesn't want to eat you. How lucky you are. Get out."

She cupped his face in her hands, her eyes pleading as tears rained down her face. "I won't leave you to your wrath. I have not betrayed you. Please, *please* don't do this."

Emerald eyes focused on her face. They took in how her lip trembled, how she shivered and shifted from foot to foot.

"Please," she whispered, searching his expression for any sign he would bend.

"Why should I forgive you?" he said, and his voice was still frozen steel. "Why should I forgive *him*?"

Calla licked her lips as her mouth opened, but words failed her at first. Her eyes darted around as she thought, searching the room for the words to say that would move his caged heart.

"Because we—we *care* about you. We didn't do it to cause you pain. We did it to set me free so I can set *you* free. Please." She leaned forward and kissed the feathers over his breast. "Please."

A low trill sounded from his throat. Calla's heart leapt in her chest and she kissed the feathers on his neck too.

"This isn't a game, Miss Renaud," he said.

"Who's playing?" she murmured.

Roughly, his hand shot up and grasped her chin. Wide-eyed once again, she stared at him, trying to pull away but his grip held firm.

"You betrayed me," he said so softly she barely heard it, despite being inches from his face.

"I'd do it again, if only to prove that no matter how many times that ghost tries, she cannot take me because I don't only belong to myself anymore. I belong to *you*."

His gaze hardened. "I told you I would not abide your recklessness. You cannot defeat the dead. They've already won."

Calla merely narrowed her eyes in defiance. If he could not see reason, she wouldn't beg him for his forgiveness. All she could do was take what he freely gave, whether that was punishment or absolution.

"Spiteful canary," she growled as his grip tightened on her jaw.

With a derisive scoff, his hand left her jaw and slid to the back of her head. With a tug, he captured her mouth with his own. And into his mouth, Calla laughed as she wrapped her arms around his neck and kissed him back.

Chapter Thirty

Infection never took hold of Godfrey. As a physician, he was easily able to inform the herbalist of how to treat his wound to avoid it since he couldn't tend to it himself.

At first when Calla tried to visit him, Delilah had refused to let her in. Aneurin offered to speak to his staff about showing her more respect, but Calla threw up her hands and said, "Absolutely not. I need to make amends on my own."

To that end, she'd spent two entire days building elaborate flower arrangements for Godfrey, Delilah, and Cresedan, the three highest-ranking members of staff.

Cresedan's arrangement was a burst of sunflowers, orange marigolds, and blue daisies. She used a yellow vase with a gold ribbon. Like a bowl of gold and magic.

Delilah's had pink roses and both purple and white tulips. She arranged them in a red box wrapped in black gauze. She used a small, two-foot wooden trellis to stack the blooms. It was the heaviest of the three and took the longest to make.

Godfrey's was a vibrant display of blue salvia contrasted with bursting red amaryllis—the salvia whispered *I'm thinking of you* and the amaryllis shouted her pride at being his friend. She hoped the message wasn't lost on him.

Cresedan eyed her suspiciously when Calla delivered her arrangement, then sighed and embraced her. "Godfrey runs things, and I know you were just doing as you were told," she sighed. "I'm not angry with you. Most of us aren't. We know the way he is. He is very commanding and always does what he thinks is right."

When she brought Delilah's arrangement to her, Calla was met with an icy stare. "He could have died," said the servant.

"I love him too," Calla replied.

Delilah gritted her teeth. "You don't know anything about us. We've been a family for five hundred years. You haven't even been alive for a quarter of a century."

Calla swallowed her frustration. "I don't know what you're arguing. Do you think I don't understand love?"

Delilah scoffed. "How could you? You don't know what five hundred years of loyalty demands of a person. *That* is love."

Shaking with rage, Calla narrowed her eyes. "If you think for one fucking second that I wouldn't give this family five hundred years, you're an idiot and all your time has been wasted for you've gained no wisdom from it."

"You've given this family *nothing*," Delilah growled. She grasped Calla's chin in her hand, and the longer she spoke, the louder she shouted. "What claim do you have to our love? To Godfrey's love? What right does a victim have to the king?

Better women than you have died for him, but you think your suicide will make you worthy of him? You'll never be worthy of him. Or worthy of us. Who do you think you are to ruin *everything?*"

Calla's eyes widened with rage. "I am nobody. And I told Aneurin I was nobody the day he made love to me for the first time. But he told me I was someone, that my life wasn't wasted, and if I don't live like I believe that, I will never be who I need to be."

Delilah gripped her chin harder. "Sarah was my friend and she *died* for a chance at what you've been flaunting for months. It's not right. Who are *you* to take what should have been hers?" Her voice lowered to a gravelly whisper. "I know she would have borne him a child, probably a son. She was twice the woman you are. A servant like the rest of us but she didn't need divine blood to have a glorious destiny."

Calla's heart sank. "I've never thought I deserve his love more than anyone else. It's just…it's just coincidence."

With a scoff, Delilah let her go. "You don't understand."

"Yes, I do," Calla said grabbing her hand as she turned away. "You have all lived for so long with nothing but each other and I came along and upset everything. And I know I had no right, but being here has given me the only happiness I've ever felt in my entire life. And I don't owe that just to the king. Godfrey gave me that happiness. *You* did, Cresedan and Mary did. Everyone. And when I break the curse, I won't just be doing it to set free the man I love. I'll be doing it to free *all* of you. So you can have the lives you want without being shackled to Aneurin's fate. So you have a *choice.*"

An expression of shock washed over Delilah's face. Her mouth opened, then shut, then opened again. "I—I hadn't thought—"

Calla offered the arrangement again. "Clearly. So accept my condolences on Godfrey's injuries and allow us to move past it. Please."

Hostility subdued, Delilah took the arrangement from her. "Thank you," she murmured. "I'm sorry for thinking the worst of you."

With a shake of her head, Calla said, "You were just protecting the memory of your friend. Are we going to be all right?"

Delilah nodded. "Yes. I think we will be…my lady."

Calla's heart shattered. Even though Aneurin loved her, she'd never be his queen. Della Mortis would claim her before she had the chance.

Godfrey sat in an armchair reading a book in the music room when Calla brought his arrangement. "I made this for you. I'm happy you're able to sit up," she said as she set it on the table beside his chair.

Godfrey peered at the flowers, his expression soft. "It's beautiful, Calla, like everything else you've ever created. Something pretty to look at while I am forbidden from attending to my duties."

Calla laughed. "Aneurin just wants you to recover well."

Eyebrows raised, the steward sighed. "I know. And I don't want him to worry about me. It's been too long since I've read a book anyway. The last five years have been so much busier than the last five hundred for *some* reason." He gave her a wicked smile.

She laughed. "Sorry to make your life so complicated."

Godfrey barked a laugh. "Oh, 'complicated' doesn't begin to describe it, Miss Renaud. But I'm grateful for the chaos. We needed it. We've still potentially got another five hundred years of tedium ahead of us."

"Not if I can help it," she said with a smile. The piano in the corner of the room grabbed her attention. She hadn't practiced in quite a while. "Would you like me to play for you? Might help you relax."

Godfrey stared at her, his lips pursed. "I'm the only one in here, Miss Renaud. Don't trouble yourself on my account."

Rolling her eyes, she leaned down and pressed a kiss to the top of his head which earned her a startled sputtering. "No trouble. I want to. Discovering my talent for music is the best gift Aneurin has given me."

She moved to the piano and opened it. She sat on the bench and placed her fingers on the keys. "You're a second father to me, Godfrey, and I love you just as much as I loved my first. Remember that when I leave and remind the king that I am glad to face my destiny so I can free you all."

He just stared at her, his bottom lip trembling. With a benevolent smile, she began to play.

A melody she'd heard in her head for months but had never seen composed on paper trickled out from her fingertips as her hands danced over the keys. At times she'd glance at Godfrey who wore an expression she couldn't decipher as his hand reached out and caressed the petals of the amaryllis in his arrangement.

The melody was melancholic but hopeful, starting low and lifting to a higher key before gently falling again. The story of the loneliness she'd come from and the love she'd leave behind.

She felt Aneurin enter the room, but she didn't look at the door. She kept her eyes closed, *feeling* the music as she played the tune she'd heard in her head since Aneurin uttered those three words that changed her life.

He'd only said them once, but she remembered the velvet sound of them as they fell from his lips. But that wasn't the only time she'd heard the melody. It became focused and lingering when Godfrey spirited her from the palace to see her father and she'd learned how much he loved her. When she'd learned that *somehow* she'd earned his love and he would give anything for her freedom just like he would for Aneurin's.

As the melody fell again, she opened her eyes to acknowledge Aneurin. After all, he was the king. His expression as he leaned against the doorframe and watched her play was the same as the one he'd worn when he'd first made love to her

I belong to you, she thought, willing the words to fly to his heart. And they seemed to; as her eyes fluttered shut again, he took a step forward into the room.

She played for twenty minutes, composing a song she didn't know if she'd ever put on paper but realized she'd always be able to play from memory.

Della Ros was the god of beauty—and that included music. So to him, she prayed for the strength to face her future when she left these two noble, beautiful men behind.

When the last trickling notes faded away. She opened her eyes again. First she looked to Godfrey, who wiped away a tear. "Well done, Miss Renaud."

She smiled at him, blushing slightly. "It's my gift to you. To both of you."

As her gaze flickered to Aneurin, he set his jaw and furrowed his brow. "Come with me," he said, offering his hand.

Calla and Godfrey exchanged a glance, but she wasn't about to disobey her king. She slid off the bench and took his hand. He grasped it tightly and led her through the house and up the stairs to his chambers.

"Am I in trouble?" she asked. "His Majesty seems displeased." Worry flowered in her heart. She couldn't *think* what she'd done wrong, but his brow was still furrowed as he closed his chamber door behind them.

"Have a seat," he said, gesturing at the two armchairs in front of the fireplace.

She eyed him suspiciously and sat in one of the chairs. "It's almost dinner time," she said. "I don't want—"

"We will miss dinner. Unless you are terribly hungry."

Calla patted the skirt of her gown as he knelt before the hearth building a fire. "Not so terribly, no. I had a big lunch while you were doing whatever it was you were doing."

In the dim light from the rapidly setting sun, she watched him coax a spark to a roaring flame. He set the flint aside and looked at her, his wings flaring.

To her surprise, instead of sitting in the other chair, he knelt before her and put his head in her lap, wrapping his arms around her legs.

"Please don't go," he said quietly. "Stay and marry me and be my queen. I cannot endure five hundred years without you."

Like a stone dropped from the veranda, Calla's heart plummeted to her stomach. "Would you still love me and desire me when I'm old and feeble?" she mused, her fingertips lightly caressing his feathered head.

"I'm five hundred thirty-six years old. I wouldn't have declared you my *rosara* if I wouldn't."

Calla smiled. "I don't want to grow old and weak knowing I could have saved you when I was young and strong. Time would become a cage just like this palace is a cage, just like my hovel was a cage. You know I cannot stay."

His arms tightened around her legs. "Please."

For a long while, Calla didn't say anything. She looked down at his feathered head as she kept touching him, hoping her ministrations soothed him, but also knowing they didn't.

After her gaze flickered to the blazing fire, she spoke again. "For twenty years, I never dared wanting anything. My father couldn't obtain anything for me because we were too poor and anything that was free could not be experienced from within the rotten walls of the house I grew up in. The only thing I wanted but never expected to have was safety. And then you gave that to me."

He opened his mouth to speak but she shushed him.

"I know I got sick. I know Loewen hurt me. But do you know what I thought of as he licked my blood from his fingers? I thought of you and how you would feel when you found my body. Because after I came here, I forgot fear. I forgot it because it was replaced after just a few months by love. I'd been in love with you for almost two years by the time you kissed me. And I know you could tell. I know that's why you kept hiding away from me, trying to protect me."

"I hid from you because I loved you, Calla. I loved you early on, though at the time I thought it was just loneliness pulling me to you. I never loved Ginny. I didn't know what the real thing even felt like. I spent those months away from you trying to understand how I felt. But it just got stronger and you held my hand on your twenty-third birthday and I was so angry with you for making me realize that *it was love*." He scoffed, burying his face in the folds of her skirt for a moment. Then he turned his head back to the side again. "I can still remember how your eyes looked under the shade of the canopy. They were glimmering with the reflection of the sun on the stone and your lips were parted and all my resolve crumbled away. You were and still are the most beautiful thing I've ever seen. And I don't want to lose you."

She bit her lip to stifle a little whimper but kept stroking his feathers. "My heart needs to go, *rosara*. I cannot watch you mire in this cage for the rest of my life, not now I know I can free you. It is because I—"

Aneurin trilled lowly, silencing her. He still did not want her to say it.

As her fear and tenderness turned to anger, Calla's eyes widened and widened. She gripped his head and pulled him up to be sitting on his knees. Then she slipped from the chair to kneel before him. Once again she gripped his face in her hands and said, "I *love* you, *rosara*. And it is because I love you that I will set you free and then wait for you in Arronet. You didn't find me for five hundred years and I would wait just as long for you. I love you." She kissed him. "I love you." She kissed him again. "I *love* you and in a few months I will free you and nothing you say can stop me because I love you so much I would rather die than watch you suffer a minute longer than I have to."

Aneurin squared his shoulders as he shook, his gaze locked on hers. "Say it again."

A breathless chuckle bubbled from her lips. "I love you."

"Again."

Her brows creased as she pressed her fingertips into the feathers on his jaw. "I. Love. You."

With a sigh he pressed his lips to hers, sliding a hand to her back to hold her as he lowered her to her back on the plush rug in front of the hearth. Her legs straightened out; her hands clenched the lapels of his jacket.

"*I love you,*" she whispered after nibbling on his bottom lip, her glimmering gold eyes meeting his.

He smiled, his emerald gaze washing over her face from eyes to mouth and back again. He unbuttoned the front of her taupe-colored dress as he leaned over her, propped on one forearm. His wings spread over them, tense with his eagerness, but as he kissed the curve of her breasts over her brassiere, they relaxed until they draped loosely behind him like a blanket thrown over his body.

Undressing Calla took almost no time compared to what it would take to undress him, but she didn't mind. She loved the tingling ache in the pit of her stomach that kernelled within her as he hurried. When she was naked underneath him, her body fuzzy from the warmth of the fire even as a cool breeze floated in from the veranda and set her skin alight.

For a while, he just looked at her prone form. Then he ran his hand over her bent knee, pressing his lips to it. "I cannot decide how I want to remember you. Like this, bare and open for only me, or the way you looked the night you tried to hit me."

Calla tittered, one of her hands coming up to cover her mouth. "Imagine if you'd let my strike find its mark. Would you love me now?"

He leaned down to kiss her thigh. "I'd love you more. You're quite a warrior despite your lack of experience." He lifted her leg and rested it on his shoulder. Her toes brushed against his wing as he changed position to lie between her legs. "I know you want to free me, but can you not give me just a few years to train you better? It would make me feel much more comfortable with your mission to duel Della Victus."

As she considered her answer, he dragged his lips up one thigh, then nibbled on the other. Her breathing became shallower, and she knew she should answer before she couldn't speak at all.

Aneurin

The layers of silk and brocade he wore were complicated to remove, but Aneurin endured her efforts with every patience even though she could see how he strained at his trousers. But even when he was nude and his black feathers swallowed the flicker of the firelight, she ignored that straining part as she ruffled his feathers on his sides and thighs.

"Finally going to make me beg, are you?" he breathed as her knuckles *just* brushed past his organ.

"Have to, I'm afraid. My king commanded it of me."

The word *king* came out more like some sort of purr, and he shivered as he gasped, squirming. "Whatever you say, Calla lily, lily mine, *rosara*."

She leaned down and breathed on him. "Beg, king."

He squirmed again, propping himself on his elbows so he could better look down at her dark radiance between his legs. "Cruel Calla, Vengeful Calla. Queen Calla. Have pity on me. I just want to spend forever with you and you're denying it to me. At least, *at least* give me this."

She withdrew. "Terrible manners," she said. "Five hundred years old and still a spoiled prince."

She gripped him a little harder and he gasped, but Aneurin swore from the pleasure of it. "*Yerna*. Please, Calla. *Please*."

Calla smiled, softer this time. Her lips brushed over the head as she murmured, "Yes, Your Majesty."

It wasn't *what* she was doing that he wanted to remember. He wanted to hold on to the way she cared for him and gave him memories of joy to hold onto just in case she failed. At least he'd have this consideration. This freedom. His heart was free even if he couldn't show it to anyone else ever again.

For five hundred years the weight of his fabricated, meaningless love for Ginny had poisoned him and broken him. So futile, such a waste of time. But then Calla had appeared at his gates.

The glass doors that led out to his veranda had been opened to let the petrichor in from the morning rain. He'd just finished dressing when he saw two people break from the tree line. It had startled him at first. The bottle of sandalwood cologne he'd been holding had dropped from his hands when he saw it was an older man and a young woman.

He hadn't dared go out all the way on his veranda. Just close enough to see and hear the woman beg Trevorn, his guard, to help them get an audience with him. When Trevorn had said he didn't know what to do, panic had settled into Aneurin's heart. He didn't want them to leave. He'd take the risk. Just hearing them out couldn't hurt. So he'd sent out a command that they were to be admitted and everyone was to receive them at the stairs. Not in his throne room. He wouldn't sit on his throne until he was free to rule the way he'd always meant to.

And then he'd seen the weariness in her face. He'd smelled her ambrosia, but she was in a dress that was barely more than rags and she was at least twenty and he didn't know how she'd survived so long.

The moment Peter Renaud had asked, he'd decided to let her stay. But when she spoke, her voice trembling…

His heart had instantly softened. And he knew he had to protect her, even if it meant a fresh hell for him. But in a thousand years of dull, aching regret, what were five years of exquisite agony?

But instead, it had turned into five years of joy. Agony only punctuated the years, like commas in a sentence.

Lunging forward, he pulled himself out of her mouth. Then he pulled her up so he could kiss her face. As he flipped them over, pushing inside of her, he touched her cheek. "Whatever happens, you are my queen. For five years, for five hundred, for five thousand. If my destiny was only to live long enough to find you, then I am satisfied."

Her eyes fluttered shut as she whimpered as his hips moved against hers. "*Rosara*," she sighed. "Aneurin."

"Calla," he groaned. But he didn't move any faster. He wanted to feel her around him forever. The urgency to hurry made the moments stretch out and he was *glad* because it felt as if he were buying more of the time he already had too much of, yet not enough with *her*.

He kept his eyes on hers whenever they opened, imagining how blessed he would be by every god if she succeeded and somehow survived and they could have a lifetime of freedom and love.

As he watched her skin flush and her lips become red and full, he clung to her, desperate to never forget the way she felt in his arms. And as her back arched and her fingers ruffled the feathers on his back, he thought over and over again: *I'd give anything for an eternity with you.*

Chapter Thirty-One

Calla

Light woke Calla, but she had only been asleep for a few hours. In the middle of April, her room shouldn't have been so bright before eight. Her eyes snapped open and took in the orange flames licking the outside of her window.

She tore out of bed just as Godfrey ran into her room holding a sizable brown leather satchel, a silver canteen with a hemp strap, a belt, a dagger, and a sword. When he saw she was already awake he sighed with relief as he dumped the load he was carrying on her bed. He rushed to her wardrobe. Frantically he began stuffing into it every article of clothing that wasn't a dress; as much as could fit.

"Ambrosia hunters. A clan from the west. Seems they heard about our escape from Senden's Branch. Dress, Miss Renaud.

Now's not the time for modesty," he thrummed as he shoved more clothing in the satchel. "Hurry."

She threw on a loose white shirt, black trousers, stockings, her tall boots, and a wool-lined jacket before running to the peg on the wall for her hooded cloak. "What am I to do?" she asked, dizzy with terror.

Godfrey slipped a wad of paper marques of various denominations into her hand and a small bag of gold coins. "Flee child. You have five days until your birthday. Go to the east; take refuge in the Solda Hills. Hide yourself well and wait for your birthday to pass."

Calla nodded. Dread made her joints lock up. "I can do that. Is the sword for me?"

Godfrey nodded and helped her tie the belt around her hips after she tucked in her shirt. She sheathed the sword and dagger, nervous about the weight of the weapons. Far heavier than the practice sword she'd used for so long.

The steward draped the bag over her shoulder so it rested across her body. He tied the strap of the canteen to it. He appraised her, then shook his head. He moved to the chest of drawers and pulled out a dark blue wool scarf and tied it around her neck, then pulled some black gloves out of a box on her vanity. Then he nodded, seemingly satisfied. "Take the saddled horse as far as you can go before stopping for supplies. They will hunt you if they detect you, but they shouldn't." He reached into the pocket of his coat and pulled out the brooch and the perfume. "He can't hide anything from me, though he thinks he can. Foolish boy."

He spritzed her with the perfume and handed her the bottle before pinning the brooch to her chest. She slipped the bottle into the satchel just as he said, "Go now, Calla. Save us."

Calla ran for the door but froze as her fingertips brushed the knob. "Does he know I'm leaving?"

Godfrey sighed and looked at the ground. "He cannot defend the palace *and* worry about you. I would have the rest of the staff protected while you flee."

Pain twisted her mouth and squinted her eyes. "Tell him I love him."

Godfrey reached over and pulled open the door. "Tell him yourself when you come home." His voice caught on the last word and an anguished sigh puffed out of him. "Please, my girl, come home."

Calla whimpered and threw her arms around his neck. "I love you, Godfrey. If I can, I'll come back. But if I don't..."

She unsheathed the dagger from her belt and cut a lock of her hair. She handed it to him, and he looked at her with gleaming eyes. "I would have this buried with him when the time comes. Whenever that is. Promise me."

The king's true father sniffed as he nodded. "I will put it in a locket and make sure he never removes it."

She kissed his cheek. "See you soon," she said.

"I hope so, sweetheart. I hope so."

Calla supposed the darkness of the forest to the east of the property should have terrified her, but then she reasoned that as long as she kept spritzing the perfume, her ambrosia was hidden, and the cloying jasmine would put off any natural predators.

Men preying on her comeliness was another worry, but the woods were silent save for the rustling of bats and the song of crickets. Sometimes an owl would call, and the sound was so familiar it made her smile.

She'd charged Lucky into the dark until he'd nickered and huffed, then slowed to a stop. It was still dark, but she knew she was going to the dawn. She wondered if Aneurin had been victorious. She didn't doubt that he would be, but she hoped no one was lost. The blood was on her hands if a single member of the staff had died.

If the day was won, Aneurin likely knew she was gone. And that was the thought that spurred her to snap the reins and go forward. She had to get out of the Vale before he could pursue her or he'd try to stop her.

Around breakfast time, she stopped to water herself and Lucky in a small stream. She refilled the canteen and fed the stallion a carrot. Godfrey had said to go as far as she could before stopping, but she hadn't even passed a small village. Her stomach grumbled, but as soon as Lucky caught his breath, she kept going.

It was around noon when she broke through the trees. About a mile ahead was a village. She spritzed herself *twice* with the perfume and headed in.

The curious glances from the villagers made her feel enormously self-conscious but her fingertips brushed against the brooch and her heartrate slowed. Not that anyone in this village knew who she was, but in case her description had been spread around by the ambrosia runners and the hunters who were their customers, she was glad to be incognito.

Calla followed her nose to the market, where she was surprised to find a bustling little center of commerce. The village, Timber's Fortune, didn't seem to be large enough to warrant such a frenzied market but she was glad of it as she purchased a hot sticky bun and a pouch of powdered gruel she could use to make food. She was just trying to survive, but she couldn't help but purchase a small box of early strawberries. She bought a tin of black tea and a kettle and a pewter cup so she could have something stimulating to drink in the mornings. She also bought some rope, a tent, and a bedroll.

An inn stood at the corner of the market, and weariness

tugged at Calla's bones, but she knew she shouldn't stop yet. With a sigh, she strapped her purchases to Lucky's back and climbed back in the saddle, pushing farther and farther east.

It wasn't until after she was on an empty road just out of sight of the village that she realized that she'd been able to buy things at the market like a normal person without anyone approaching or accosting her or chasing her or hunting her. She'd left the village more invisible than she'd been when she'd entered.

It was invigorating. A taste of the freedom she'd always longed for.

She kept going until the terrain turned rocky and looming hills of shale and shrubs rose around her. She turned to go between them, hoping to find a creek or lake to water Lucky and herself, but all she found was a small, tepid pond buzzing with mosquitos.

With a sigh, she returned to the road and kept going.

Almost twenty-four hours after she'd last slept, she heard the rush of water. She followed the sound to a copse of woods near a swollen river. With a sigh of relief, she set up camp and built a fire. It took her an hour to do that because the only knowledge of *how* came from books. Papa had always ignited the hearth in Senden's Branch, and either Aneurin or Godfrey or Cresedan did it at home.

Home. Aneurin's palace was home to her. No, *Aneurin* was home.

She tiredly looked over the map she'd found in the satchel as she ate her gruel. By her inexperienced estimates, she'd pass through three more towns until reaching the start of the Solda Hills.

Calla knew that the hidden, magical valley that was home to Della Victus had its entrance one mile from the sea on the northern end of her first destination. With a smile, she rolled up the map and kicked dirt on the fire to hide her presence from the rest of the landscape. Maybe she'd see the ocean first before she ventured to face her fate. Just once.

With one final yawn, Calla curled up and fell asleep, truly alone for the first time in her entire life.

Tomorrow, she'd leave the Vale.

Chapter Thirty-Two

Aneurin

The king slammed his foot down on the jaw of the ambrosia hunter who called himself the clan leader of the *fifth* clan of outlaws who'd assaulted his palace in quick succession. It had never been about Calla. There were dozens of Ambrosius born every month. Hunting the only one in the Vale under royal protection was never the point, as tantalizing as the thought of her potent blood had no doubt been.

According to this final clan leader, it had been about claiming control of the Vale from a king who dared to show his face after five hundred years. That nameless clan lord had set about uniting the most powerful ambrosia hunters the day he'd learned about the party for Calla's twenty-second birthday. "Enough talking," Aneurin said as he scuffed his boot in the dirt to wipe the blood and gore from his sole.

For two days his five hundred soldiers had fought. No food. No rest. Godfrey had barricaded the doors to the palace as soon as Della Petricha had blessed them with rain to put out the fires in the gardens and woods. Blessed king, indeed.

He needed to see Calla. There was nothing on earth he wanted more than to wash the blood from his skin and sleep for days with her in his arms.

"Trevorn," he said, sliding off his pauldrons in front of the entrance to the palace.

The guard stepped up. "Yes, Your Majesty."

"I want these bodies burnt by nightfall. Then I want everyone to eat and rest and then I want one hundred men to march into Senden's Branch and arrest the mayor and the sheriff and anyone in their direct employ. They've been allowing hunters to spoil their streets for years and I've had enough of it."

Trevorn looked at the ground, hesitating just a moment too long before bowing. "It will be done, Lord Aneurin."

The Strix Lord glared at him. He knew what he was thinking. *Aneurin* had allowed hunters to take over his kingdom and it was only after he fell in love with an Ambrosius that he was going to do anything about it.

He knew what he looked like. But he couldn't let this stand. If they were so set on claiming the throne, they must be dealt with.

With a shrieking trill to let Godfrey and everyone else know the threat had ended, Aneurin flew to his veranda.

He stripped himself of his armor, piling it in the corner for Godfrey to clean. The sun was setting. He didn't even know what day of the week it was.

Godfrey appeared just as he began to run his bath. Running water hadn't been innovated when he'd inherited the throne, but he was glad he had it now as he soaked in the tub designed to accommodate his wings.

"I'll clean your armor then bring you dinner, my lord," Godfrey said, placing a towel on the edge of the tub.

Rubbing bleariness from his eyes, Aneurin nodded. "Bring a plate for Calla too. I'm sure she's worried sick."

Godfrey hesitated. "The armor will take a while, I think," he said, leaving the washroom.

Aneurin's feathered brow furrowed.

He finished his bath and dressed in silk sleep pants and waited at his desk for Calla and Godfrey to come to him.

They didn't.

Aneurin had never appeared before his staff undressed, except for Godfrey. So he dressed in simple trousers and a plain white shirt and pulled on socks and boots.

Every member of the staff averted their gaze as he passed them. Terror gripped his heart. Something had happened, but he didn't know what, but his staff was *afraid* of him. As afraid as he was of finding out what they were hiding.

Godfrey sat on the stairs. His elbow was lifted so it rested against the bannister and his hand covered his eyes, massaging them.

"Where is Calla?" Aneurin said in a low voice from the first landing.

Godfrey took a deep breath, then blew it out. "She's gone. I sent her away because if she'd been abducted in the night a grisly fate would have befallen her and you would have been wretched."

Shaking so violently he thought was going to be sick, Aneurin took a step down the stairs. "You *what?*"

Godfrey sighed and stood up, turning around to face his son and king. "I gave her the brooch and the perfume and a sword and a dagger and enough money to supply her for months. She left during the first attack."

Aneurin unleashed a shrieking roar so pitched and anguished the enormous panes of glass behind him exploded sending a shower of crystal shards raining onto the steps. Two sliced Godfrey's face, but he did not wince. He stood his ground.

With a terrified groan, Aneurin shot into the sky out from where the glass had once been. To the east he flew, searching the ground for any sign or trace of his queen.

He sped through the sky, but sometimes he dipped low under the canopy of the forest to search for tracks, but it had been too long. Travelers and caravans had turned over the dirt and there was no sign of her.

It was the middle of the next day when he arrived at the Solda Hills at the border of the Vale. Hills—the Solda made up a mountain range that spanned for miles. Miles, miles, miles of treacherous terrain and snow and woods and crevasses. Glacial and unforgiving.

But there were still towns nestled in that range, and that was what Aneurin feared. He knew the bottle of perfume had only had five spritzes worth left. There wasn't enough, and there were still two days left until Calla's birthday.

He didn't find her in the first town at the foot of the mountains. But he found a young hunter peddling bottles of ambrosia. Despite having no weapon, Aneurin lashed out with rage, crushing his throat with his bare hand.

No one intervened.

In the second town, higher up on the road Calla would have taken, he smelled ambrosia and found a group of hunters in a hovel with twenty ambrosia-hunters in the lust phase of their high. They, too, he killed with his bare hands.

Bare hands and a wood stake he pulled up from the ground, setting a freezing dog free to find warmth.

Before he killed the last hunter, he asked about an imperious blond traveling alone.

"Only one traveler in the last nine months, save us," the man rasped. Aneurin sneered at his yellow, chipped teeth. "She left yesterday. Very pale, sickly thing. Probably down the other side by now if she didn't fall down dead. Spare me, my lord. I'll never touch ambrosia again."

"I know you won't," Aneurin said through gritted teeth, gouging out his eyes with his fingers.

He didn't bother with the third town. He flew to the border of the Vale.

No sign of her.

No sign of her.

No sign of her.

He knew it was coming but dared to hope he could shatter the barrier between kingdoms as he flew straight into it at full speed.

An earth-rending quake echoed throughout the wooded valley that marked the border between Lorana Vale and Rynthia. The air seemed to shiver; prisms of color vibrated along the barrier as Aneurin's body slid five hundred feet in the air down to the ground.

"*No*," he wept as he launched himself into the air and flew a mile back toward the Solda.

Again he launched himself at the barrier, shrieking in agony as he collided with it, sending another quake through the valley.

He returned to the foot of the closest Solda hill and tore through the air toward the barrier. "Calla!" he screamed, praying to all of the Twelve that she could hear him. That she would turn around and come back to him.

He didn't get to say goodbye.

He needed to say goodbye.

To kiss her one more time and *god*, why hadn't he allowed her to sleep in his room? Would it have changed anything?

Again he attacked the barrier and again the valley shook with his rage and terror.

"Calla! *Calla!*" he cried as he slid down the wall of shimmering translucent air.

Calla called the palace her prison, but she did not know the agony of having an entire kingdom be a prison meant just for you.

His staff could cross the barrier. It wasn't Della Ros's magic that prevented him from doing so or it would confine them too. He knew there was a way.

Weeping, he flew into the sky as high as he could climb, until his wings- already so close to breaking- ached unbearably. His tears turned to ice that fell back toward earth only to melt and evaporate before ever reaching it. Could he go over the barrier?

His blood turned sluggish and he fell back to earth.

But still, King Aneurin was not dissuaded.

He slammed into the highest point of the barrier he could reach, but still slid toward the earth, glittering friction slowing his fall.

Aching and broken, he lay at the base of the barrier as it exploded in color around him as he leaned against it. For a full day he recovered his strength, or what little of it he could grasp. On the day before Calla's twenty-fifth birthday, he pushed himself to his feet and began his weeping anew. He wouldn't give up. Even if he ended up escorting her to her death, he would say goodbye.

From morning until dusk, he slammed into the barrier, screaming her name.

As the sun set on April twenty-first, Godfrey and a contingent of soldiers rode up from the west.

"Aneurin!" Godfrey called as the king barreled into the barrier again.

He did not hear him. Or if he did, he ignored him.

But his body was too broken from the days of battering the holy barrier, and on Aneurin's last drive toward his queen, his left wing cracked and broke and he tumbled out of the sky to the earth.

"*No!*" Godfrey cried as he leapt off his horse and ran for the barrier. His son's twisted body collided with the earth like a meteor, unhindered by the friction from the wall, a crater twenty feet wide dented the earth around him.

Godfrey slid down the tragedy-tilled earth into the center of the zone of impact to the body of his son.

Sitting in the earth, the steward clutched Aneurin to his chest. "No, son. You have to let her go. What happens now is up to her."

Aneurin shivered with the shock of his pain, but then he shook like the valley did every time he collided with the walls of his prison. Sobbing. "She's going to duel Della Victus. No one survives that, even if they win."

Godfrey choked back his own sobs. "I know, my boy. But maybe she will. You can't know the future. If you knew five hundred years ago what you know now, would you make the same choices?"

Aneurin's eyes squeezed shut. "I'm sorry, father, but I would. I would sentence you and Trevorn and Delilah and everyone to this hell with me. I wouldn't change a single fucking thing because every choice led me to her. I have to—"

He tried to get up, but the pain was too great, and Godfrey was able to overpower him. "No, son. All you need to do now is go home and pray and wait. Pray to Della Sorvis that fate will not be so unjust as to take her from you. The god of justice hears all prayers."

"The gods don't care," Aneurin wept. "It was not a god, but a devil that cursed me. I've looked upon the face of Della Ros, but I must have been mistaken. Not the god of beauty, but the god of wretchedness. *Della Yerna!*" The name of the most reviled god came out like the braying of a spirit.

The summoning of the god of wretchedness failed.

"I cannot do this. Not five hundred more years, father. I can't—"

"Yes, you can. But I don't think you'll have to. I think she will succeed. And I pray she will come home. But if she doesn't, she'll await you in Arronet. Perhaps she'll visit you in your dreams."

"A dream," Aneurin whispered, his pain all-consuming as the shock began to wear off. "I'd sleep forever to chase such a dream."

Chapter Thirty-Three

Calla

At the base of the southern-most part of the Solda, Calla squinted her eyes. Even from where she stood, the path looked treacherous. She could have gone around, but she knew Aneurin was likely already in pursuit.

"Sorry, boy," she crooned to Lucky, patting his neck. "I have faith in you, and I'll reward you with all the carrots once we are on the other side."

Lucky snorted, pawing at the ground.

Not far up the road, almost still at the base, she found the first town of three she had to get through to get to the border. She pulled out the bottle of perfume and spritzed herself, but the spray was weak. She began to shake when she tilted the amber bottle in the sun and saw there were just a couple drops left.

She stocked up on food and bought two extra canteens. There was plenty of snow higher up to use for water, but she didn't know how far she'd have to travel without water on the other side before she'd get to Della Victus. The map Godfrey had given her was only of the Vale.

The town had a shop specializing in gear for traversing the passes, so she bought a coat lined with Rynthian ram wool and gloves lined with fur. She bought more rope, an ice pick, and a tent with long sturdy iron stakes. Finally, she bought a blanket to cover Lucky if it snowed, which it likely would. It was April.

That first night on the mountain was the most dreadful experience of her life. The wind howled, Lucky sneezed and snorted with terror and it took all her strength to keep him from fleeing into the night. She knew in the dark he wouldn't make it, so she fought hard to keep him calm. When the blizzard ended, she fed him a carrot and put the blanket over him, begging him to rest so she could.

The bottle of perfume was almost empty. She had *maybe* one spritz left.

Terror filled her heart when she came upon the second town and realized there was no way around it. She'd have to go through it.

She waited outside of town, hiding by some rocks. She hoped the snow muted the scent of her ambrosia, so potent now, like it silenced sound.

"Just have to wait until dark, and then I'll go," she whispered, huddling behind a boulder.

"What the fuck?"

The man's voice was close. Calla, leaning against the boulder dozing, sat up straight. She hadn't heard anyone on the road in hours.

"Was Darkpeak expecting a new shipment of blood whores? I can smell them from here. They haven't paid us in weeks; said supply was low and they couldn't make the money," the same man said.

Calla started to shake.

"Nah, couldn't be. We've been watching the pass. Only solitary travelers, sometimes a caravan, but no one we do business with."

Calla heard a slapping sound, flesh on flesh. "Do you not fucking smell that, Marl? There's either a flood of ambrosia in Darkpeak or there's a twenty-four-year-old Ambrosius nearby."

"Don't fucking strike me, or I'll slit your throat. I'm telling you, there's been no blood whores taken into town. Not since the last time we were here."

Calla closed her eyes, praying to the Twelve that the men moved on.

Lucky chose that moment to whinny, anxious to move around after being stuck in one place for so long with nowhere dry to lie down.

Calla winced and drew her sword. She could barely land a blow on Aneurin who she was able to distract by flirting with him or yelling at him. And he never wanted her blood. These men did, and those who have tasted ambrosia will always do whatever it takes to get more. But she knew she couldn't take on two enemies.

What was she *doing* here?

She heard the crunching of snow as the men left the road in her direction. She could use the last spritz of perfume now. She should. But what if they still wanted to have their fun with her, to violate her? She was a woman alone on a secluded mountain road.

She was trained by the man the world knew as King Aneurin Roran. If she could defeat these monsters, she had no doubt she'd win her duel with Della Victus.

She jumped out from behind the boulder, hoisting her sword. "If you leave me be, I won't tell the king about the ambrosia operation you have running here." she said. "Just turn around and go back the way you came."

The men eyed her hungrily. "Not a chance, sweetheart. If there's only one of you, you must be turning twenty-five soon. We can smell you," the one called Marl said.

"Stay back!" she cried as they drew closer.

They drew their own swords. "The king is busy, little one. Five clans, including ours, are at his pretty little palace. When they're done with him, there will be no king. And blood whores like you will be put in your place." Marl smiled. "Not just an unseated king, but unseated gods. The Twelve can have no champions. We'll drain them all dry."

Marl and the other glanced at each other, nodded, and charged her.

Calla whirled, slicing at the other's midsection, but he dodged her attack. Marl took his chance to lunge for her shoulder, but she parried it.

The sword was off-balance compared to the evenly weighted wooden one she'd used. Unwieldy. Aneurin should have let her practice with real weapons.

"Don't kill her, Reggie," Marl taunted as she parried another vicious thrust, this time from the other. "We can have our fun with her until her birthday."

Reggie laughed. "Oh, we'll have fun."

Calla had to get out of there. She had to flee. Desperate, she tried to do what she did with Aneurin when she was so angry with him. She lunged for Reggie's stomach, hoping her brazenness would catch him by surprise. The terrain slowed her steps but adrenaline surged her forward anyway, the snow sloshing and crunching under her feet.

And to her shock, it did.

His eyes widened as her sword impaled him. "Feast on your own blood," she said, yanking her weapon free.

Marl stood staring at his friend, and Calla took her chance. She ran for Lucky, but her exhausted arms couldn't haul herself into the saddle quick enough. Strong, heavily veined arms wrapped around her.

She pulled out her dagger and stabbed at the arms, not caring if she cut herself. Reckless, like she always had been. But no matter how many slashes she cut into Marl's arms, he just laughed. He kicked her, bringing his knee to the small of her back. With a cry, Calla sank to her knees.

Marl took the rope from where it was latched to her saddle and tied her up. "Luckily for me, I hated Reggie. And now there's more of you for me to taste," he said, tightening a knot. "Darkpeak is under the control of my clan, and no one will save you. It is in your best interests not to scream when we get there or else more of the town will know you're there."

He draped her over Lucky's back, then climbed in the saddle behind her, helping her sit up. "There you go, gorgeous." He put his lips to her ear. "If you can survive until your birthday, I might marry you. Hope you don't mind the cold."

Calla turned her head away, nestling her chin in her unwashed, tangled hair. It was not fear that made her weep, but sorrow. She should have stayed in that copse of trees until her birthday passed. She should have sought out Brenna and asked her to hide her stepdaughter until it was safe. She should have been cleverer, smarter, stronger, better.

But as men jeered at her as Marl paraded her through town to a dirty ambrosia den, she furrowed her brow. This wasn't the way she'd die. Marl knew nothing about her—she could trick him. She only had one more day until her birthday. She could do it.

Marl would never let her live. Even after her birthday, if she weren't drained dry, he'd still keep her to use her body. That was the way of things for women without a partner to protect her. Even in Senden's Branch, with the presence of Aneurin's soldiers so close by, things were that way.

Even though she loved Aneurin with all her heart, she couldn't help but resent him a little for abandoning his people. For letting all *this* grow and fester in what could have been the most vibrant, bountiful kingdom in the world.

They arrived in front of a dilapidated, two-story house. Marl slid off of Lucky and hitched him to a post then heaved Calla onto his shoulder and carried her inside.

The ambrosia den was dark and rotted. But even though the reek of mold and soggy wood permeated the air, the ambrosia of other people lit up Calla's nose. It didn't appeal to her—it couldn't. She was immune to the lustful, violent effects of magic blood.

Philosophers had never reached a consensus whether or not a Destined's call to glory was because of the magic or because of the years of fortitude it took to survive until twenty-five. After all, living in fear for a quarter of a century was bound to make a person feel entitled to the glory promised. A Destined paid for that glory with years of their life.

Marl carried her through the living room where drugged men masturbated with their heads rolled to the side, lost in their haze. But as she passed, they sat up, jerking their hands more furiously. Calla glared at them, refusing to look away.

"Give me some," one man cried, scrambling to get up from the sofa.

"No, she's mine, and I'll gut you and drink *your* blood if you come within ten feet of my bedroom," Marl spit at him, not stopping.

Upstairs in what was the cleanest area of the house Calla had seen, he tossed her on a moldy mattress.

"I will untie your legs, but not your hands, whore," her captor said. "If you try to run, I'll slit your throat and spill your blood in the living room where every one of those deviants can taste you and do what they will with your corpse."

Calla said nothing as she stared at him. He was rather ugly. Her age, dirty but not stringy blond hair. Not very tall, but taller than she was. She couldn't tell what color his eyes were in the dim orange light from the setting sun reflecting off the snowy mountains around the town.

Marl seemed to be waiting for an answer. When minutes ticked on with none forthcoming, he shrugged and sliced the rope around her ankles.

"Are you going to rape me?" she finally asked.

"Probably, but maybe not. Depends on what your blood does to me. Your birthday can't be more than a few days away," he said. He peeled off his coat and gloves and set them on the cheap-looking dresser. He sat on the edge of the bed near her feet and took off his boots. "You were stupid to hang around so close to town. Where were you going?"

Calla didn't answer the question, but she said, "I won't try to run if you untie my hands. I'll be good."

Marl chuckled. "You'll be good because I will *not* untie your hands. Where were you going? Why were you not sheltered inside a fortified house to ride out your potency?"

Again, Calla didn't answer. He turned around and sat cross-legged on the bed.

He sighed. "Why were you alone? A potent, female Ambrosius alone in the Solda. It makes no sense. You're either very stupid or very desperate to get out of the Vale. Which is it?"

Tired of sitting in an awkward position, Calla fell back against the thin, probably lice-infested pillows. "Looks like I'm both. You're doing a terrible thing, you have *been* doing terrible things. Have you drank the blood of a child, *Marl*? How do you live with yourself?"

The corners of Marl's lips quirked upwards. "I have. But you'll not judge me, whore. It was my own brother, and I did it to keep him safe from my father. A nine-year-old doesn't have the strength to take down a grown man without magic."

Calla froze, staring at the ceiling. "You were nine?"

"Yeah."

He didn't say anything else. The longer Calla stared at the ceiling, the worse the waiting got. Why hadn't he cut her open yet? He just sat there. She didn't know if he was looking at her or the ratty quilt on the bed or the floor.

"Did he find his destiny?" she finally asked, afraid to twist her body to see him. Afraid it might remind him that she was helpless.

"Didn't get the chance," Marl said quietly. He took a deep breath. "But it wasn't me that drained him, so get that idea out of your fuckin' head."

Calla winced. A mistake. He'd cut her now for sure.

But he didn't.

"I don't want to die," she said. "I want to claim my destiny. I won't tell the king about you if you let me go. I'll owe you that much if you spare me."

Marl said nothing, and the room got darker and darker as the sun set.

"Untie me, please. Did you hear me? I will *owe* you a debt—"

"—Are you familiar with the king then? Let me guess, you're the king's pet Ambrosius, the one he killed three hundred hunters to protect."

Heart thudding in her chest, Calla twisted to try to see him, to look in his eyes. But when she did, he glared at her.

"That's right," she said, taking a chance. "Which is why you should believe me when I say I can get him to spare you."

Between one second and the next, the room became too dark for her to see him. But she felt him move.

Marl pressed her down onto the bed, his face buried into the crook of her neck. "He killed hunters who hadn't tasted ambrosia in years just because they associated with ones who had. I tasted ambrosia *yesterday.*"

Calla squeezed her eyes shut. His hand cupped her breast, and even though she was still fully dressed, she felt as if she wasn't. "Please," she whispered shakily.

"You're very pretty," he said. "I bet it was Della Ros who enchanted your blood. Did you fuck the pigeon tyrant or were you just a meal for him?"

All of his weight was on her; she had no choice but to spread her legs a little to make room for him. He gasped as he fit right between her thighs.

"Let me go," she whimpered. "Please don't do this. You're not… you're not even in the lust stage. You haven't tasted me."

"Yet," he said into her ear.

"If my ambrosia was on your tongue, it would still be monstrous. But if you don't even need it to do this, your entire existence is a violation of the Twelve."

He scoffed, and his hand moved to her hip. "The Twelve. Absent gods, like our absent king."

Calla didn't even know who the gods were anymore. It had been so long since she'd prayed with any belief that someone was listening. The only proof she had that the gods—if they even still existed—weren't evil, was Aneurin's beauty.

Della Ros had chosen not to make him ugly. Just different. Different so that eventually, someone would love him.

And if he was the one who enchanted her blood, he'd made her so she *could* love him. That was either a great cruelty or a great kindness to both of them. More than ever, as she was groped by this stinking, desperate ambrosia hunter, she had to believe that there was a purpose behind the way fate had aligned.

Taking one long whiff of her skin, Marl growled and sat up. He roughly flipped her over onto her stomach.

"Please!" Calla screamed. "Please, don't!" She sobbed into the pillow as Marl moved behind her.

But her weeping cut off abruptly as the rope binding her wrists was cut and her hands were freed.

Not hesitating, she scrambled to a sitting position, backing away from Marl to cower by the wall.

"You're going to do exactly as I say. If you don't, both of us will die," Marl said.

Calla nodded, wiping tears from her face.

"First, I'm going to cut you. Just a little, to get the smell out into the rest of the house."

Calla nodded again, looking skeptical.

"Then you're going to pretend I'm doing exactly what you thought I was going to do. I want you screaming, I want you panting, and I'll do the same, but we will *just* be sitting here. Are you a good actress?"

Calla nodded, then shook her head. "I don't know."

Marl shrugged. "Best hope you are. The smell of your blood will get every one of those hunters down there excited and frenzied. Which makes the next part the most dangerous, and it will not happen until dawn. But if you do what I say, and if you're half as good an actress as I need you to be, you'll get out of here alive. *Do you understand?*"

"After we've had a few hours of 'fun', I'm going to drain you. Not all of it, but enough to make you look like you're on the brink of death. I'll bottle a few vials of your blood and give it to them to satisfy their appetites, then I'll tell them it's your birthday so you're of no more use. Hopefully it will be enough to get you out of here."

Calla could only stare at him. She didn't know why he was going to free her, or what made him inclined to do so. "It will work for certain if you can get me the brown satchel. Tell them I have money in there. I do, and you can have all of it if you just bring me that bag."

Marl looked skeptical. "I can't leave you in here alone. The second I appear on the stairs, someone will slip in here to have their turn with you."

Calla pressed her lips together. "So take me with you. I—I'll put on a good show. I'll cry and beg and you can…" She winced at the thought in her head, but she had to be brave. "You can kiss me and fondle me in front of them. Exert your dominance, show them I'm at your mercy."

"Well, you are," Marl said, smirking.

She frowned. "I know. And I don't know why you're doing this. But I need my bag."

Marl was still uncomfortably close to her, so she could see his unwillingness to retrieve her bag, but she knew that the one spritz left in her bottle was her way out. She had to have it.

He didn't say anything for a long while. Then he sighed and got off the bed. He put on his boots and lit a candle. Then he settled on his back on the bed, folding his hands over his stomach. "Well, no better time than now," he said. "I set my knife on the table. Slice your arm or something and let's put on a show."

Calla eyed him suspiciously, worried that if she made a move for the knife, he'd tear out her throat with his teeth. Despite his offer of help, she didn't trust him, nor had she forgiven him for feeling her up.

He raised his eyebrows at her. "The sooner we get started, the longer we can do it, and the more believable it will be, sweetheart," Marl said, his impatience louder than his voice.

Calla set her jaw and reached over him to the bedside table. She glanced down at him as she did, and saw he was smirking again, her chest inches from his face.

"Why are you trusting me with a knife?" she said, snatching the weapon from the table and sitting back against the wall.

He chuckled. "So you know I'm not going to hurt you. Believe me, I want to. I've never tasted anyone more potent than a twenty-one-year-old."

"Then why?"

He closed his eyes. "Because the king's Ambrosius was worth killing for," he said. "And if she was able to draw him out of his nest for the first time in hundreds of years, maybe her destiny is to save the Vale from itself." He rolled onto his side facing her. "There's no reason people like me should be allowed to exist, not in a place as beautiful as the Vale. And I think the fact that I am not inside you right now with my teeth buried in your throat is proof that you were put here to inspire change. That maybe it was my own sin that made me faithless, not the absence of cruel gods. All I ask from you is that you make sure your royal lover puts down everyone like me in every corner of this kingdom. Don't imprison us; kill us. There are some things that cannot be forgiven."

Shock made Calla's face feel numb. "Why did you bring me here at all?"

Marl snorted and rested his head on his arm. "Because Reggie drank my brother right in front of me. And I've never had the courage to defy him, to leave, to try to make a life somewhere better than this, and I have hated myself for twelve years for it. You'd never have made it through this town alive, and I knew it. I was conflicted about what I should do with you, but when I saw how scared you were even after that bravery you showed on the road, I knew I couldn't do what my baser instincts are *still* demanding I do." He sniffed the air, his eyes fluttering shut. "I want you to let me taste it when you cut your arm. It will make me stronger in case they don't buy your performance."

Calla shook her head, gripping the knife. "The lust stage will overwhelm you."

He rolled his eyes. "You can keep the knife up your sleeve just in case. I didn't rape my brother when I tasted *him*, you know."

With a scoff, Calla relaxed just a little. "You were *nine*."

"I've seen other children of hunters do worse. I won't hurt you, I swear it," Marl said placidly. "You're armed. No matter how high I get, I won't have a death wish."

It seemed too good to be true. Calla couldn't allow herself to hope—the pain of failure would be too great. But she had to try. She owed Aneurin and Godfrey and herself to try.

She rolled up her sleeves and put the knife to her arm. "You make one wrong move and I'll put this through your eye," she said.

Marl smiled, pushing himself onto his back. He put his hands behind his head. "I won't move at all. Make the cut and put the knife to my throat. I'll open my mouth and you can let just a few drops in."

Calla glared at him. "You're just lazy."

"Do you want me to touch you?"

"No!"

His smile grew broader. "I know. Hey—"

She gripped the knife again, pointing it at him as he turned his head to face her.

"What's your name?"

She relaxed again. Perhaps if he knew her name, his bravery would hold, and he'd keep his promises. "Calla," she said.

He looked back at the ceiling. "Gorgeous name for a gorgeous girl. Of course you're destined for the bed of a king."

"Better than the bed of a murderer," she said, then instantly regretted it.

"You're right and I am that. But you're still in my bed anyway."

Calla sighed. "I think you could have been a good man if your father was a better man," she said.

"I could have been a lot of things if your lover had done his job," Marl sneered, so aggressively Calla scooted away from him. "Unfortunately for everyone, he didn't, my father wasn't, and I am not. Worry about fixing the *future*, Calla."

She nodded. "I'm going to do it now."

Marl seemed to relax at that, as if he was just glad to get back to the plan. "Go ahead."

Full of foreboding, Calla sliced the back of her wrist.

The moment she did and the smell of her blood filled the air, Marl moaned. His hands flew up to cover his mouth. "*Yerna,*" he swore, "what a fucking mistake that was."

Calla pointed the knife at him, but he didn't move. He started to shake, his fingertips pressing into his cheeks hard enough to bruise.

She couldn't help herself. She looked down to his hips and saw that the lust stage was already starting.

"Stay away," she said.

"Shut *up!*" he shouted, clenching his fists and digging them into his eyes. "Just shut up! *Do what I said now!*"

Calla suddenly realized this plan wasn't thought out. To get her bag, she had to go downstairs after making them believe he was having his way with her. Which meant she needed to be in a state of undress. And so would he.

Something they should have attended to *before* he became high just off the *scent* of her blood.

"I said moan for me, *whore!*" he shouted. He lifted his arm and wrapped his hand around the headboard. He made it hit the wall again and again.

Calla had no choice. She stood up and took off her belt, wincing as she moaned softly.

"Like you mean it," Marl growled. Tears flooded from his eyes as he held himself back from attacking her.

Calla sighed, hating every single thing about what was happening. "Stop!" she shouted, unbuttoning her trousers. "Please don't!" She moaned, cringing at the sound. She hoped she didn't sound so ridiculous when actually doing such things.

Marl was full on weeping as more blood dripped from her wrist. His moaning sounded more real than hers, but that was because he wept for grief and regret and a large amount of self-loathing. Calla knew it. She knew that sound. She'd wept like that every time her blood had put her in danger.

With another feeble protest, she crawled onto the bed and put her hand on his shoulder. His eyes snapped open and immediately focused on hers. "Please," he whispered.

She nodded and lifted her arm over his face. Precious rubies dropped into his mouth and freckled his pale cheeks. With a whimper as desperate as any Calla had ever given Aneurin, Marl touched his face and wiped the spilled drops with his fingertips. Then he stuck them in his mouth.

"You're a stupid whore," he said. "What made you think you could come into *my* territory and get away with it? I'm the lord here."

Someone thumped against the door, and Calla jumped from the bed, whimpering.

With a less enthusiastic moan, Marl lunged forward and grabbed her wrist, pulling her back to the bed.

"What are you *doing*?" she whispered hoarsely.

"They can't see your feet when they look under the door,"

he whispered back. Then he buried his face in her shoulder, gripping her. "Stupid whore," he cried, his fists clenching her clothes as he fought the instinct that told him to destroy her. "Stupid, useless king," he wept some more.

She needed swollen lips, tangled hair, a love mark. But the thought of obtaining those things made vomit rise in her throat.

"Can I trust you?" she whispered, then pretended to moan again.

"No."

"Well, I have to. Kiss me and bite my neck." She dug the knife into his stomach. "But restrain yourself from doing anything more than that."

With a moan that *wasn't* fake, he kissed her hard enough to bruise. Calla's eyes squeezed shut. She didn't dare allow herself to think of Aneurin. What if he thought this was some betrayal? But she would never have done it if she'd had any other choice.

"Let me move," he whispered. "I'm *chafing*."

With a sigh, she pulled the knife back a bit and he adjusted his position before putting his mouth to her neck.

The moment she thought he might have left a bruise on one side, she took the knife and tapped him on the head with the handle so he moved to the other side. "One more," she said quietly. "Then you better get the fuck away from me."

He sighed but did as she said. She didn't have to warn him this time. He moved away not long after he started.

"I can't take much more of this," he grumbled, sniffling through his tears. He groaned theatrically and buried his face in his hands.

Laughter erupted from behind the door. "Our turn, Marl," one voice said. "You know the rules say to share."

"Fuck the rules!" Marl shouted back. "*My* captive, *my* rules!"

"Fuck you, Marl," the men behind the door shouted.

"I'll fuck *her,* and you can just listen, you impotent degenerates!" He sat up on the edge of the bed. He rested his elbows on his thighs and tangled his hands in his hair.

Calla sat up but didn't move otherwise. Her heart was sick with what she'd allowed him to do, but somehow she knew he was suffering just as much. She *knew* that through the haze of his intoxication, he'd hated every minute of the time they'd known each other.

And she knew, in all truth and certainty, that if Aneurin had been a better king, Marl would have amounted to something far greater than that to which he'd ever aspired.

As much as Calla loved Aneurin, as willing as she was to die for him, she understood why Marl hated him. Why *everyone* hated him. Before she'd met him, *she'd* hated him, even if just a little.

So many dead children. So many wasted childhoods. So many dead ends.

That was Eugenia's curse. He'd been beloved by his people when she'd died, when Ambrosius first started being so aggressively hunted. And he'd loved them, had wanted to be the king they deserved after the reign of Octavian.

Sarah, Aluard, Calla, Godfrey—they were all just collateral damage of the world created when Aneurin fell apart. No one was immune to the curse because *everyone* was cursed.

Not Aneurin Twice-Cursed.

Aneurin, King of a Cursed People.

"I need my bag," she whispered after a time.

Marl looked over his shoulder at her, clenching his fists. "We need to pretend a little more. They're still out there," he said quietly. Then, louder, "I'll have you again, whore."

They sat on opposite sides of the bed for an hour, both pretending to be violated—her by him, him by ambrosia. And in a way, it was true. But as they cried and whimpered and moaned, they watched each other. Both of them understood that after she left, they would never see each other again. And for that, they were both relieved.

When Marl stood up, Calla did too.

"You got money? And you want one of your ladies cloths to clean up the blood? All right, Your Highness, let's go get your finery. But I'll be giving those cloths to my men, rest assured," Marl bellowed.

There were no cheers from behind the door. They'd either fallen asleep or they were downstairs sinking into their stupors.

Marl wrapped his arm around her shoulders. "You'll have to put on a compelling show this time," he whispered in her ear. "If they've drank more blood, they're probably still jerking off downstairs. They'll try to take their turn with you."

Calla glowered. "No one will be having any turns."

"Yeah, well, we'll see about that. As I said, you've got to be good." He reached into his pocket and pulled out another blade.

Calla backed away from him with a gasp. "You tricked me! You were armed the whole time!"

He grinned and said, "You're fine. Even after this."

He knelt on one knee and pulled down her trousers. Before Calla could stumble away, he sliced a one-inch gash on her thigh. Then he helped her pull her clothes back on.

"What the hell was that?" she gasped, backing into the wall.

"They'll expect to smell blood from between your legs. Unless you'd have preferred it if I made the injury more authentic?"

She swung her knife at him. He caught her wrist and peeled the knife out of her hands. "You walk out of here with that and they'll know it's a farce. They've always thought me soft."

He held her furious stare as he set the knife on the bed they'd mussed up. "It'll be here when we come back to finish our fun."

She curled her lip at him but didn't flinch when he returned his arm to her shoulders. "Start weeping, Calla," he said. "Beg for your life until we're back behind this door."

The instant he opened the door, Calla began wailing. "Please just take my money and let me go," she mumbled, slurring her words.

"Let's talk about it after I'm done with you," Marl jeered, leading her down the stairs. As he'd predicted, ten of the men in the room were pleasuring themselves again, but this time their eyes were on the other four men who were pleasuring each other in various ways.

Three of the spectators jumped to their feet as Marl dragged Calla into the room. "Our turn," a man with black hair said.

"I'm not finished," Marl sneered.

"You aren't the boss, boss. Not for real. Where'd Reggie get off to? He didn't come back with you."

Marl extracted his knife again. "He went to find a girl, mate. Get the fuck out of my face, and the lady's face, or I'll end you."

The hunter stepped away as he averted his gaze, but another one stepped forward. "You don't usually care so much for the females you take upstairs. Usually by now they're dead and wrapped in a curtain." He eyed Calla up and down, appraising her like she was livestock. "This one must be something special."

Calla was going to vomit and her tears weren't fake when she said, "Please let me go."

"Not yet, little one," he crooned. Then his knife flew to the cheek of the man preventing them from getting to the door. "If a single other person talks to me or the Ambrosius, this knife will go through Linden's eye. A single word, or, fuck," he laughed, tightening his grip on Calla as the fornicating men finally stopped moving and started to listen, "if anyone even thinks a coherent thought beyond the *urgency* of your silence for the next five minutes, I will set the entire *fucking* warehouse on fire and lock you all inside of it. After all, I now have my own private supply." He kissed Calla hard, and while she didn't dare push him away, her whimper was real. Marl pulled away, his eyes wild.

Eyes Calla now noticed were green.

"Get the *fuck* out of my way," Marl spit at Linden, who backed away.

Marl pushed Calla toward the door, but she was suddenly torn out of his grasp by the first hunter, who pressed his own knife to her throat.

Calla shook violently as blood dripped down her neck and the man holding her shuddered. "She's potent. Birthday coming up," he rasped. "You can't keep that to yourself, Marl. It isn't right."

Marl's eyes couldn't get any wider if he wanted to keep them in his head. "Give her back," he said quietly. "The only way you will ever leave this house alive is if you give her back *right now*."

The man dug the point of his blade into Calla's throat. Calla tasted blood. "Marl—" she said, but already her voice was ragged and gurgling.

"Roddick, give her back *now* or I swear Della Victus himself won't be able to free you from the *torment* I will unleash upon you. *Now*." Marl's eyes were glimmering, from fear, from regret, from sorrow, or just because he hadn't blinked in almost a minute, it was impossible to know. Perhaps all of them at once.

Roddick licked her neck and Calla closed her eyes. But Loewen's face swam before her, so she opened her eyes again to focus instead on Marl, who was her only hope.

The hunter pulled her to the sofa as the lust stage flared in him. "You can have her back when I'm done," he said. He threw her onto the furniture, his hand digging into his trousers which were still unbuttoned.

"You are a very stupid man, Roddick," Calla heard Marl say. Before she'd finished turning around, he plunged his knife through the hunter's throat. The tip of it shone even in the dim light, dripping red.

"Traitor," the men in the room grumbled, all standing now. And they all stepped toward Marl.

Calla wished she had her knife.

Marl laughed and Calla realized he still hadn't blinked. Maybe he hadn't even breathed until then. "Traitor?" he asked, his tone incredulous. "I'm the one who decides who is a traitor." With a whirl, he dug his knife into Linden's eye. As *that* hunter fell to the floor, he looked around the room. "Who will hear my judgment next?"

No one moved.

No one spoke.

"Come, whore," he said, dragging Calla to her feet. She prayed to every one of the Twelve that no one else heard his voice break on the degrading word.

Marl pulled her outside. "Get the bag," he rasped. "Now, woman!"

Calla rushed to Lucky's side and grabbed her satchel. Marl grabbed her arm tight enough to bruise as he hauled her through the living room and back up the stairs.

Once they were back in his room with the door locked, Marl whimpered and collapsed onto his bed. "*Yerna*, I'm going to die."

Calla knew he was right. Aneurin *was* coming for her and he would kill any hunter he found.

Should she warn him? As she looked upon his haggard face, she wanted to spare him. Wanted to tell him that she, as the lover of King Aneurin, granted him clemency.

But she couldn't bring herself to say it.

"We should drain me now so I have a chance to recover before dawn," she said.

Marl nodded and moved to his dresser. He pulled out a box clinking with empty glass vials.

"Might I have a taste?" he asked as she settled onto his pillows and pulled her sleeve up to reveal her arm.

"You had to fight so hard not to violate me after just a few drops," she said. "I don't know if you'd be able to stop yourself if you had any more."

Marl smiled softly as he uncorked the vials. "I had no desire to violate you. Did I desire to *have* you in some way? Oh yes, Calla. Do not think I am a rehabilitated man. But rape was far from my mind."

Despite the fact he, an ambrosia hunter, was holding a knife to her arm, Calla wasn't as afraid as she thought she should be. "According to your friends down there, it's never far from your mind." She winced as his knife cut her open and blood began pouring out of her wound. She knew he wasn't bothering to protect his linens so he could lick them later. But still, less fear than she expected.

"Do you know why they think I'm soft?" he asked.

She shrugged.

"You're not the first Ambrosius I've tried to save. The others I did drink from, and some I did fuck, but I never raped them. I tried to reason with them, like I did you, but most of them didn't bother to argue with me. They were ready to die. They asked me to ensure that the rest of them didn't get their chance with them. Most of the people I've killed asked for it. And I don't mean that to imply some sort of philosophical vagary. I mean they begged me to kill them as gently as I could so that someone else couldn't be cruel about it."

Calla began to shake as he began to sweat. Vial after vial was filled with her blood, and she was dizzy. "It's not your place to kill anyone, even if they ask for it. Not unless they were threatening you," she said softly.

"I thought I was being merciful. I thought…"

He laughed quietly.

"I thought that even if I couldn't be a good man, I could do a good thing. Unfortunately what makes a thing good is a lot different from what makes a man good. Sometimes it's not so easy to know the difference between right and wrong. Not for me, anyway."

He wiped his brow with his sleeve. Calla could see how hard he struggled not to upend one of the vials into his own mouth.

"It's never too late," she said, her speech slurring with her lightheadedness. "Tomorrow is a new day. A clean slate. Aneurin…called me his queen. And I…"

Marl looked down on her, his pasty, hard features tight.

She sighed. "I find you guilty on all counts you can think of. But I sentence you to…time served," she said. "I spare you…the gallows. I declare you free to become the man you want to be, not the man you think you're doomed to be."

Marl said nothing. He exhaled sharply through his nose. "You're going to be the best queen the Vale ever had, Calla. Just remember what I said. Make sure he kills all of us. Even me. I don't deserve absolution."

Far away, she heard him pretending to do the very thing he said he had no desire to do. And she believed him. The last thing she saw before her eyes stayed closed was the anguish on his face.

"Rise and shine, Miss. Might be your last day on earth, but it's time to go. You're of no use to me now." Marl shouted the words. "Whore! Just leave! Get out! Go die in the mountains where I don't have to look at you."

Calla opened her eyes to find Marl fully dressed and waiting. He had her sword and dagger in his lap.

She pushed herself to sitting. Her head ached monstrously, and her arm did too. "My bag," she whispered. "And some water."

"Just have ale," he said, tossing her a canteen that reeked of cheap alcohol. "But I packed some snow into your canteen. I gave everyone a vial of your blood to ensure they stayed out of my room while you slept."

She nodded. She stood and sheathed her sword but kept her grip on the dagger. She caught her reflection in the cheap mirror hanging from the door. She barely looked human. In fact, she looked so sick she doubted she would make it to Della Victus.

But at least she had a chance to try.

"Bag," she said. He handed her the satchel and she reached inside and pulled out her perfume. She looked at it for a moment, then took a deep breath before spritzing herself. Then she stood and put the bottle on his dresser. At his curious stare as he sniffed the air, she said, "A magic gift from the king. I was saving the last of it until I got into Rynthia."

Patting herself down one more time, she realized she wasn't wearing the brooch.

She turned to Marl, who pursed his lips. "I was going to sell it," he said. He reached into his pocket and pulled out the brooch. "But then I saw it was magic. But I'm glad I saw your real face." He offered the adornment to her. "Come on. They're sleeping it off. I fed your horse and even brushed him. Do not stop until you're off the mountain and over the border. Please, Your Majesty."

The honorific chilled Calla's bones even more than the cold did. She would never be truly queen. She was more certain than ever that she was hunting her doom. She fastened the broach to her breast and hoped she was wearing her true face when she greeted Della Mortis.

Outside, Marl helped her onto Lucky's back. She wasn't strong enough to do it herself. "Remember what I said," he pressed as he handed her the reins.

"Okay," she said. But before she dug in her heels, she looked down at him. "Marl."

He raised his eyebrows at her.

"If the king has defeated the clans, he is probably already on his way here. He will kill any hunter he finds."

"Good," Marl said, and the relief in his voice was evidenced by the way his shoulders relaxed.

"No," she said. "My first act as queen was to pardon you. Don't let that be in vain. I want you to flee." She reached into her bag and pulled out the rest of her money. "This is enough for three months on the road. Stay out of trouble. And if Aneurin should find you, give him the perfume bottle and tell him that Calla Renaud said both of you could be good men if you tried, and that's what you're doing. Trying."

Marl shook his head. But all he said was, "Gorgeous name for a gorgeous girl. Get to Rynthia before the sun sets."

"Goodbye, Marl."

"Goodbye, Calla."

It took everything Calla had not to look behind her as she sped her horse down the mountain. Even long after she left him behind, she wanted to look to prove he wasn't still standing there, awaiting his violent death at the hands of her lover. But she didn't.

At the border of Rynthia, she held her breath as she crossed out of the Vale, and out of Aneurin's reach.

She had just entered the tree line when she heard her name. That was when she looked behind her and saw the sky illuminate in rainbow streaks as Aneurin slammed into the barrier between the Vale and Rynthia, screaming her name.

"Come on, Lucky," she said, her face crumpling with her longing to go to the king she loved. But she had a meeting with Della Victus, and not long to live. She had to win her duel before she succumbed to the darkness. Not just for Aneurin's sake, but for the sakes of Marl and every nine-year-old boy forced to kill to survive in the world Aneurin abandoned.

Chapter Thirty-Four

Calla's eyes drooped as Lucky plodded toward the northeast. Rain fell hard around her, and she was soaked through. Her thin blood could not warm her as her body temperature dropped dangerously low.

Even through the rain, she knew that the salty clarity she smelled was the sea.

Magnetic water pulled her east. The road stretched on, and Calla followed it. Her heart surged. So close. She could taste the salt. She just wanted to see it.

Before the pine forest ended, she reached a crossroad. One road led straight, and she knew it led to the sea.

Another road stretched to the south. The marker pointing in that direction read *Orlyne*. A major city in Rynthia, but not the capital.

The road that led to the north was overgrown with vines.

Calla knew that was the way to Della Victus.

She urged Lucky forward, but he shied away from the eastern road. Snorting and stamping his hooves.

Calla's throat was dry. She could barely keep her eyes open. She unlatched her canteen full of melted snow and sipped it, but her stomach hurt.

Marl had taken too much blood. She was dying.

The Ambrosius had six hours until midnight on her twenty-fifth birthday. She was so close.

But the ocean called her. She'd always wanted it. Just to see it. It had been her dream since she first saw a map of the continent.

To see the blanket of water and the far horizon. The endless world spread before her. A place where she could imagine a world better than the one she lived in.

She turned her head to the north. That world could not exist unless she broke Eugenia's curse. Not in the Vale. Not beyond it. Ambrosius were hunted everywhere on the continent. Even if somewhere existed where the Twelve did not reign, did not bewitch the blood of infants, the world *she* inhabited was cursed and fallow.

"Your death comes upon you swiftly," said a cool voice.

Calla whipped her head around to see the source of it, but her vision was so blurry. Someone tall, impossibly so, the black horns on their head stretching and curving twelve feet in the air. Their skin was pale. Even with her vision so obscured, the contrast between black and white reminded her of Aneurin.

"What are you?" she asked.

The figure drew closer, but their steps made no sound. "I am the one you truly seek though your destination is my brother's domain."

As he drew closer, Calla could see shadows whispered off the spirit's shoulders and around his arms and legs. Specters, whispering and hissing. He was dressed in strange clothes—silk but shimmering with diamond dust. The rain didn't seem to touch him.

"Divine…divine death," Calla said. "The lord of death. Della Mortis. But I am not ready to die just yet."

"I know. I am not here to claim you. But I am your destiny, Calla. You need to decide the nature of our inevitable embrace. Will you die by the sea, collapsing in the sand before you touch it? Or will you die defending something you know could be saved if someone was willing to fight for it?"

She felt him draw even closer, and the air cooled around her. Della Mortis stood so close the rain stopped touching her too. She could see better.

The god of death was beautiful in a devastating way that made her want to tear out her eyes. Black hair, silver eyes, a narrow mouth that she knew would look cruel on a mortal man but looked only severe and ancient on a god.

She stared at him and he stared back, a patient benevolence in his eyes. A wagon trundled by from Orlyne, but moved down the eastern road, passing right through her and Della Mortis as if they weren't there at all.

Calla didn't understand.

"You hover between life and death even now," Della Mortis said. "I can give you enough strength to get where you intend to go. Decide where that is, and I will bless you. But time will run out eventually. You cannot reach the ocean *and* free the Vale."

Disappointment and regret flooded every corner of Calla's soul. There was only one choice to make.

"I am afraid," she said.

"I know," Della Mortis replied. "You will be until the moment you die. But then I will escort you to Arronet."

Calla looked down the eastern road, though she couldn't see far. "Will I free the Vale if I take the northern road? Or will I lose having given up my only chance to see what I've longed for my entire life?"

Della Mortis lifted his hands in a strange gesture. "I do not know the future, Calla. I only know your destiny because it is intertwined with my strongest, and weakest, champion. You know him as Aneurin Fontaine. He is my calamity on a world desperate for justice. He *is* my justice. The moment Octavian chose to allow the Destined to die, I sent his wife a Destined child to pass my judgment."

Calla closed her eyes. It couldn't be true. "Aneurin never claimed his destiny."

"Yes, he did. By abandoning the world, he did. Eugenia never cursed him, Calla Renaud. His bad luck and yours was borne of the ambrosia that once flooded his veins and runs through yours now. Godfrey Fontaine would have met me next. Without the source of his code of honor, everything Aneurin did would have been cursed to fail. You see, Calla Renaud, his great destiny was to destroy the Vale so a better one could be rebuilt when the time came. I am the god of death. The one who blessed you is, indirectly, the god of life. And that time has come."

Calla couldn't breathe. It would break Aneurin to know his fate was to destroy the kingdom. It would break Godfrey, who was so proud of his son even when he made questionable choices.

A ruinous fate. Great and terrible. "Della Sorvis is the god of justice. It wasn't your right to punish the Vale."

Della Mortis smiled. "If that is true, I will be punished. But you haven't cared about the gods for a long time. Who are you to tell me what I may or may not do? Make your choice now, mortal. It is time to go."

Lorana Vale needed to be rebuilt. There was only one choice Calla should make, though it broke her heart. But maybe… maybe knowing that Della Mortis himself thought she would succeed was enough to strengthen her. She'd win the duel and Aneurin could save the Vale, even though it would come at the price of *everything*.

"I will go to Della Victus," Calla said.

Della Mortis sighed as if holding his breath. "You choose life, though yours will be taken. You are everything a champion of Ros should be. He will be proud of you."

Like a flash of lightning, Della Mortis clutched her face in his hands. Freezing cold radiated out from his fingertips, flooding her veins with ice. She thought she screamed, but maybe she didn't. When the god of death released her, her vision was clear but her body still ached.

Without a word but with a heavy heart, Calla spurred Lucky to the northern road.

The overgrown road led through the forest and out of it. Calla passed through meadows illuminated by moonlight. She counted the fireflies dancing in the night; she listened to the cries of owls and nightravens.

Eventually, the path led directly to a cave that was green with moss. No one had visited Della Victus in hundreds of years. Perhaps not since Miriam Bells.

In the darkest hours of night, Calla unsaddled Lucky and piled all her supplies on the ground. She took off her cloak. She took off her jacket. She slammed her boot into the brooch, shattering it. Then she kissed Lucky's snout and said, "Thank you for aiding me. Go home and tell them I said goodbye." She struck his flanks and he ran off back down the road.

At eleven o'clock, Calla entered the cave.

She had no lantern, but she pressed forward, her hand on the wet stone walls fuzzy throughout with moss. She slipped quite a few times, but always steadied herself.

Deeper, deeper into the dark.

It was a holy place, but that just meant the dread was more sinuous, writhing in her belly and blood like smoke from a blown-out candle.

When she turned a corner and saw light ahead, Calla's heart thudded so loud, she would have bet anything that Della Victus could hear it. Did he know she was coming?

It was a stupid question. Of course he did.

She turned one last corner to set eyes on the massive, thirty-foot high crack in a wall that would have been a dead end if not for the rift. Through it, Calla could see a ripe, fertile field, green and bursting with life. The colors were more vibrant than she'd ever seen. Even under the cloak of night, the blossoms of gladiolus spires and daffodils shone as bright as if they sat in direct sunlight.

The rift was *just* wide enough for Calla to squeeze through.

Birds cawed as they soared overhead, unhindered by the fallen night like mortal birds tended to be. Wolves lay in the meadow to her right, but they did not growl or bite. To her left, rabbits and deer frolicked and tumbled, unafraid.

And yet…a wolf had blood on its maw.

A bright blue light shone from an amphitheater not too far ahead. Calla headed straight for it even as her eyes searched her surroundings, drinking in the beauty of the place.

Della Victus stood in the center of the dirt arena, bathed in moonlight. His skin was pale like Della Mortis, but a pale sort of blue. His hair was also blue, darker, and his horns were an even darker blue still, reaching high above his head.

"Mortal women do not come here anymore," he said.

Calla licked her lips. "If I had any other choice, I wouldn't be here. But I am not a Forsaken like Miriam. Destined to die I may be, but you will grant my wish, Lord Victus."

In his hands, with the point buried in the dirt, Victus held the handle of a sword almost as tall as Calla was. "I do not grant the wishes of weak women."

"Yes you do. That's why you cannot wait to strike me down. My love is pure, unlike Miriam's."

She drew ever closer to the god of liberty, who smiled. "Miriam betrayed me and failed to pay the price for her lover's freedom. I do not desire your pain, Calla Renaud. I desire only for our transaction to be mutually completed."

Calla unsheathed her sword. "I notice you didn't say 'fair.'"

Della Victus laughed. "Life isn't fair, even for the gods. You know that. Nothing about anything you've endured in your miserable ambrosic life has been fair, but here you are, alive and breathing and ready to pay the price for the freedom of others. *Fair* is subjective. *Fair* means whatever the ones who pay the price for it say it is."

Calla nodded. Then she smiled.

Fear had evaporated. She was meant to be in that arena. She was meant to serve her king and her country. Even Della Mortis knew she would succeed.

"I say fair is you breaking the curse on Lorana Vale," she

said.

Della Victus nodded. "You should have seen my brother Sorvis if your quest is so simple."

"And I say fair is you erasing the enchantment Della Ros put on Aneurin Fontaine. Only you can break two curses. Justice has nothing to do with the way Aneurin looks, because he is beautiful no matter how many feathers adorn his face. Let him live the life he wants to live."

The god of liberty nodded again. "Pay the price, Calla Renaud. Land a blow so I may rule the Vale again." He chuckled. "*Liberty* at last. But there is one aspect of the enchantment I will not break."

Calla lifted her sword. "What is that?"

Della Victus lifted his own sword. "Aneurin may not leave the Vale. I will rid him of immortal life, but however many years he has left will be spent fixing what he broke."

Calla's heart sank. But…it was a small price to pay for the salvation of the kingdom. She hoped Aneurin could forgive her for allowing his imprisonment to continue.

But it didn't matter anymore, for Della Victus swung his sword and Calla had to leap out of the way.

Calla spun around the arena dodging the attacks of the giant god. He was too tall, his reach too long, his sword too big. She couldn't get close.

"How can you expect to strike me if you keep running away?" Della Victus taunted her, chuckling as he swung his sword again.

"It's *cheating* if your sword is as tall as your enemy is!" Calla protested, jogging away.

"It is proportionate to my height, as yours is for you. Don't you think that's *fair*, mortal?"

With a grunt, Calla rolled out of the way of his next attack and used the time it took for him to lift it again to charge at him.

Della Victus laughed and picked her up by her throat. "You told your lover you needed to land *just* one blow, didn't you?" he sneered before tossing her across the arena.

Every notion of breathing was knocked out of Calla upon her impact. But she didn't have time—Della Victus was already striding toward her. She pushed herself to her feet and spit out dirt as she ran out of his reach.

But the intimacy of his hand around her neck gave her an idea.

Instead of dodging his next swing, Calla prayed to Della Mortis for more cold strength and instead lifted her sword to meet his.

Shock washed over his divine features and he wrinkled his pointed nose. "Brave, but foolish," Della Victus said as his strength bore down on her, his blade drawing closer and closer to her face.

"I just wanted to see if I could withstand it," Calla said. She pushed with all her might, then dropped her sword and dove out of the way.

Della Victus chuckled as he spun to see where she'd run. "Do you think you'll get close and scratch me with that little dagger?"

"I'm not stupid," Calla said.

"No, but you're uneducated. Naïve. Blinded by your love."

"Emboldened by my love," Calla countered.

Then she felt it.

At the stroke of midnight, Calla absorbed her magic and glory made her eyes glow. Her moment of triumph had come.

She gritted her teeth, baring them, and glared at Della Victus

He smiled as her golden eyes shone on him. "Come earn it," he crooned.

Calla ran in a circle around him and slid in the dirt to pick up her sword. "I would have thought the god of liberty would understand that *true* love is about allowing others to make their own choices. You tried to force Miriam to love you. You broke your own laws," she grunted as Della Victus brought his sword down on her.

He hesitated, but that whisper of a moment was all Calla needed. She swung her sword at the legs of Della Victus. Her blade sliced his blue skin the moment he grunted and plunged the tip of his mighty sword through her heart.

He left his sword inside of her, pinning her to the dirt as he crouched next to her. "Brave," he said softly, "but foolish."

"Free..them…" Calla said.

"I already have. Rest now. My brother awaits you." Massive fingertips brushed her skin, forcing her eyes closed.

I love you, rosara. *Live freely.*

The last thing Calla Renaud heard before she died was the sigh of Della Victus.

Chapter Thirty-Five

Aneurin

The first thing Aneurin noticed when he opened his eyes was that he was flat on his back. He turned his head to the side and didn't see his massive, bandaged wing. He saw nothing but mattress and bedsheets.

His eyes widened. His hands flew up to touch his face. Eyebrows and skin, skin, skin.

The king of Lorana Vale tore out of bed and staggered to his mirror. Shock made his jaw slack as he touched his face. No feathers. No wings. Nothing at all but his smooth, unlined face and unobstructed green eyes.

"Godfrey!" he shouted, still staring at himself. *"Father, please!"*

He stared at himself until he heard the pounding of footsteps. Then he turned and met the matching gaze of his steward, father, and friend, whose face collapsed.

"She did it," Godfrey whispered, stumbling into the room. "My boy, I told you she would."

Aneurin wept and fell into the arms of his only living family member. "That means she's gone," he sobbed. "She's gone but the world is still here. How can the sun still shine if she's dead?"

Godfrey patted his back before tangling his hands in the soft black waves he'd missed so much. "She freed you. She freed all of us. Don't mourn her victory. She wants you to *live*, Aneurin. We have much to do now to make the kingdom safe again."

But Aneurin was inconsolable. His knees gave out and he sank to the floor. "She never saw my face except in the painting. She loved the worst of me. What gives *me* the right to live and her to die?"

Godfrey kissed the top of his head. "You are king. And you must rule now. You must return to the world and lead it. That was her wish. Don't betray her by giving up now."

Aneurin groaned but nodded. "You're right. You're right. I have to be worthy of her sacrifice." He got to his feet and wiped the tears off his face. "But I want to retrieve her. I will go to Della Victus myself and claim her body. *Then* I will lead."

Godfrey nodded as he, too, stood. "Yes, Your Majesty. I will send word to the barracks. You need a guard now that you will be out in the world."

Aneurin waved his hand. "Small contingent only. I don't want the Rynthian queen to think I'm declaring war on her by marching an army to her borders. Mary and Cresedan must start inventorying supplies to see what we can take. And I need wagons. Commandeer any in the area and tell the owners I will give them two *new* wagons for every one I take. I want to leave at first light tomorrow."

"Yes, my king," Godfrey said, but he couldn't hide the pride in his voice. And it made Aneurin smile just a little.

The first stop Aneurin made was in Senden's Branch. As his procession consisting of guards and supplies and Godfrey and Cresedan made its way into town, the villagers crowded the streets to take a look. All were wary and weary, haggard from a hard-lived existence under the brutality of his negligence.

"You dare show your face now?" a young man shouted. Aneurin stopped his horse and turned to find a scruffy, black-haired man around Calla's age standing on the wide base of one of the lampposts. His hand held him aloft as he glared at the king.

Aneurin folded his hands on the pommel of his saddle. "I have not been a good king," he said. Hoarse agreement sounded from the villagers. "But I *am* the king. I am here to do my job."

"Why should we let you? You abandoned us! You're a coward!" the young man spat.

The villagers agreed. Godfrey drew his horse closer to Aneurin's.

Aneurin bowed his head and said, "I want the mayor and sheriff brought to the street. I did not do my job, but they did not do theirs either."

The young man sneered but watched as four of Aneurin's men went to the small prison to fetch the men who had been elected to steward the village.

Haggard and blotchy from lack of sleep and malnutrition, the men sank to their knees before Aneurin's horse. "Please, my king, it was an impossible task to keep the runners out. There are too many of them," the sheriff wept.

The weight of the crown on his head made Aneurin grimace as he slid out of the saddle and approached the two men. He looked down on their dirty, tear-streaked faces. They feared him. And he was glad of it. He'd cultivated the fear of his people for centuries to avoid their deaths, but this was a benefit too—they would heed him now even though it pained them to do so.

"I relieve you of your posts," Aneurin said. "You have not done what you were supposed to do. You did not protect the people of Senden's Branch."

"*You* didn't protect the people of the Vale!" the young man from before cried.

Aneurin raised his hand to silence him without looking at the boy. He continued addressing the kneeling prisoners. "I will not execute you. I know your job was made more difficult by my own actions. But you are banished from Senden's Branch. Find your livelihoods elsewhere. You may return in five years if you have proven yourselves to be an asset to your new communities."

The men wept and kissed his boots, which only made Aneurin grimace even more. He did not want their supplication.

Someday, he hoped to be loved.

He turned to the young man who still stood attached to the lamppost. "What is your name?"

The challenger jumped down and approached the king but stood a good distance away. "Rhyser Howe, Your Majesty. My sister is dead because of you and my mom and pop are sick because there's no way to make enough money for food. Again, because of *you*."

Aneurin did not bow his head or apologize. He needed to show the strength that would make his people have faith in him again. "I need good men to steward this town. Men I can trust so I can focus on fixing the Vale. What has plagued Senden's Branch has plagued my entire kingdom, and I am going to clean it up. But that will take time. I will not shame you by throwing coins at your feet as if money can make up for what has happened here. But I would like to pay you fairly for your service as the new sheriff. And I have coin I can give you right now if you can promise that in two weeks you will come to the palace with twenty trusted men and women that you think I should appoint in other roles of service to Senden's Branch. Do you accept?"

Rhyser's brow furrowed and he leveled an icy stare at the king. "Why have we known you as the Strix Lord if you have no feathers or wings? Three years ago you hosted a party and the people who attended saw you. You were a bird, but you are not now."

Aneurin squared his shoulders. "There was an Ambrosius from Senden's Branch who lived with me for five years. Calla Renaud. She fulfilled her destiny and broke the curses upon me so that I might be the king you deserve. If you cannot find it in your heart to forgive me, you can and should be grateful to her."

A woman pushed through the crowd and fell to her knees before him. "My name is Brenna, my lord," she said, breathless. "Calla was to be my stepdaughter. I met her on the night her father died. Where is she?"

Aneurin looked at Rhyser and held his gaze as he said, "My queen is dead. She gave her life to Della Victus to save us all."

Rhyser's lips pressed into a tight line. "I accept your offer. I will come in two weeks." He dipped into a low bow and turned away, disappearing down a side street.

The woman called Brenna wept on the cobblestones. Godfrey appeared beside Aneurin and murmured, "Calla loved her despite hardly knowing her. She would want you to comfort her."

Aneurin knelt before the woman, lifting her chin with one

hand. "Do you have money and food?" he asked.

She nodded, gasping with her sobs. "Calla saw to it. She gave me permission to sell Peter's business and make a life for myself. But it's lonely without him. I'd hoped after she was of age, her and I could be a family."

Aneurin sighed. "My love for her was great as well, Brenna Renaud. I would like you to come to the palace. You don't have to serve on my staff, but you can serve as my first courtier in the new court of King Aneurin of Lorana Vale."

Brenna's wet eyes widened. "That's generous, my lord."

"It's a genuine request, Mistress Renaud."

Brenna nodded, gasping once more as she rose to her feet with Aneurin's help. "I will settle my affairs here in town. I'll come in a week."

"Very good."

Aneurin climbed back into the saddle. To the rest of the assembled townspeople, he said, "Change is coming. Some of you will say it is too late, and I agree with you. But I am the king, and I will rule. Be prepared to live a different life."

The people of Senden's Branch bowed. But they did not cheer.

As he passed through the towns he'd all but destroyed while searching for Calla, Aneurin fought the urge to hide his face. A late April thaw made the passes easier to traverse, but he felt strange wearing soft wool and silks instead of armor while being amongst his people. Stranger still was the feeling of the gold crown on his head and the black kohl around his eyes and the diamond dust on his cheeks. The adornments of a contemporary king in a contemporary age. A present king. A ruling king.

He supposed it was a good thing he was an attractive man.

While there was a hardness to the way everyone stared at him as he passed through each town, there was a reverence too. A reverence that had been lost the moment Eugenia cursed him.

He supposed the couriers with bags of gold for every town probably had more to do with his safety than anything else. Word had spread quickly—King Aneurin had been freed from whatever bird had confined him in his avian prison and he had left his nest.

At the base of the Solda, Aneurin and Godfrey passed a haggard blond man with dirty hair and a shadow of patchy facial hair. He wore a flimsy hat and had two knives and a sword at his belt. When the man's eyes met the king's, his face collapsed in some anguished emotion. "My king," he called.

Aneurin stopped the procession. "Yes?"

The man did not step forward, but he took off his hat. "You're wearing all black. Are you mourning?"

Aneurin and Godfrey exchanged a glance. Godfrey nodded.

"I am. The Ambrosius who broke the curses that confined me to my palace gave her life so I may free the Vale from the despair that plagues it. I am going to Rynthia to recover her body so she may be buried at my palace, where I can visit her. I owe her…everything."

The man twisted his hat in his hands. "We all do, Your Majesty. We all do." He sank to one knee before the king and kept his eyes on the ground until Aneurin moved on.

Aneurin felt the worst of his guilt as they passed the ambrosia den in Darkpeak where he'd slaughtered so many people. But he did not avert his gaze from the house nor from the people who probably lost loved ones in his rampage.

They bowed to him. And in return, he made them a silent promise to rebuild Darkpeak first so those left wouldn't have to suffer much longer.

At the border, Aneurin slid off his horse, determined to take his first steps into the world on his own two feet.

But an invisible wall blocked him. He collided right into it, staggering backward with a look of confusion.

"What witchcraft is this?" he sputtered. He turned to Godfrey who was still astride his horse. "Why am I a man but still imprisoned?"

Godfrey shrugged, shaking his head with wild eyes. "I cannot tell you, Your Grace."

Aneurin spun around and put his hand on the barrier. Rainbow light flared around his hand as he furrowed his brow. But there, about halfway to the tree line, a pop of color appeared. Then another. Then another. An explosion of black smoke, then one of red smoke, then one of yellow smoke. When the smoke dissipated, Aneurin's eyes widened as Della Mortis stood before him accompanied by two of his brothers—Della Sorvis, the god of justice, and Della Ros, the god of beauty and life.

And in the arms of Della Ros was the bloodied body of his dead queen.

Aneurin sank to his knees.

As a quarter of the Twelve approached the wall, Godfrey came to stand beside him. "On your feet, Your Grace. You're in the presence of divinity."

Della Sorvis, whose hair and horns were bright golden yellow and complemented his dark brown skin, raised a hand in greeting. "You have come for your bride," he said.

"Y—yes," Aneurin rasped. "Why can I not come claim her?"

The mouth of Della Sorvis turned down. "It is unjust that

you are still confined to the Vale because the enchantment holding you there was lifted. But she—" he gestured at Calla "agreed on your behalf to the terms of Della Victus. He would free your people, remove the enchantments, but you cannot leave the Vale until you have brought prosperity to your kingdom. Until you—" he sighed "—free your people from the chains of poverty with which your neglect shackled them. That is a just sentence, but I do wish it would have been your choice to accept."

Aneurin nodded. He—he could live with that. If he must live at all without his beautiful queen…he could live in service so losing her *meant* something.

Della Mortis spoke next. "The champion of Della Ros, the god of life, died for love of the champion of the god of death."

Aneurin's eyes widened. It couldn't be. "No," he whispered.

"Yes, mortal. You are mine. Your destiny was to destroy the Vale. Hers, to save it. That is why she found you beautiful from the moment she first saw you. Her destiny was to save the Vale by saving *you*."

Della Ros spoke. "I have brought her here as a token of trust."

Aneurin looked at her face. She didn't look like she was sleeping, but he could tell her body had been preserved for the days it took for him to get to Rynthia. Divine protection.

"Why does it matter if I trust you?" he asked. His gaze snapped back to the pale face of Della Ros. "Have I not given you enough?"

The god of beauty smiled and tilted his head. "My brothers and I offer you her life so she may be queen. But if you accept, you will once again become immortal. You will rule the Vale forever unless you are slain—by your own hand or another's."

Aneurin's face went slack. He could have her back. But at

what cost? His staff…he couldn't do that to them. Five hundred years of servitude was already too much.

"My—my staff. I do not want them enchanted. Do not sentence them to my fate." He put his hand back on the barrier. "Once, I told Calla that I would rather have a few decades of love with her than face all but five of a thousand years without her by my side. If you spare my staff, I will accept."

Della Ros smiled. Della Sorvis sighed. Della Mortis nodded.

"Your staff's fate is tied to yours," Della Ros said. "But here—"

Della Mortis pulled a small vial out of the pocket of his black robes. Inside the vial was a swirling, shimmering pink liquid. He offered it to Aneurin, his hand reaching through the barrier. "The contents of this vial decide the nature of your fate," the god of death said. "One small sip taken by any member of your staff will free them from immortality. They will age and someday die, mortal again. But if your queen drinks the entire thing, she will join you in immortality to rule the Vale with you for eternity."

Aneurin began to shake as he took the vial from the cold fingers of Della Mortis. He couldn't make that choice. He *wanted* to make the choice, but he once said that immortality was not a gift.

He needed to think.

He put the vial in his pocket and said, "I accept your terms, Holy Ones. Give her back to me."

Della Sorvis peered at him strangely and Aneurin thought it must be because he knew he would not force the decision of whether to drink on anyone. The god of justice looked relieved.

Della Mortis put his hand on the shoulder of Della Ros and Della Sorvis did the same on the other side. All three of them closed their eyes. A flash of rainbow-colored light flared over the valley, temporarily blinding everyone, everywhere, whose eyes were open.

Aneurin whimpered as Calla's eyes fluttered open.

Della Ros set her on her feet. She stumbled at first, but the god who chose her steadied her. She stared at the ground as if trying to remember where she was. Her mouth opened as she frowned. Then she lifted her head to look at Aneurin, whose heart surged as recognition washed over her face.

"*Rosara*," she breathed and fell forward through the barrier to collapse in his arms.

When Aneurin opened his eyes again after breathing in the smell of her hair, the gods were gone.

Chapter Thirty-Six

Calla did not regain consciousness until the day after they returned to the palace. Aneurin held her in his own saddle the entire way, his arm nestled under her breasts so he could feel her heartbeat.

He bathed her himself. He tipped water into her mouth himself. He dressed in the most comfortable clothes he owned and laid beside her unsleeping. He wished he could have asked the gods why she was sleeping, but he hoped it was just weariness. After all, she'd been dead for days when the gods gave her back to him.

He was watching her when her eyes opened. A smile spread across his face and he kissed her before she said anything.

Calla smiled into the kiss, her hand reaching up to touch his stubbled cheek. "I miss your feathers," she said softly as he pulled away.

Aneurin scoffed. "What a horrid thing to say."

"I do," she pressed. "They were soft and pretty. I've never known you without them."

He pressed his lips to her forehead. "You knew me," he said. "I saw in your eyes that you knew me before you succumbed to whatever made you sleep so long."

She sighed and rolled onto her side, burying her face in his chest. "My birthdays are always so exciting for you, aren't they?"

He laughed. "I will pray to every single one of the Twelve every single day that your twenty-sixth is uneventful and, dare I say it, *boring*."

Calla laughed into the soft cotton of his shirt. "I don't like being bored. I was bored for twenty years."

"I was bored for five hundred years. But you're right. I don't think it will be boring. If we're together, how could it be?"

Calla frowned as she heard the steel sorrow in his words. She leaned back and looked at his face. "What's wrong?"

Aneurin pressed his lips together to stop them from trembling as the magnitude of his immortality washed over him. He touched her face with his fingertips. His eyes creased and his brow furrowed. "You were dead, Calla. And I knew you were dead, and I came to get you. But I was met by Della Mortis and Della Sorvis and Della Ros, who carried your corpse in his arms, and they offered to give you back to me. I was ready to face the rest of my life without you even though I did not want to, but I was not ready to reject an offer of more time with you. I told you almost four years ago—five years was not enough time."

Calla's eyes widened in terror. "Tell me you didn't make another deal. You cannot, *cannot* have made another deal," she whispered.

"I had to," he pleaded. "I *had* to. I'd have given anything, killed anyone, spared anyone, and built anything, taken anything to see your golden eyes open again."

"No," she whimpered. "What did you give them? Whatever it was, I wasn't worth it, Aneurin." She grasped his head in her hands and her voice rasped with desperation as she cried, "What did you do?"

"Eternity," he said. The word just...fell out of his mouth. "I became their eternal king. But you—you will not rule with me for so long. Unless..."

Calla stared at him, shifting her gaze from one of his emerald eyes to the other. "Unless?"

He bit his lip and sighed, wrenching away from her, and leaving the bed. He moved to his cabinet and unlocked it, pulling out the chest in which he'd locked away the brooch. He opened it and pulled out a shimmering, glowing vial. "If you drink this, you will be my immortal queen."

Calla tilted her head skeptically. "That seems too easy."

Aneurin laughed. More of a scoff, really. "Seems so. Philosophically? Not so easy. If I give this to my staff, they will no longer possess eternal youth. They will age and eventually die. But you must drink every drop to join me in eternity."

The sorrow Calla felt was so black and twisted, she couldn't bear it. She got out of bed too and wandered slowly out of his bedroom, through the rest of his chambers, and out onto the veranda. She walked all the way to the balustrade and looked out over the property which was still covered in scorch marks from the clan attacks. Scorch marks—and blood.

She felt Aneurin behind her as she put her hands on the stone rail and gasped, her head bowed. "I would die a thousand times to be able to drink that potion," she said. "But I cannot do that to them. I promised Delilah I would free her when I freed you."

"You did," Aneurin protested. His urgency made her wince. "I'm the one who undid that. You don't owe her, or anyone, anything at all."

Calla shook her head. "You know I cannot drink it. Not unless they, too, refuse to drink it. But we must offer it to them, *rosara*. You know it's the right thing to do. I *died* so you would be free to do the right thing."

Aneurin's eyes squeezed shut and he clenched the vial in his hand. "I know. As always, you're right and I am weak."

"No," she sighed. She turned around and threw her arms around his neck. She kissed him again and again. "You're a good man, *rosara*. I've died once, I'm not afraid of doing so again. The only thing I fear is your passion for me dying too."

"*That* will never happen. Even when you're a hobbling old woman wearing a crown heavier than you are, I'll still love you."

Calla laughed, tears pricking her eyes. "What a ghastly image for everyone who works for you when that time comes— you so beautiful and me so old and ugly."

"Old—maybe. Ugly? Never." He kissed her again. He held her in the sunlight for a long time. Could have for minutes or hours or days.

But eventually, Calla sighed. "Let's get me dressed and go save your servants. We should offer it to Godfrey first."

Aneurin nodded.

When Calla was clad in the first dress Aneurin had ever chosen for her, she went to the dining room, the vial in her hands. She sat at the head of the table and took a deep breath before she studied the potion in the sunlight pouring in through the windows. Magic in a bottle. Liquid salvation.

As Aneurin found each member of the staff, they trickled into the dining room. Delilah arrived first. When her eyes met Calla's she smiled. So did Mary and Cresedan. Everyone did. A couple of them reached out and touched her shoulder, murmuring their gratitude for what she did.

Godfrey arrived last. He stood at her side, a hand on her shoulder, as she lifted the vial for everyone to see.

"One sip of this potion and you will be mortal," she said.

She felt Aneurin enter the room. She saw his head over everyone else's as he leaned against the wall. And she was comforted.

"I don't think she would have told you, but I promised Delilah that I would free you all from eternity when I freed the king. I did free the king. And I did free you. But another deal has been made, and you are once again shackled to time though it will pass right through you. If you wish to live a normal life…take this vial from me and drink," she said.

Godfrey's grip tightened on her shoulder.

No one said anything. Delilah lifted her chin and Calla could see her swallow, but the servant said nothing.

She turned to Godfrey after two minutes passed in silence. "You are the oldest," she said, offering him the vial. "You lead these people. If it is your choice, drink."

Godfrey cleared his throat. "And what happens if none of us choose to drink?"

Calla's face heated. She looked to Aneurin, but he shook his head. He wouldn't tell them. He couldn't. They would hear his desperation in his voice and feel obligated to give up their chance to please him. By keeping his silence, he let them decide for themselves.

But Calla couldn't answer either.

So Godfrey did. He plucked the bottle from her fingertips and held it up before answering his own question. "If none of us drink from this vial, the woman who saved the kingdom will drink it. And when she does, she will become immortal like the king. Like us. She will join with us and be shackled to the same fate, be it dark or light. Whether we greet hell or Arronet on earth, she will stand with us. And that is something both she and the king have longed for since the day of that confounded *party*."

A low chuckle sounded from around the room.

"I will not drink," Godfrey said. "I will stay by my son's side until he no longer needs me and then I will stay by his side until he kills me himself." He laughed breathlessly. "Because of *this* woman, I can name Aneurin as my son. His true name is Aneurin *Fontaine* and he is the king and he is *my* son and now I can tell *everyone* because *she* died for my freedom to do so. I will not drink. Will you?"

Calla heard mumbled denials from around the room. But she didn't dare hope. She didn't dare look at Aneurin either because she didn't want to see his hope.

Trevorn, the captain of the guard, stepped forward. "What if we don't want to serve for eternity? Do we have to choose to either drink and leave or stay and serve? Can we choose to forego the potion and still leave?"

"Yes," Aneurin rasped from the back of the room. Everyone turned to face him, dipping into bows and curtsies. "You may go and live your eternity elsewhere. I will even give you money to take with you to start your life. But it may be that if you leave, you will no longer be part of my staff and therefore not shackled like the rest of us. The choice is yours. Drink and stay. Drink and leave. Don't drink and stay, or don't drink and leave. Your lives are your own now, thanks to Calla."

"So choose," Godfrey said.

No one said anything, but Calla could hear a roar in her head as if she heard the racing minds of everyone faced with such a crucial decision for the first time in centuries.

Finally, Delilah spoke up. "We all swore an oath of service to Lord Aneurin before he became the Strix Lord," she said. "And we all swore to protect Miss Renaud when he allowed her to stay here. If we drink, we are honorless oathbreakers." She turned around, staring down everyone in the room. "*He* protected us for five hundred years by letting everyone hate him so we could be pitied, not reviled when we went into town. And because of *her* he can now protect the kingdom. How many of us want families of our own? There's no reason we couldn't have them, but none of us have tried because of how dangerous the Vale has become. Because of Calla Renaud, we can serve our king until he makes it safe, and then we can do whatever we want. I will *not* drink."

Godfrey smiled.

"I will not drink," Mary said. She looked at Calla and smiled with tears in her eyes.

"Nor will I," Cresedan shouted. She grabbed Mary's hand and brought it to her lips.

One by one, the rest of the staff declared they would not drink. Calla's eyes met Aneurin's and he flew out of the room into the hallway where all five hundred of his soldiers were lined up. From beyond the door, Calla heard each and every man say they would not drink.

When Aneurin ran back into the room, his mouth was open,

and his breathing came in shallow. His eyes were wild, *wild* and terrified with the scale of his hope.

Godfrey leaned down to whisper in her ear as he wrapped her fingers around the vial. "Thank your staff, girl. Thank them and go to him. You should be alone when you drink."

Calla nodded and pushed herself to her feet. She could barely hear him over the sound of her ambrosia-less blood rushing through her head. She kissed Godfrey's cheek. "Thank you, Mister Fontaine," she whispered.

"My love for you both is eternal," he said. "Go."

"Thank you," Calla murmured to everyone she passed. "Thank you. Thank you."

By the time she made it to Aneurin's side, she was weeping.

On the veranda, Aneurin cradled Calla's face in his hands. His eyes gleamed with tears he had not yet shed. The sky was a glorious canvas of violet and orange and royal blue as the sun set. All around them, the lamps glowed, casting a golden light over the stone.

"I love you," the king said.

"I know," Calla replied. "You made a stupid, reckless bargain to bring me back from the dead."

He pressed his lips to hers, then smiled. "Blah blah, something to do with gods and destiny, blah blah," he murmured. Then he kissed her again.

She stifled an unladylike snort as he laughed into her mouth.

"You're happy." She lifted the hand that wasn't holding the vial and touched his face. She brushed her fingers past his mirthful dimples and to the corner of his joyfully creased eyes.

"I will be when you drink," he said. "When you drink and become my queen. When the passes through the Solda are safe and Senden's Branch has been cleaned up, I'm going to throw the most lavish wedding and coronation for you, *rosara*."

Calla blushed.

Aneurin grinned. "*I* will bring in courtiers and royals from every nation to witness the start of your reign. And then as I clean up the estates around the Vale, I will invite any living descendants of my old dukes and earls to come reclaim their titles. And we will have a *court*. And sometimes we will have *parties*. And every day, hundreds of people will see you with a crown on your head and they will know that finally, all is right in the world."

Calla couldn't help but smile even though her eyes watered. "When will you rewrite the history books in between all that housekeeping and decadence?"

"Godfrey will do that. Did you hear him? He's going to tell everyone that he is the true father of the king. Will you allow me to steal some of your light at your coronation to add a small ceremony naming him Warden of the Vale? I'd like to see him wear a crown too."

Calla erupted into laughter and wiped away a tear. "Of course. He'll never consent to wear one but if you can get him to agree to wear it for just one day, I'll cherish the memory."

He kissed her again. "That settles it. Now drink, *rosara*. Once you're immortal and I can feel secure knowing we have *both* conquered time, I'm going to make love to you until you beg me to stop. I don't care if we're in bed for *months*."

Calla scoffed, averting her eyes with embarrassment. She couldn't understand how she could feel so happy. She'd *never* felt such joy. It had never been an option—not with poverty and destiny and curses weighing upon her.

She was free. Aneurin was free. Everyone she ever cared

about was free.

She'd won. And the smile that hadn't left Aneurin's face in hours reminded her every time she looked at it that her victory was worth every moment of agony it took for them to claim it.

So she took a deep breath and uncorked the vial. "After I do this, you'll never be able to get rid of me. Are you sure you want this?" She held her breath as she waited for his answer.

Aneurin chuckled. Even as frustrated as he was, she knew he couldn't help it.

They'd won.

And no ghost would come between them ever again.

"As King of the Vale, I order you to drink, Calla lily mine," he commanded as she got lost in her thoughts yet again.

"Pigeon Lord," she retorted. "Canary Prince." She stuck her tongue out at him.

"Not anymore, thanks to you." He tangled his hands in her hair. "Drink, damn you."

With one last shuddering breath, Calla closed her eyes and poured the potion down her throat.

When her golden gaze fell upon him again, Aneurin's smile broadened. "Forever, *rosara.*"

"Forever," Calla promised.

Acknowledgements

First, I want to thank my Patreon supporters. Thank you so much for your monthly support. You have helped make this dream a reality for me. Your contributions have kept food in my pantry, purchased this cover for this book, and every dollar helps me so much. I love you all so deeply. My inbox is always open for you. So thank you to Brittanie Wing, Lauren Chiasson, Demelza Clearwater, Jamie Aron, Jacqui De Landelles, Darrian Costello, Sierra Gibson, Brittany Lowe, Clarissa Oquendo, Chester, and Joseph Crollard.

I also want to thank my beta readers. You have been so supportive of me, and I honestly wouldn't have published this book without you. You have convinced me that I have what it takes to be an author, and I know it was hard to do that. Sometimes I think you could be more constructive in your criticism, but if you really believe my books are as good as you've told me they are, that just… blows my mind. Thank you so much.

I also want to thank my editor Danielle. Your help with this has been absolutely essential in making this happen. I am so immensely grateful to you, and I'm excited for you to read and edit my future books.

Finally, I want to thank my children. Momo, for being the absolute perfect child. I don't mean that you never make mistakes, or that you're perfect in school. I mean you are perfect because you are you. Everything that I am loves you so completely and unconditionally. I know I've told you this five thousand times, but there is no problem or situation you find yourself in that I won't help you with. Even when you're an adult and potentially living hundreds of miles away, I will come to you if you need me. Always. And to my son, Colin, you're still too little to read, but someday when you're an adult, if you ever pick up this book and take a look at it, I hope you know that I love you. My unconditional love goes for you too. If you ever need me, I'm just a phone call away. I will always be there for you, no matter what it is you need, be it help, answers, or just the love of a parent.

I love you, I love you, I love you.

About Author

Ren Sylvain is a nonbinary autistic writer who lives in California, even though their heart resides in the Northeast. They are so passionate about writing, they are quite obnoxious. They also quite enjoy Romantic-era poetry, Dostoevsky, anime, and One Direction.

For exclusive AU content, sneak peeks, and the chance to become an alpha or beta reader for future books, support them on Patreon at patreon.com/rensylvain

They can also be found on Twitter at twitter.com/rensylvain and on Facebook at facebook.com/groups/rensylvain

Be on the lookout for more books in 2021.

CPSIA information can be obtained
at www.ICGtesting.com
Printed in the USA
LVHW020056230321
682109LV00011B/367